"When are you going to admit how much you want me, Kate?" Alex whispered. "Call an end to this ridiculous charade and invite me back into your life, into your bed?"

Kate trembled under the slow caress of his hands, the determination in his eyes.

Alex kissed her lingeringly, the gentle seductiveness of the embrace stealing the breath from her lungs. Shuddering with sensation, Kate whispered his name. Tenderly, she explored Alex's back, the solid warmth of his shoulders. He countered wordlessly, with a searching foray from breast to thigh that left Kate breathless and aching with desire. . . .

Touch
of Fire

CATHY GILLEN THACKER

A Love Affair from
HARLEQUIN
London · Toronto · New York · Sydney

First published in Great Britain in 1985 by
Harlequin, 15–16 Brook's Mews, London W1A 1DR

© Cathy Gillen Thacker 1984

ISBN 0 373 16037 2

18/0185

Printed and bound in Great Britain by
Richard Clay (The Chaucer Press) Ltd,
Bungay, Suffolk

To three very special people –
Julie, David and Sarah

Chapter One

The sleek red Mazda cut in and out of traffic on Springfield, Missouri's crowded central thoroughfare, changing lanes and zipping around cars in a way that was guaranteed to wake up even the sleepiest of commuters. Twenty-six-year-old Kate Ryker sat at the wheel, routinely commandeering the sporty RX-7 through the early morning mists. She was testing an article for the January issue of *Missouri Woman* magazine, but in order to get a valid reaction, she had to hit a few more tedious traffic lights. Slowing her pace abruptly, Kate poked along at a carefully calculated rate. Much to the consternation of the drivers behind her, Kate's sports car rolled to a languid stop just as the light turned red.

Step two on the notepad at her side read: *Apply mascara*. Kate groped for the container, careful to maintain a steady boot-clad foot on the brake. In the sedan in front of her, a car pool of four businessmen turned around to stare as the willowy blonde thickened her dark gold lashes to even more luxuriant proportions. When the light changed, Kate whipped the container back into the purse at her side and zipped on ahead, fully aware that one set of lashes was thicker than its twin. What she sacrificed for *Missouri Woman*!

At the next light, Kate managed to even the appearance of her eyelashes, then applied blush with quick, deft strokes. Consulting the proposed article for instruction, she whisked tawny shadow on her lids during the third stop, applied a bit more gloss to her lips at the fourth. The drivers following her were less than patient. Ignoring the blasting horns and irate catcalls from open windows, Kate jotted down the time and number of stoplights it had taken her to complete the offbeat beauty routine and her reaction to it. Just as suddenly, Kate became aware of a steady stare.

Glancing up, she looked to her right, left, then eventually into the rearview mirror to check out the person in the Jeep behind her. That driver, too, had been watching her with more than the usual interest, but Kate was unable to discern much in the seconds that followed except that the man was dark-haired and attractively built, probably tall. Tinted designer sunglasses completely camouflaged his eyes.

The lights changed. Her task finished, Kate resumed her customarily reckless style of driving and zoomed on ahead to the next light. The man in the blue CJ-7 kept pace, switching lanes every time she did. When Kate reached Commercial Street, she decided to lose him.

For a time it seemed she did, but then several lights later he was there again, two car lengths ahead, in the lane to her right. Curious, Kate studied the man from a distance. Jet-black hair, rugged masculine profile, dark business suit and tie, starched white shirt. It seemed every virile man she encountered these days reminded her of Alex and the marriage that had lasted only one year. A managerial expert and corporate "fire fighter," he made a living solving other people's disputes and restoring order into their work environments. Kate had founded, owned, and edited a regional woman's magazine. It had never been easy for the dynamic duo to form a partnership. From the first they had argued about everything from the idealistic way Kate did business at *Missouri Woman* to the slavish devotion he gave to his career, sometimes to the exclusion of all else. Initially, Kate had understood Alex's deep need to prove himself, but when it meant accepting a lucrative assignment on the Southwestern Oil Company compound in Saudi Arabia, she had rebelled. Besides the fact that she could not go with him for the required three years due to her work at the magazine, that section of the world was constantly under siege. Kate had argued that it was too dangerous and begged him not to go. Alex had insisted that was exactly why he was needed in Riyadh. Kate had parried with the remark about the comfort of Iranian prisons and subservient women and they were off. Two days later he was packing.

"This isn't a marriage, it's a battlefield!" Alex had exclaimed. Tossing his suitcase and clothing out the door after him, Kate had agreed. The next weeks brought crushing loneliness to them both and several witty but acerbic written and verbal transatlantic exchanges. Pride and the stubborn conviction that each was correct soon put things at an even larger impasse. Eventually, communication had broken down between them entirely. After six months of silence, Kate had felt compelled to do something, and had written to ask him to cooperate in a no-fault divorce. For whatever reasons, Alex had failed to reply, further confirming Kate's heartbroken assumption that the marriage was over. Anxious to get on with her life, Kate had instructed her lawyer to send Alex the necessary papers along with a letter explaining her position. That had been three weeks previously and guilt had plagued her ever since. She knew she should have waited and faced Alex personally instead of taking the coward's way out, or at the very least telephoned, but she couldn't. There were too many memories, too much stored-up emotion whirling around inside her. Pressed, Kate knew she would recklessly say even more things she didn't mean and she didn't want that to happen again. She wanted the hurting to stop.

Traffic moved ahead slowly. Kate tapped her foot impatiently from gas pedal to brake, anxious to get to work. Switching lanes again, she steered her sports car towards the next exit. Again, the CJ-7 cut in behind her. Thoroughly irritated, Kate switched again, this time even more dangerously. He didn't. When the vehicle finally coasted even with hers, she knew why.

Sunglasses slid down over the bridge of the driver's nose. Seven months to the day, Kate thought, and he hadn't changed a bit. Still holding the wheel with one light hand, Alex Ryker directed her towards the next exit. Kate refused. Alex Ryker pointed again, even more vigorously. Kate mouthed "Get lost!" She hadn't followed her estranged husband blindly before and she wasn't about to start now. If he wanted to meet with her it would be on her terms and not at the direction of some macho command.

Downtown Springfield had never seemed such a

maze of lights and treacherous one-way streets. Kate dodged one obstacle after another, always precariously aware of the careening jeep behind her. Three shortcuts later, she had lost him. Breathing a sigh of relief, Kate headed for Durst Park alongside the Medical Center. Ten to one, Alex would expect her to go to the magazine, was probably already there waiting for her. Here at least she could relax and collect her thoughts, before going on to work.

Leisurely, Kate drove around the park grounds, finally settling for a parking place on the less traveled south side. No sooner had she turned off the motor than she became aware of the purring mechanical vibrations behind her. Before she could even reach towards the ignition, the CJ-7 had rumbled abruptly to a stop, the high silver bumper resting cozily above the license plate on her Mazda.

Kate was trapped. And by the look on Alex's face as he climbed down out of the jeep and tossed off his sunglasses, it was not going to be a pleasant meeting.

Well, so much for doing anything on her terms, Kate thought wryly. Tawny gold hair slid riotously over her shoulders. Her skin was fair, cheeks stained even pinker than her blush. Wide amber eyes flecked sun gold in the morning light.

Always conscious of the business she represented, Kate made a point of dressing chicly. Her slender torso was encased in a long-sleeved blue, lavender, and rose plaid shirt, dusty rose cinched pairie skirt. Custom leather boots protected her feet. A cream-colored shawl-necked wool blazer kept her warm. The pulled-together look gave her an added boost of confidence as she climbed from the car.

Mouth taut with fury, Alex Ryker approached. Kate noted his thoroughly masculine appeal dispassionately. The dark blue of his business suit molded the athletic lines of his body, emphasizing the rugged width of his shoulders, the trimness of his taut, lean waist. The thighs were powerfully fluid beneath the flatteringly tight European cut of his pants, his eyes as cobalt blue as ever. It was the grim set of his chin that alerted her, the proprietorial angry way his gaze raked over her slender form.

"If you ever pull another stunt like that again, Kate Ryker, I'll break your lovely neck!" He skidded to a halt just two inches short of her nose.

Kate stepped back defensively, but maintained a glacial demeanor. "Hello, Alex."

"What were you trying to prove out there?" Reaching up, Alex jerked loose the knot of his tie. Equally taut gestures undid the first two buttons on his pristine white shirt. "Don't you realize you could have been killed!"

Kate refused to let him make her feel guilty. "Need I remind you who started it?" she purred. "As I recall, Alex Ryker, I never asked *you* to follow *me* anywhere!"

A muscle worked convulsively in one cheek. "Charming to the end, aren't you?" Masculine anger dissipated into a commendably lazy drawl. "Damn it, Kate—" Unwillingly, his stormy regard strayed to the parted, shimmering surface of her mouth. He drew nearer.

But Kate refused to let herself be drawn into his sensual spell. "I assume you received the letter from my attorney."

Exasperation hissed through clenched teeth. "I'm glad you brought that up." Alex jerked his tie down another notch. His frown returned even more dangerously.

The early morning sun drifted down through the shelter of trees, burning away the spiraling autumn mists. The air was fragrant with the scent of crushed leaves and recent rain, but Kate could take in little of either as her husband drew perilously close.

Kate started back. Alex followed, his one measured stride overpowering her every backwards two. Kate recalled Alex never had been very good at controlling his temper. Pushed the way he had been earlier, as adverse as he was to losing, she doubted he would have much success at all now.

"Wait a minute, Ryker!" Kate raised her palms like a traffic cop ordering him to halt. "Just because you've been away—"

"You're damn right I've been away," he retorted, pushing past the flimsy barricade of her hands. "And it's not very comforting to find out what you've been up to behind my back!"

Kate swallowed. So he was a little riled about the way she'd gone about asking for a divorce. Pausing to steady herself against a nearby tree, she contemplated making a fifty-yard dash for the car. But even if she could have reached it, a physical impossibility considering his vantage point and speed, she still couldn't have gotten past the blockade of his Jeep. No, with his bumper resting cozily over hers, she would just have to stall it out.

"Well? Don't you have anything to say for yourself?" Mockingly, Alex circled to the opposite side of the tree. Hand extending flatly against the bark, he faced her in mirror image symmetry, waiting.

Kate knew any in-depth discussion of their differences would make her cry, the reasons for them would make her shout. She glanced away at the sky and the trees and the ground. Finally she met his extremely unreceptive gaze. "Were the papers in order?"

What little control he had left snapped. "Oh, they were in order all right. So letter perfect I tore them up." Reaching into his jacket, he pulled out the crumpled blue remains and placed what was left of the confetti in her hands.

Kate leaned weakly back against the base of the tree. Hand still covering hers, Alex refused to let her run. "I take it this means you didn't sign them," Kate surmised wearily, exhibiting a nonchalance she could not possibly feel.

"Sorry to disappoint you, but no I didn't. Why did you do it, Kate?" Without warning, both grasp and tone softened, and Alex pulled her closer, so her cheek brushed the wool of his coat. The clean scent of his aftershave assaulted her, mingled with the unique fragrance of his skin. "Why did you ask me for a divorce?"

He knew the answer to that better than anyone. "Because I couldn't take the uncertainty of a separation anymore," Kate said. Because she couldn't stand the loneliness, couldn't function as a woman or a wife with him halfway across the globe. "I wanted a clean break."

"No legal action is going to end things between us, I don't care how many lawyers you see. Marriage is

forever, Kate. You can't tell me you didn't feel that
way when we exchanged our vows.''

Kate reminded herself it was he who had walked out
on her. Ignoring the sudden stiffness in her frame,
Alex brushed at a stray lock of hair at her shoulder, ran
his finger beneath the curve of her chin, tilted her face
up to his. "You knew I'd be back. I had vacation coming," he reproached. "Another five months and—"

"That's just it, Alex." Kate straightened resolutely.
"I didn't want to wait another five months. I wanted it
over." She couldn't stand the strain of a long-distance
marriage, knowing their careers would always come
between them. Even one more month would have
been too much.

"I see." Alex interpreted that to mean Kate no
longer cared. Gaze icy beneath the slit of his dark
brows, he drew back. "And you think it will be just
that simple. Papers signed. The marriage over."

Kate had hoped. "Alex, I—"

"Think again, Kate," he snapped. "Think hard."
Pivoting on his heel, he stalked towards the jeep.

"Alex, you can't just walk away now! As long as
you're here, I want this settled!"

But as far as he was concerned the conversation was
over. Alex climbed into his jeep and turned toward
her, his hand tightly clenched on the door handle.
"The next time you want my attention, Kate, try
picking up a phone. It's a lot easier and a far sight
more economical." He slammed the door, winked at
her rakishly, and drove off.

"I hate to tell you this, Kate, but if trying out that
'Making Up in Morning Rush' article did that to you,

then you'd better pitch it and fast!" Liz Shaw quipped as Kate straggled into the office. "Do you realize it's almost ten o'clock?"

Kate glanced in the mirror behind her door. Liz was right. She did look devastated. "I was in Durst Park."

"Doing what? Testing out an article about jogging in a dress?"

"Very funny." Kate tossed her briefcase and notepad onto the already overflowing desk.

Red-haired, hazel eyed, Liz never failed to be perfectly coiffed or prepared. And though the managing editor lacked Kate's talent for scrutinizing and editing material, she was a first-rate businesswoman, as well as the only female confidante Kate had.

"Alex is back." Sighing, Kate threw herself down into the comfortable beat-up swivel chair behind her desk. *Missouri Woman* might just have moved into new offices, but their equipment was largely the same. Secondhand and renovated, thrift shop cheap.

"Oh." Tactfully, Liz walked over to pour them both a cup of coffee. "You know if I had some whiskey, kiddo—"

"Forget it." Kate waved off the empathetic gesture. "I doubt even a hundred proof could counteract the effect that man has on me."

"Yes, but what a handsome gorilla!" Liz sighed. Twice divorced, Liz had a very forgiving, pragmatic attitude towards men. Kate envied her ability to enjoy.

"Well, you can have Alex, cage and all," Kate muttered, remembering his parting smile.

"Oh, no, honey." Liz tossed Kate a packet of cream. "Alex Ryker is all yours, whether you realize it or not."

Kate frowned, still lost in thought. "If I don't do something to stop him, Alex will be chasing me all over town." She knew there was nothing he liked better than a challenge, whether in work or women.

Liz grinned. "You could lead him around the block twice, and then give in!"

Kate looked at her. "Can we get on with this morning's business?"

"Sure." Liz went back over to check the magazine calendar and fill Kate in on all she had missed. "The covers for the December issue are finally in and need approval. There's a writer wanting to see you about excerpting a book. I told her we usually don't do fiction, but she wanted to see you anyway. Max Collins called this morning to remind you about lunch." Liz scrambled through the stack of messages, searching for the appropriate one. "The Hilton at noon. One of our regular writers, Tamara Johnson called, and wants to know about the fate of her zucchini article. I told her we haven't had time to spot test the recipes yet but she's pressing."

Kate made a note to call the home economic professor at the University of Missouri's Columbia campus. "Anything else?"

Liz grimaced. "Gavin Hayes. He wants a meeting with you as soon as possible."

"Next century would be too soon for me," Kate muttered, thinking of the seedy used car dealer. "Anything else?" Perusing her mail, Kate scribbled a note to herself about an overdue article for the January issue.

"Just lunch." Liz was already wandering off to make her own list of calls and appointments.

"If anyone needs me, tell them I'll be at the Hilton," Kate said. Hopefully, the afternoon would go a lot better than her morning.

"Kate, you're looking wonderful as always." Thirty-two-year-old Max Collins rose from his chair to greet her. As usual his brown hair was rumpled, his shoes slightly scuffed. The striped red and blue tie did not quite match either his tweed sportscoat or navy blue trousers.

"Thanks, Max." Kate leaned forward to return the casual kiss. A friend since childhood, Max was the one man she could always depend on. "How are things in the Senate?"

"Don't ask!" He made a woeful grimace as he gallantly helped her into her seat. Kate knew he had been working on a bill to increase state aid to dependent children.

"No luck, hm?" Kate reached over to brush a speck of lint from his arm. Max covered her fingertips briefly with his own. So engrossed were they in the mutual exchanging of sympathy neither noticed the grim-faced patron in the door.

"None whatsoever, Katie. What do you think about running a vote-getting article in your next issue of *Missouri Woman*?"

Kate leaned back to study the menu, fingers still absently curled around Max's arm. If only she could get her mind off the earlier run-in with Alex. "Sure, Max. Just send me a copy of the specifics. I'll run it under the State News section." Max had done lots for her in the past. He was also one of the truly concerned young politicians in their state.

A waiter appeared with a carafe of wine. "I hope you don't mind," Max said. "I took the liberty of ordering a drink for you."

Kate watched Max fill two glasses with fragrant Chablis. "Don't be silly. Now, about this article I want you to do..." Heads bent together, they studied the points Kate had outlined.

"Sounds simple enough," Max concurred, tousled brown hair pressing close to her cheek. Kate jotted down working title and word length. "When do you want it?" Max asked.

"Any time would be too soon for me," a third party drawled unexpectedly. Kate felt the warmth of a large strong hand curve around her shoulder, linger carelessly at the juncture of shoulder and neck. Only one man could generate a heat like that.

"Alex." Kate's breath escaped waveringly. *Not another confrontation*, she thought.

"That's right, sweetheart." Alex circled warily around to face her. Max awkwardly disengaged his hands from the papers he and Kate had been sharing.

"You didn't tell me he was back," Max murmured.

Alex's eyes were metallic blue chips of ice. *So this is how you've been spending your time*, the accusing look said. *This is why you're in such a hurry to divorce*.

"Honestly," Kate began, more flustered than she wanted to admit.

"So sorry you have to go, Senator." Speaking loudly, Alex captured Max's hand firmly and pulled him from his chair. Other diners in the plush dark surroundings turned. "Kate and I were so looking forward to your joining us, weren't we, Kate?"

More heads turned. "Yes, we were," Kate agreed,

sending Alex an irate glare only he could read. Still pumping Max's hand wildly, Alex gave the senator a clap on the back and started him on his way. Max turned, started to speak, and then evidently decided against it. Waving, smiling, he bowed pleasantly out of the dining room.

"How dare you send Max packing," Kate began as soon as the attention had turned away.

"Sweetheart, I'll dare anything when it comes to protecting my interests." Alex lazily drew up a chair.

"That was a business lunch!" Kate reprimanded.

"Well, this isn't." Alex leaned forward slightly on his elbows, his amused look just daring her to make a scene.

Kate sat back. Obviously the man was determined to have his say. "What are you doing here?" she asked coolly. But this time he wasn't buying her frosty reserve.

"I have to sleep somewhere." Alex signaled the waiter for a drink. "I'll have a scotch."

"Coffee and shrimp salad for me, please," Kate said. She had a feeling if the day continued status quo she was going to need all the strength she could muster.

"Nothing to eat for me," Alex dismissed the waiter summarily.

"When *did* you get back?" Kate sipped her Chablis.

"Last night." Alex's hands slid across the tablecloth to twine with hers.

Reacting nervously to the sheer confidence of his azure gaze, Kate laughed. "I'm surprised you didn't come crashing in then." Heaven knew it made a lot more sense than chasing her all over town.

"I tried, darling." At her stunned look, Alex's indolent grin widened. "There was a small matter of my keys no longer fitting any of the locks."

This time Kate's amusement was genuine. "I did that after you left. I'd forgotten." Unfortunately, it hadn't made her feel any better at the time.

"I assume that was after your string of good wishes," Alex went on dryly, accepting his drink from the red-coated waiter. Kate leaned back to allow her lunch to be placed in front of her, the hot coffee poured. "Surely you remember a few of them," Alex smiled. "The flying leap in the bubbling vat of lye? The short drive over the edge of the earth? The directive to build myself a cozy little nest in a Saudi Arabian snake pit?"

Kate blushed. She had never been known for her lack of passionate advice during a fight. "I was angry."

"We both were," Alex said softly. "Come on, Kate. Let's get this squabble straightened out once and for all. I'm only going to be here two weeks."

The magic words. Kate froze and pulled back. "It's over, Alex."

"A second ago you didn't think it was." Grimness permeated his voice.

That was before she had known he was leaving again. "I'm sorry, Alex," Kate got up resolutely. "But to drag this out would be pointless. Your work is wherever the company sends you. My work will always be here in Springfield. Face it, our marriage is never going to work, not on any real, viable level."

Alex passed on the opportunity to disagree. Leaning back in his chair, he studied her quietly; then did absolutely nothing to stop her as she stalked out of the hotel dining room through the lobby to her car.

Kate spent the rest of the afternoon going over photo layouts, *Missouri Woman* editorials, and potential story and article ideas submitted from their list of preferred freelance writers. Quitting time came and went. At seven o'clock, Kate finally decided to call it a day.

Alex obviously was not going to get back to her about signing the papers or having a new divorce agreement drawn up. Nor was he going to be inclined to work things out easily, if only for reasons of pride. Kate supposed she would just have to let their lawyers hassle it out.

The house was dark and quiet when Kate pulled into the drive. To her relief, Alex's car was nowhere in sight. Kate parked in front of the garage, too tired to get out and lift the door, and, toting her briefcase and small bag of groceries, went into the house. The quad-level, nestled in a quiet residential area north of the city, brought back ambivalent memories for Kate. Back in the days of their courtship, she and Alex had jointly selected every piece of furniture, wallpaper, tile, and paint. Realizing they'd never agree exactly on anything, they had compromised on color schemes and done all the rooms in different tones. Inundated with books, plants, and fondly collected memorabilia, the house was an open storybook of both their courtship and early marriage. That sometimes made it very difficult for Kate to go home.

Kate walked up the steps to the third level where kitchen, living, and dining rooms were located. Humming softly, she strolled into the kitchen, flicked on the overhead light and methodically began putting groceries away. Coffee, juice, frozen dinners, and Pepsi.

Stretching wearily, Kate walked back into the living room and flicked on the stereo. New Orleans jazz floated through the room, soothing, relaxing. Stopping on the arm of the sofa, Kate yanked off a boot, then kicked the other off with her stockinged foot. Her blazer was left across the silky cushions of the sofa, her skirt was tossed off mid-hall and left lying across the wicker hamper reserved for dry cleaning. Kate was down to apricot silk teddy, pantyhose, and blouse when she reached the bedroom door. Not bothering to switch on the light, she started familiarly across the darkened room, her mood already lifting in anticipation of a nice hot bath. She was just about to reach for a towel when she saw the masculine form draped across the bed.

For a moment, Kate couldn't decide whether to scream, run, or simply stand there and continue to hyperventilate. The problem was solved for her when it appeared her feet were glued to the floor. No matter how many times her brain sent the appropriate electrical impulses charging down her legs, her toes refused to budge.

Without warning, "Goldilocks" mumbled himself slowly into wakefulness. The voice was all too familiar. By the time Kate stomped to the bed, Alex's eyes were open and he was staring sleepily towards her.

"What are you doing here?" Kate demanded irritably. She thought she had made it quite clear he was no longer welcome in her life.

Alex pretended not to notice her annoyance. "I fell asleep waiting for you." He'd also hidden his jeep. "What time is it?" Alex yawned sleepily again.

"Eight thirty."

"Do you always work this late?"

"No. Sometimes I go out."

He let slide the opportunity to react jealously. "What'd you do to your hair?" His voice dropped caressingly as he took in the tousled tawny length of it, wildly rumpled from her habit of raking restlessly through it while she thought. "I noticed it was different earlier."

"I had it layered in one of those carefree cuts that is supposed to make it a breeze to fix." Kate answered his question dryly. "What that means is it does its own thing regardless."

Alex grinned, reaching out to cup a hand about her slender waist. "It's very sexy."

"It's unruly!" Kate adeptly sidestepped his attempt to reel her in to his side. "And you didn't answer my question. What are you doing here?" *She* hadn't given him a key.

Alex yawned again, looking bored. "Trying to get new keys made for one thing." Lazily, he folded both hands behind his head.

"Obviously, you managed." Chagrined, Kate realized that was something that should have occurred to her before. It wasn't like Alex to let her have the last say on anything. A matter of carefully tended masculine pride. Which meant, of course, there would be no divorce until *he* decided it was time. Then it would be acted upon posthaste.

"Yeah, I managed," Alex grumped, resenting the inconvenience she had caused him. "But it was one hell of a pain."

"Well, then that makes us even," Kate retorted. "Because you scared me half to death!"

"It's not my fault you're not used to having a man in your bed." Alex shrugged.

Kate was glad the darkness hid the extent of her blush as she studied his indolent form through partially lowered tawny gold lashes. Curiosity made her wonder if his muscles were still as powerful and well-conditioned as she recalled, his kiss and touch just as devastating. What would it be like to make love to him again and be loved in return? Would the old spark still be there? Had she lost her mind? The man had left her, walked out cold! One *Adios, amigo* and that had been it!

Noticing her scowl, Alex chided, "You know you've really lost your sense of humor." His contemplative glance said he had all sorts of ideas for helping her regain it. Sitting halfway up on the bed, he plopped a pillow behind his back. "What's for dinner?"

"Nothing," Kate said. If he thought they were going to play house again he had another think coming.

"The refrigerator did look pretty empty."

Kate deliberately didn't tell him she had just restocked it—at least with beverages. Food was still pretty slim pickings unless you were wild about Stouffer's Lasagne. "Actually, I haven't been home most evenings long enough to eat."

Grinning with unsuppressed amusement over her failure to provoke even the slightest hint of jealousy on his part, Alex let his eyes rake lazily over her figure, lingering particularly on the curves that inter-

ested him most. Knowing she had to get out of
there, Kate looked backwards over her shoulders towards the bedroom door and the relative safety of
the hall. If only she hadn't stomped so close to the
bed. And the fact that she'd already taken off most
of her clothes was not helping to erect any additional
barriers.

Unexpectedly, a long supple finger reached out to
draw a line across the apricot silk teddy from sternum
to waist.

"That looks new, too," Alex murmured. "Or at
least I don't recall it. But as for what's beneath it, now
that I remember very well." As he spoke his fingertips traversed up to lazily cinch and measure her waist.
Kate was unable to stop the involuntary tightening of
muscles beneath his hand, to deny the heat transmit-
ting itself down through the sheerness of the silk.
Prickles of sensation engulfed her from head to toe.
Kate swayed towards him traitorously despite the
open rebellion of her mind.

Still studying her sensual reaction to his touch,
Alex lifted a second hand to join in the maneuvers.
Both hands cupped loosely about her waist. After a
second, the measuring, testing hold moved treacherously upwards.

"You've lost weight," Alex murmured, caressing
the leanness of her ribcage.

"Stop mothering me!" Kate slapped his hands
away before he could proceed further. What was
wrong with her, for heaven's sake? The man had
broken her heart!

Alex moved languorously from the bed before she
could flee, and towered above her. "Believe me,

Kate," he drawled confidently. "There is absolutely nothing maternal in what I want to do to you."

Alex was still wearing the blue trousers of his suit, having discarded the jacket on the bed behind him. His collar was unbuttoned, the tie whipped off altogether. Shirt-sleeves had already been rolled casually to the elbow. Kate was close enough to count the fine black hairs whisking across the sinewy length of his arm when the gentleness of his fingers closed compellingly over her wrists.

"Alex, don't." Suddenly, she was desperate for him not to kiss her.

"If I really believed you meant that..." Alex murmured softly, lowering his head to hers.

Kate told herself it was curiosity that drove her to accept his kiss, that she wanted to know for a fact if he still had the power to turn her world upside down, set her adrift in a splendid sensual sea.

Wounded pride, however, refused to make it easy for him, to simply let him take up where he had left off months before. When his lips coaxed hers apart, she turned her mouth away. When his tongue sought entry into her mouth, she closed it, haughtily denying him entry. And when his hand dropped lower to the curve of her shoulder, she pressed it away deliberately, refusing him access to the bare velvet of her skin. In wordless defeat, Alex lifted his head. From the hall a rectangular shaft of light spilled a quarter way into the room. Where they stood, there was only darkness.

"You're still angry," Alex said softly.

"Yes. I guess I didn't realize how much." Relieved to be given an out, Kate started to pull away. He let her get a distance of two steps and then the warmth of his hands curled tenaciously about her waist. Ignoring her defensive cry, he pulled her back into his arms, against his chest. "Then I guess it won't hurt to make you furious, because God knows I need this even if you don't!"

His mouth lowered swiftly to hers, robbing her of breath, taking her with a total command that demanded response. Unrepentantly, his tongue slipped into her mouth, parted her lips and teeth and ravishingly explored every honeyed crevice. Kate was flooded with white-hot burning, and a desire that was suddenly as potent as his. The kiss grew even more thorough, Alex's lips gliding across hers in a caress that was both expert and devastatingly tender. Once again, she knew the rough possessiveness of his caress, the feel of his hands twining through the length of her hair, the solid warmth of his hard lean body pressed against hers.

Weakened, swaying slightly, Kate laced her arms about his neck. Drawn together, her soft breasts crushed against his chest, Alex tightened his embrace until even their heartbeats seemed to blend. The hands wound around Alex's neck curled upwards, laced in the inky black darkness of his hair, then trailed lingeringly down his back to draw him into the swirling maelstrom with her.

When the long soul-searching kiss ended, Kate could barely breathe. It was harder than ever to stand. It was the uncertainty reflected in his eyes, the control, harsh and relentless on the rugged planes of his face, that hurled her swiftly back to the present, the painful reality of their separation and impending divorce.

Kate swallowed, fighting the ache in her throat that always preceded tears. "One brief night of lovemaking won't change the stalemate between us," Kate whispered raggedly, running a hand agitatedly through her hair.

"Come away with me then," Alex implored. "Spend the next two weeks alone with me."

"And then what?" Kate demanded.

Alex shrugged. It was an old argument, one he had no wish to replay. "You go back to your job. I go back to mine."

"No, thanks." Kate knew she couldn't bear another year alone, particularly if there was no end to the dilemma in sight. "I want more out of life than a long-distance marriage." And a husband who was hers only for a week or two every year.

Alex's mouth tautened into a thin line devoid of compassion or coaxing. "Meaning I can quit my job in the Middle East or forget about staying married to you? Not much for compromise, are you, Kate?" Grabbing his jacket, Alex started angrily towards the door. He paused for another devastating glance. "If you think this is the last of us, Kate, you're wrong." And on those words, he walked quietly down the hall and let himself out.

Chapter Two

Kate slid neck high into the frothy array of scented bubbles in the sunken marble tub. How like Alex to think he could simply waltz in and sweep her off her feet! No doubt like every other predatory male over thirty he figured it was just a matter of a few well-placed kisses and a rousing tumble or two in bed before he'd have her eating out of his hand again. Well, this time he had another shock coming. Kate was not going to sleep or vacation with him, no matter how much he persuaded or enticed, until they had established whether they could have a future together. And at that point she had to admit sadly it didn't seem likely. Not with him going back to Riyadh for another lengthy stint as a consultant for Southwestern Oil.

Stepping out of the bath, Kate toweled herself dry and smoothed on scented lotion. Rummaging through the huge closet in the master bath, she selected a silky emerald green caftan, lacy green and blue jungle-print panties. She slipped them on, and then sat down at the mirrored vanity to run a brush through the wild curls. Reknotting her hair loosely on top of her head, Kate padded out to the den for a book and a glass of wine. Halfway there, she noticed the scent of charcoal permeating the air, which was odd, because she hadn't started the grill.

In the hall was a trail of clothing that matched her earlier discarded ones item for item. Trousers lay artistically next to the skirt she'd left lying on the wicker hamper. Shirt, socks, brief black jockey shorts lay littered across the guest bath. Strewn across the sink were shaving utensils, shampoo, toothpaste, and contact solution and case. The air was scented with a distinct smell Kate knew only too well. Walking in, she capped the bottle of aftershave, grimaced at the wet towel on the floor and walked out again.

The living room offered more of the same. Next to her boots were Alex's discarded shoes, lying at precisely the same angle as her cast-off footwear. His jacket was also thrown carelessly over the back of the sofa. His tie and wallet lay next to her purse. Kate was almost afraid to go on.

"About time," called a droll voice from the kitchen. A comical figure in apron and chef's hat approached. "I was certain you had drowned."

"Not very likely." Kate took in his snazzy new apparel. Trying hard to suppress a grin, she stalked barefoot to the kitchen. "I see you're making yourself right at home." He had changed into a yellow polo shirt and tightly fitting jeans. The shirt-sleeves were pushed up past the elbow, the front placket of buttons completely undone. A curling mat of dark hair sprung out of the casual V-shaped opening. He too was barefoot. Done with the apron and the hat, he dispensed with both items and walked back over to the cutting board at the sink.

"Actually, I'm running a shelter for wayward wives and magazine editors who won't eat." Turning a radish upside down, Alex examined it for pithiness in the light.

"I'm serious, Alex." Now that the shock had worn off, anger was beginning to set in.

"So am I." His eyes raked the length of her silk-clad figure desirously. "Initial calculations indicated you'd lost at least ten pounds since I left." His mouth curled in anticipated pleasure as he put down both radish and knife and stepped forward, palms spread obligingly. "Of course if you'd like a more exact accounting..."

Kate picked up a carrot peeler and held it in front of his nose. Alex went sedately back to chopping celery. "Have it your own way. But they don't call me the miracle worker for nothing."

Kate was all too well acquainted with his sensual skills. It was precisely what she'd been trying to avoid. "Okay, Alex, fun time is over. What are you still doing here? What do you want?"

"You know what I want, Kate. And as for the other"—he paused deliberately, dark brows drawing together warningly—"it is half my house."

So the tiger had teeth after all, Kate thought. Wisely, she opted for time-out to recover and directed her attention to the meal set out before them. Thick porterhouse steaks were marinating in trays beside the sink. A loaf of crusty golden brown French bread and a liter of good red wine stood next to that.

"When did you do all this?" Kate asked. Was he hoping the way to her heart was through her stomach?

Alex stopped chopping cucumbers long enough to pour her a much needed drink and answer her question. "While you were drowning. I like to keep busy. And as for the next query, some of us do eat, even if we don't reside permanently and perennially in the States. Help me with the salad, will you?"

Kate took a sip of her wine and walked over to the sink to stand next to him. Like it or not, Alex was there, and she was hungry. She could kick him out later, before bed. "I thought you were staying at the Hilton," Kate mused, tearing leaf lettuce into a large wooden bowl.

"For one night. And then only because I didn't want to wake you or the neighbors by banging on the door."

"You didn't mention you planned to stay here at lunch." If he had, Kate would have moved out.

"I didn't think I had to."

Silence. Kate took another sip of wine, grimaced at the strong, dry lukewarm taste. Strolling over to the refrigerator, she extracted a couple of ice cubes from the freezer and plopped them wordlessly down into her drink. Alex rolled his eyes heavenward, but made no verbal comment about her lack of gourmet attributes. Which was good. Because Kate thought there was nothing sillier than running about a room trying to find the perfect place to let the wine breathe.

The silence between them continued, more fraught with tension than before. Trying not to reveal her thoughts, Kate reached for a tomato and began slicing it into salad-sized sections. The tenuousness of the situation prevailed. Kate couldn't think of anything but the earlier passionate kiss, the way he had gently but persistently coaxed her to respond, her after-bath freshness and his, the inviting nakedness beneath her snugly cut emerald green silk caftan.

The knife in her hand slipped. Only by a fraction of an inch did she miss cutting off two of her fingers. Muttering invectives between tightly gritted teeth, Kate grabbed the wounded appendages and held them over the sink. Well, she'd missed the salad, that was something.

"That'll teach me to let you help!" Dropping everything, Alex took the injured figures in his hand and turned on the tap. Kate closed her eyes tightly, afraid to look lest there be squirting blood.

"It's not *that* bad." Alex pushed her stinging fingers underneath the flow of icy running water.

"I have this thing about gushing blood," Kate moaned, lashes still tightly shut. "It only bothers me to the fainting point when it's mine."

"Well, then don't look."

"I'm not. You couldn't pay me to look." Bewailing her general ineptness, Alex wrapped her hand in a wet paper towel and settled her blindly onto a nearby stool. "I'll be right back."

"Let's hope so," Kate sighed. Or she was doomed to a rather dark night. He returned eventually with a bottle of antiseptic and a couple of adhesive bandages. "Your medicine cabinet is a mess. I took a minute and organized it for you."

Kate choked. "Gee, thanks." How could she have forgotten his penchant for orderliness? "You must think I'm an awful sissy," Kate hissed as the sting of antiseptic hit raw skin.

"Only about blood," Alex murmured. Gently, Band-Aids were wrapped around the injured fingers. "Good as new," Alex pronounced. Still holding the wrist of the injured hand, he pulled her up off the chair.

"If only hurt marriages were fixed as easily," Kate sighed impulsively, momentarily allowing wistfulness to invade her tone. "A Band-Aid here, a Band-Aid there."

"It doesn't have to be as hard to work things out as you sometimes make it," Alex countered softly. Thumbs tilting the edge of her jaw, he lifted her face to his. If the first kiss had been gentle, this one was shatteringly tender, inundated with months of longing. Without reservation, Kate opened her mouth to his. But this time when she would have prolonged the kiss experimentally, he withdrew abruptly. "I'm no saint, Kate." The words were harsh with frustration. "It's been a long time and I'm not going to be put on hold again, not on a whim."

Kate turned away, face suffused with heat. So now it was he who was delivering the ultimatums. Ante up or forget it. "If that's the way you feel, why are you staying here? Why did you come back?"

"Because it's my house too, and I don't intend any childish temper tantrums on your part to run me out." Abruptly Alex turned back to the counter, then walked over to slide the salad into the refrigerator to chill. Silently, he finished what was left of his wine and then poured himself some more.

Kate stared steadily at the microwave beside him. The tensions would only rise unbearably if he stayed there with her. But unlike Alex, Kate was not drawing

a six figure a year salary. She did not have the money
to go elsewhere.

There had to be some way to settle it in a calm and
sensible manner. They were two adults. Surely he
would understand if she just explained. "Alex, this is
my home now," Kate began reasonably. "I'm the one
who's paid the mortgage the past seven months."

"Check with the bank," Alex retorted tautly. "It's
been paid double." He elaborated at her shocked reaction. "I wanted to make certain you were taken care
of."

Or maintain his stake in the property should their
dispute come to a divorce, Kate thought cynically.
"No one told me that."

Alex switched off the bright overhead light. The
kitchen was lit now only by the muted lamp over the
stove. "I asked them not to."

"I'm the one who's taken care of the upkeep, cut
the grass, cleaned the windows." Kate was the one
who would live there after he went back to his job
assignment in the Middle East.

Still, he had no intention of turning the property
over to her. "The trim at the back of the house needs
painting," Alex interrupted archly. "I plan to see that
it's taken care of before I leave. And as for the rest, as
long as you're married to me, the property will be
jointly owned, shared, and paid for."

"Oh, you're impossible!" Kate swore, wondering
desperately what she was going to do next.

"Look who's talking."

That did it. Kate went at him, not knowing precisely
what her intentions were. The next thing she knew
she was pinned roughly against his chest. "Let me

go!'' Palms splayed across his chest, she shoved with all her might, and didn't succeed in moving him one lousy inch. "Beast!" she yelled when he laughed.

"Ah, Kate, you make such an easy target."

Alex had meant only to silence her in the simplest most effective way possible when he pulled her into his arms. But desire swiftly entered into the passionate embrace. His restraint fled. Unable to resist, he drew her nearer still, brushed his lips softly across hers, then again when he felt her breath catch, her pulse quicken. The silk of her caftan, the familiar essence of her perfume, the imprint of her breasts against the cloth all added to his arousal. With an impatient oath, he let his mouth move over hers hungrily, let himself taste, experience, demand more and more.

There seemed no way Kate could escape either Alex or the driving pressure of his mouth. If she were honest, she would admit she didn't really want to. His sinewy length pressed against her, igniting a wildfire of sensation wherever contact was made. She tasted the sweetness of the wine on his tongue, felt the muscular cradle of his arms as he moulded her even more precisely against him. His free hands circled possessively over her hip and breasts, nipped in at the waist, and then gently explored the smooth hollow at the nape of her neck.

"God, how I've missed you," Alex murmured, holding her close.

Hungrily, Kate nibbled at his lips, suffusing with warmth as she felt the augmenting pressure of his masculine response. The admissions Kate had longed to hear for months got lost in the provocative beckoning of the kiss. She forgot her reservations, forgot the future, let herself shift against him until they achieved an achingly erotic fit.

Instinctively, his hands curled around the fullness of both breasts, but when he felt material beneath his palms, he brushed the crumpled silk of the caftan aside. His lips closed over the petal soft tip, then claimed the roundness of her flesh. Kate shuddered with desire, then winding her fingers through his tousled black hair pulled him to her. Eyes pressed shut, her fingers dug into the shirt-covered muscle of his shoulders and a low moan of pleasure escaped her throat.

Alex paused, body tensing in reaction to her passion, and then as if shaking himself awake, released her. Kate stumbled upright, the hem of her silky green caftan floating whisper-soft to the floor. She quickly righted the deep-cut neckline.

Grimacing with the effort of the self-imposed control, Alex turned and walked past her. The distance between them physically was minuscule when compared to the emotional chasm caused by his abrupt withdrawl.

"I'm sorry. I thought that would be enough," Alex swore softly, face etched with the rough possessiveness he felt. "But it's not. I want all of you, Kate. Your love, your devotion—both physical and emotional, and, yes, even your promise that you'd follow me to the ends of the earth *if* I asked, especially if that were the only way we could be together. I'll never be satisfied with just your hesitant surrender to my physical love. Under those circumstances, it's not fair to either of us to continue."

As if to prove his strength of character, Alex dutifully and chivalrously kept his distance the rest of the evening. They drank wine and charcoaled steaks on the gas grill out on the deck, but at bedtime it was a chaste peck on the cheek and a completely willing retirement to the guest room for Alex. Kate had to admit that despite her reservations she had never been so frustrated in her entire life.

"Well, don't you look like something the cat dragged in!" Liz Shaw handed Kate Ryker a stack of unopened mail and followed her into the cramped executive office.

Kate tossed her briefcase onto the cluttered desk top, loosening the collar of her white silk shirt as she went. "Don't hassle me, Liz. I've had one rotten night!"

"Alex?" Liz sat down on the edge of Kate's desk, pretty features softening sympathetically.

"Who else?" Kate tossed off her navy suit jacket and ran her hands through her hair, still damp from her morning shower. "I swear that man's got me twisted in knots!"

"I take it that means you saw him again last night." Liz riffled through a stack of messages and memos thought Kate should see, placed them front and center on top of the younger woman's briefcase.

"Spent the night with him." Kate poured herself some coffee and scalded her throat on the first hasty gulp.

Liz's eyebrows shot up in amazement. "And I thought I worked fast!"

"In separate bedrooms," Kate finished dryly. Restlessly, she paced over to the storyboard on the wall and studied the article assignments and deadlines for the next month's issue. "He wouldn't leave. Something about possession being nine-tenths of the law."

"So you wouldn't leave either." Liz grinned. "Get much sleep?"

"No!" Kate admitted. She'd spent half the night mentally dissecting their earlier lovemaking, unfinished though it had remained. The other half just waiting for him to try and sneak in. The fact that he hadn't, and had apparently slept soundly only increased her ire. Only Alex would be able to start and stop and still exercise common sense about getting the requisite amount of sleep while she worried herself gaunt about the problems still existing in their relationship.

"What'd he say this morning?" Liz handed Kate a copy of the agenda for the morning's staff meeting.

"Nothing." Kate frowned over yet another puzzle in the mire. "He wasn't there when I got up."

"Any idea where he went?" Liz asked. At 6 A.M. there weren't many alternatives.

"None." Frowning, Kate raked a pencil behind her ear.

"But you have a suspicion, don't you?" Hands on her hips, Liz regarded her boss with amusement.

"Alex may be unpredictable, but certain things are constant. He's never given up on turning me into the perfectly dutiful corporate wife, the kind that would follow him to the ends of the earth. Ten to one this—"

A knock on the door cut into their conversation. "Hello, Mr. Hayes." Kate faced their unscheduled visitor with brisk politeness.

Liz offered the routine pleasantries, and then departed. Clad in a lime-green leisure suit, the fifty-year-old businessman followed Kate to her desk. "You've been avoiding me, Mrs. Ryker," Gavin Hayes scolded.

"*Ms.* Ryker," Kate corrected. "And you're right, Mr. Hayes, I have been busy. Is there something I can do for you today?"

"You can run that ad for me in your next issue, like I asked."

Kate affected a businesslike smile. "Mr. Hayes, we've been all through this. And *Missouri Woman* and Hayes Heaven Used Cars do not mix. The truth of the matter is, I don't advertise any used cars in my magazine."

"But you ran an ad on the Honda Civic," Hayes complained.

"Because of the EPA rating," Kate admitted. "And because the advertising was basic, nonsexist, nondiscriminating copy."

"What was wrong with the ones I proposed?" the heavyset entrepreneur demanded. "I liked those ads. Matter of fact, the woman was real pretty."

Kate shut her eyes and counted to ten. "I have no quarrel with pretty women, Mr. Hayes—"

"Well, you ought not," Hayes interrupted, arching his brows reproachfully before he broke into a dazzling smile. "Because you're sure pretty enough."

The false compliment didn't even go to Kate's toe. "Your ad was sexist, Mr. Hayes. Discriminating, a real put-down to women." She quoted part of the copy he had proposed. "'Hayes Heaven Used Cars. Takes the Worry and the Complication out of Buying

Wheels for Women.' A pretty young woman and a couple of hot-to-trot salesmen. What are you selling, Mr. Hayes? Carburetors or afternoon rendezvous?''

"I resent that!" Hayes blustered. "After all, business is business and—"

"And I resent your attitude, Mr. Hayes." Kate got to her feet. "Everyone's seen your commercials on television. Springfield, St. Louis, Hannibal—they're all over the state. You make buying a used car seem like a trip to the moon. Poor lonely depressed housewives out for the terrifyingly difficult decision of selecting a car. They come into the lot, wearing their hair in a ponytail, nervously chomping their nails. They leave looking like Farrah ready for a night out on the town. From housedress to the triumph of a sequined gown all in one afternoon."

"It sells cars, Ms. Ryker."

"Not in my magazine."

"Then you still won't run the ad?" Hayes breathed as if here were finishing a marathon.

"I'm sure there are other publications who will be glad to oblige," Kate retorted coolly, though in reality she wasn't at all sure. His string of dealerships had been brought up on fraud more than once.

"You're going to be sorry you refused me, *Mrs.* Ryker." Hayes glanced at the pocket watch chained to his vest as if to symbolize that her time was indeed running out. "And that is something I can guarantee."

Kate was still reeling from her confrontation with used car king Gavin Hayes when Alex strolled confidently in the door. "Good morning, darling." Hands spread flat across the surface of her desk, he leaned forward to give her an extremely familiar kiss on the cheek. "What time's the staff meeting this morning?"

Kate froze, hands still on the paper on her desk. She had three more articles to check and a photo layout to supervise before the scheduled session began.

"Why do you want to know?" Her tone was as wary as her glance. After what had gone on between them at the house the night before, he couldn't be up to anything good. More, he was looking his professional best. Alex had showered and shaved, dressed in a double-breasted business suit of pearl gray. His black hair shone, his tan was sexily evident above the muted gray of his shirt. "Or should I say what are you up to?"

"Now, sweetheart." Alex perched comfortably on the side of her desk. "Why so suspicious? I simply want to attend."

Kate regarded her estranged husband thoughtfully, not at all dissuaded by the innocent glint in his dark-lashed gaze. Alex had never been interested in the magazine before. True, he had bailed her out of a tight spot financially—twice—but that had been the extent of it. He'd been too busy with his own work to do more than offer occasional pefunctory advice, most of which Kate promptly discarded.

"You must have a reason for wanting to be there."

"Need I remind you I co-own sixty percent of the stock?"

Kate fervently wished he'd go back to work.

"... Under the community property laws of this

state, what is yours is mine, and I intend to hold you to that."

Why hadn't Kate insisted on a premarital agreement discounting *Missouri Woman* from such claims?

"... Beyond which, it's been brought to my attention you need all the help you can get."

It was clear from the unsympathetic curve of his mouth he knew about the magazine's fiscal difficulties. "You talked to the lawyer?"

"Just this morning. Why haven't you done any of the things I told you to do before I left?"

Kate resisted the urge to tell him what he could do with his organizational charts and graphs. "We have enough problems just trying to run in the black without you barging in here, spewing advice."

"I could have helped you," Alex interjected. "You know my experience as a troubleshooter in the business world is specifically geared to difficulties such as *M.W.*'s True, I've been working in oil the last three years but before that I worked with a management consulting firm, a data processing company, and three other firms in the Southwest, all of diverse interests. I've got a bachelor's in accounting and finance, a master's in business management."

"No one's ever accused you of being an underachiever, sweetheart," Kate said dryly, mocking his earlier tone, "but the answer is no. *Missouri Woman* is my domain. If I need help, I'll go to the magazine's legal counsel."

"Darrel Hendrix doesn't have time to take care of the financial affairs anymore," Alex said calmly. "And with the emotional, idealistic way you've been doing business lately—"

Kate assumed he was referring to the amount of advertisements she refused weekly, on the basis of unsuitable or sexist copy.

"What time is the staff meeting?" Alex repeated.

Kate thought swiftly. Much as she may have wanted to, she didn't have the time to settle his gripes. She was pushing deadlines on every count. Nor was he likely to take "maybe later" for an answer. No, Alex would hang around, curiously questioning, auditing, until Kate and her staff were farther behind and more over-worked than ever before.

"The staff meeting is at two o'clock this afternoon." Kate took a deep, cleansing breath. "All in all I have no objection to your sitting in. Providing of course you keep your consulting opinions to yourself."

The way Alex was looking at her told Kate he knew she was lying about that much. Lazily, he got up from his perch on her desk. "I know I'm only going to be in the States a short time, but I can help you, Kate," he stated bluntly.

He would also drive her insane. "I'm fully aware of the extent of your personal investment," Kate said tightly. Fifty thousand dollars worth. "If I had the money to buy you out now—"

"You don't." Alex paused, splayed his hands across lean muscular hips. "Not that I want out. I will, however, probably insist on at least a few structural and/or financial changes."

"For the good of the magazine," Kate said sarcasti-cally.

"And you."

Kate picked up a pencil, twirled it thoughtfully round and round. "You realize your interference here, warranted though it may be from your stand-point, is bound to make things much, much worse between us." Kate couldn't even accept gentle instructions from the man at home. If he were in earnest about wanting to reconcile, maybe that would be the deciding factor.

No dice. Alex smiled, not about to be blackmailed into or out of anything. "Then think of it this way, Kate. At least you'll be financially set when we do divorce."

"All right, what's first on the agenda?" Kate had two hours in which to wrap up business for the day before Alex got back to harass her.

"'101 Ways to Cook Zucchini,'" food editor Fran Wilson said. "I don't know about the rest of you, but I'm not particularly wild about some of the author's combinations, however innovative. "Still, the—"

Without warning, the door to the conference room opened quietly. Alex Ryker strode in with all the grace of a mountain cat, danger reflected in every move. Evidently, he did not appreciate Kate's effort to misinform and get rid of him. She swallowed, glanced fitfully at the ceiling above her as she waited for the usual calm of the room to return.

Smiling perfunctorily at the staff, Alex lazily folded his tall frame into a notoriously rickety wooden chair at the other end of the table. Kate only hoped it would hold his weight the duration. To add injury to insult at this stage of the game...

"You were saying?" Liz prompted, turning to cast a meaningful look at the food editor. "Fran? About the zucchini article?"

"Ummm—", Fran suddenly seemed incapable of coherent speech. Kate wondered how much of it had to do with Alex's arresting blue eyes and ruggedly virile profile.

"The squash article as written is out," Kate interjected quietly. "I tested a few of the recipes myself the other night. And though unique, most of them fell far short of appetizing."

"The Maple Baked version was good." Fran recovered enough to inject. She flushed slightly as Alex turned to look at her. This time Kate couldn't help it. She rolled her eyes heavenward. This was exactly the kind of disruption she had been afraid of. Fran continued, flipping agitatedly through her notes. "I think there were about six or seven other recipes we could probably use, too, though..."

Kate didn't hold out much hope Fran would find what she needed, not with Alex glancing negligently over her shoulder.

"Tamara Johnson is a regular contributor, Kate." Liz remarked drolly, apparently rather amused by Alex's appearance and Kate's chagrin. The gazes of the two women met. Again, Liz seemed to be saying: *Give in*! But her tone was serious as she continued. "Her recipes alone carried us through half of last year. and if we're to go with that 'Summer Recipe Cook-Off' as planned, we're probably going to need home ec professors from the university where she teaches to help judge."

"Good point." Kate sent Liz a grateful glance for injecting business back into the meeting. "Fran, why don't you see if you can't uncover ten usable recipes from the batch Ms. Johnson gave you. If they all test

out well, we will run them in a small section near the
back of the food section." Kate frowned, hoping su-
perstar Johnson would not protest too much. Zucchini
just wasn't that popular an item, particularly not in the
dead of winter when the article was proposed to run.

Fran Wilson murmured her satisfaction with the
squash arrangement and then went on to self-
consciously get approval for a collection of fast and
easy skillet suppers for working mothers.

"Keep in mind we want to use cheap readily available ingredients that will appeal to children and grown-
ups alike," Kate cautioned, determinedly scrawling a
similiar note to herself.

Alex sent her a quizzical look. Kate continued,
"Generally speaking, our reader response has shown
that single and/or married-but-childless couples either
eat out or stick to lean meats and salads most of the
time. Any big culinary efforts on their part are usually
gourmet and not in our domain. Hence, these casser-
oles will be geared towards families with children, but
kept sophisticated and spicy enough to appeal to
adults too." Not an easy task. But Fran had proved
capable of handling the challenge. Probably because
she was the mother of two teen-age boys.

"Interesting," Alex demurred, as if coming to the
realization of how and why they did business at *M.W.*
for the very first time. Kate couldn't help wondering
what motivated his current interest more—the magazine's worsening financial difficulties or his desire to
reinstate himself in her life.

Kate flipped through to the next page of her notes.
"The 'Making-Up in Morning Rush' article is also going to have to be revised. Probably to some sort of

speedy beauty routine complete before the reader leaves the house.''

Swiftly, Kate went on to review several other items, including the photo layout and accompanying article and evaluation of a nearby daycare center.

"Do you always study the centers on such a detailed, critical level?" Alex asked.

"The ones that agree to be written up and evaluated by us, yes," Kate answered calmly.

"How do they feel when the evaluation printed is a negative one?" Alex asked.

Apparently, he had been studying the back issues.

"Dismayed, I imagine," Kate said dryly. There was an undercurrent of laughter from the staff, but Alex did not smile. The conference room narrowed to just the two of them. Kate was reminded what a formidable opponent he could be in business situations. "Our license to evaluate freely is provided for in the release form the centers sign upon agreement. Naturally, they're unhappy if our findings are not good. On the other hand, at the centers we have investigated and reviewed positively, enrollment is a hundred percent with lengthy waiting lists to get in. The ones we do fault are given a ninety day extension period to make improvements or revisions on policy. If they do that, and pass a second surprise investigation by one of our licensed investigators, then we print that too. And at the head of the daycare review section of the magazine, not just on some obscure back page.''

"How do your readers respond to that section of the magazine?" Alex asked, interest genuine.

"It seems to be one of the main selling points," Kate replied proudly. "We don't just generalize at

Missouri Woman, Alex. We identify specific problems as well as triumphs, and try to solve what we can. If we lose a few advertisers or potential subscribers along the way so be it." They would never be able to please everyone.

"Idealistic," Alex murmured, tapping a pen against the palm of his hand. "But is it any way to do business?"

Kate bristled at the note of censure in his voice. "It's the only way we're going to." And on that note, the staff meeting was adjourned, and Alex joined Kate as she walked toward her office.

"You know injecting yourself into my staff meeting was really a rotten thing to do. But to sit there and actually comment on the way we do business was unforgivable!" Kate stormed, punctuating her sentences with swift, angry strides.

Alex shrugged his shoulders indolently. "Calm down, Kate. I merely asked a few well-informed questions."

Kate was so furious she could hardly speak, but out of deference to the other staff members just outside her private office, tried to keep a handle on her emotions. "The point is you had no right even being there."

Alex admitted to that unrepentantly. "Under normal circumstances, I would agree with you there. But these aren't normal circumstances, are they, Kate?"

A shiver of unease traversed the length of her spine. Kate stopped pacing. "What do you mean?"

"I looked at your books. It appears I'm about to lose a substantial personal investment unless someone does something fast."

"And you've drafted yourself as savior," Kate ascertained dryly.

"No one else is going to do it for free."

Kate was silent, thinking of how much it would cost to hire a professional managerial consultant to bring the magazine to solvency.

"Okay, so I'll be more careful," she promised. "Cut expenses even further back."

"Unless I miss my guess, you're already doing that." Alex appeased gently, strolling near. "In fact, how you've managed to keep *M.W.* operating this long on that shoestring you call a budget is something short of a miracle. The problems go much deeper, Kate. If you want *Missouri Woman* to survive and grow, you're going to have to make some changes. In copy, in ads placed, in—"

"No." Kate would rather die than sacrifice her principles for Alex's idea of a commercial publishing success.

His jaw tautened at the open animosity in her tone. "Read the agreement we signed at the time of the last loan, Kate. It specifically states in time of fiscal crisis I am authorized to act in the best interests of *Missouri Woman* with regard to the financial and or managerial structure hereof. Or in other words, if you mess up with the money I loaned you, and you have, I'm free to act in any legitimate manner to get it back."

"Only with our attorney Darrel Hendrix's approval," Kate parried smugly.

"I got it this morning, in writing." Reaching into his coat pocket, Alex waved a sheaf of official-looking documents beneath her nose. "Now, do you want to tell the staff I'm temporarily signing on as publisher or shall I?"

"I'm running the show here, Alex. I'll decide who does what, where, and when."

Too late Kate saw the error in that approach. It was equivalent to waving a red cape in front of a charging bull's nose.

"You know you handle yourself well under pressure," Alex said calmly, hands moving to splay resolutely across lean, well-trousered hips. "And it's a good thing too. Because I have a feeling in a few minutes things are really going to start to boil."

"Out!" Her command could have been heard in the next block. But the shouting did not last for long. Alex was already stalking to her side. A wounded panther would have been safer.

"Get used to having me around, Kate." The words were gritted out like shards of steel. "I intend to be here a lot."

"Over my dead body!" At his dangerous look, she lowered her voice to an obliging hiss.

Alex turned away uncaringly, already bored with the whole exchange. "Where are your files on expenditures, Kate? Ten to one they are nowhere near the *E*'s."

About that much, he was correct. "Alex, I don't want to get rough, but if I have to, I'll have you thrown out of here." At the childishness of her threat, his gaze darkened. They both knew his loan and partnership agreement were ironclad. "With a court order," Kate added. Maybe there was some way to have the whole procedure reversed.

Alex stared at her silently. "That's your solution to

everything, isn't it, Kate?" he grated through his teeth. "Court orders and attorneys. Well not this time. Not with *Missouri Woman* and certainly not with me!"

Kate bit her tongue mutinously. She wasn't handing over or agreeing to anything until she had seen the magazine's legal counsel.

Alex went on in a tone meant to scathe. "When it comes to what goes on in this office, I am only interested in the money I invested, trying to recoup some of the financial loss your haphazard methods of management and organization have brought about. Fight me on as much as a paper clip, and I guarantee you, you will lose." And on that note, he walked cheerfully over to study the files, leaving Kate to observe him in abandoned, furious dismay.

Chapter Three

"Personal differences aside, Kate, I would think you would welcome any help Alex has to give." Darrel Hendrix faced Kate solemnly across his legal-brief strewn desk. "Your books are a mess. And I'm not talking about sloppy handwriting."

Kate blushed, thinking of the inept way she kept tabs on her own business expenses. "I know, Darrel, and honestly everyone's trying. But we've been so busy with the editorial side of the business—"

Crisply, *M.W.*'s financial advisor cut off her excuse. "Consider this your chance to get caught up."

Kate scowled at the plant in the corner. Darrel was right, but she knew Alex. When he was done with it, *Missouri Woman* would be unrecognizable. He'd throw everything distinctive about the award winning magazine out the window and end up with a very commercial piece of nonfeminist hype, complete with women in aprons on the cover. The account books, however, would be neat and precisely balanced.

Kate got restlessly up to prowl the carpeted office. "Look, even if I were amenable to Alex's direction, which I'm not, it would never work. Alex would just use the magazine to try and control or reform me. He has this fifties' idea of what marriage should be like. Hearth, home; dutiful, submissive wife."

Darrel grinned at the irony lacing her voice, for the first time revealing his personal closeness to them both. "Having second thoughts about the divorce?"

"No!" Kate said stubbornly, shooting her attorney an irate glance. But she knew she was, that she'd never really get over Alex no matter what happened. He'd been her first real love, her only love. And her passionate reaction to his embrace the night before proved she was still far too susceptible to his sensual spell.

Kate raked a hand wearily through her hair. "I don't know how I'll put up with him for two weeks till he returns to Riyadh."

"Oh?" Darrel looked surprised. "I had the impression he intended to remain until the whole mess was put to rights."

Knowing Alex, that wouldn't take long, at least not in his opinion, Kate thought. "Alex has never been known to vacation for more than two weeks at a time, if that." She guessed she could endure a little meddling, then just put everything back the way it was the minute Alex left town. "Is Alex going to work directly with you on the financial restructuring?"

For the first time that day, Darrel hesitated unhappily. "Naturally, Kate, given the stormy circumstances between the two of you, I offered to act as liaison."

"He refused." Kate's stomach contracted unbearably.

"Alex feels the only way to really familiarize him-

self with the way you do business at *M.W.* and hence
come up with long-range plans towards saving the
business or turning it around is by being there personally.''

Kate allowed that a moment to sink in. ''What happens if I don't agree with the changes Alex wants to
make?''

Darrel viewed her even more sternly than before.
''Don't you still have your copy of the partnership
and loan agreement?''

''It's in the files at my office.'' Probably under *Finance*. Then again, maybe *Alex*. ''I'd appreciate it if
you'd go over it with me again.''

Darrel sighed and slid his glasses back up to the
bridge of his nose. ''There's hardly any power you
didn't give him, Kate. He has access to every facet of
your organization, and the power to hire and fire as he
sees fit.''

''Hire and fire!'' Kate exclaimed.

''We went over this at the time,'' Darrel reproached.

''You bet we did!'' Kate exclaimed irately. ''And
Alex said naming him publisher was more or less a
token title or simple gesture of faith. He promised me
he would always be a *very* silent partner.''

''Well, let's just say he found his vocal cords,'' Darrel replied facetiously. ''Sorry.'' He apologized at
Kate's glare. ''But let's face facts, Kate. Your fiscal
affairs at *M.W.* are competely disorganized and hap-
hazardly recorded. Paper, postage, and production
costs are up. Your circulation has increased to over
twenty-five thousand—a phenomenal accomplish-
ment for a regional magazine. Add to that the prob-

lems of an insufficiently paid staff, an unsatisfactory agreement with a computer billing firm, and my inability to devote the necessary amount of time. You need a full-time business manager or publisher, Kate. Not just an attorney who doubles as an accountant.''

Kate knew Darrel hadn't been paid nearly enough for his services. ''I'm sorry. I didn't mean to give you a hard time. It's just that the past year has presented us with one fiscal headache after another, despite our increasing editorial and critical success. It's all a little dampening to the spirit.''

''Exactly why you need Alex,'' Darrel advised.

Wrong, Kate thought. That was exactly why she didn't need him. Alex would never be able to resist playing bossman to her slave, if only to get back at her for systematically failing to conform to his image of the perfect corporate wife. ''What's the bottom line, Darrel? How much power does Alex have at *M.W.*?''

''If he chooses, carte blanche.''

Kate walked out of the Springfield law office with a migraine the size of Mount Rushmore. Vaguely, she recalled signing all the clauses Darrel Hendrix had just dutifully reported on. At the time it had seemed such a silly formality to her. Nothing bad was going to happen to the magazine. Certainly at that point in time Alex would have done nothing to upset her world. He had been intent only on helping her, in any way he could. But that had been before the separation, her erroneously handled plea for an immediate no-fault divorce.

It was after six by the time Kate returned to the office. The staff had long since dispersed. Only the

lights in her room remained on. It didn't surprise her
to discover who was holding siege.

Alex Ryker was seated at her desk, feet propped up
negligently over the edge. In his hands were a dog-
eared bunch of files marked *Miscellaneous Financial*.
"Quite a filing system you have here," he murmured
disconsolately. Pausing to give her only the briefest
glance, Alex went back to examining the disjointed
group of papers.

Kate fought the resentment simmering just below
boiling point. She was there to sweet-talk him into departing, not start World War III. Taking a deep breath,
Kate sashayed across the room. Once his attention was
caught, she moved lithely around the desk and draped
herself languidly across the front of it, palms splayed on
either side of her. "Forget the files, darling. I have."

Alex glanced up as if he'd just wandered into a time
warp by mistake. There was a lengthy pause. Straight-
ening slowly, Alex tossed the *M.W.* paperwork aside
and put his feet flat on the floor. Before she could
draw a breath he had pulled her swiftly down into the
center of his lap. "I'm game if you are."

"Stop!" Kate put a hand firmly against his powerful
chest. "First, I want to work a few things out."

"Like my noninterference at *Missouri Woman*?"
Propelling her off his lap, Alex set her gently but
firmly aside.

After seven months' separation and all the hot and
heavy necking they'd done the night before, Kate had
expected him to be a little more interested. Alex
leaned back in his chair and waited for Kate to go on.
The audacious glint in his cobalt blue eyes dared her
to try and proposition him again.

The determination to save her magazine from his meddling kept her firmly in place, her tone deceptively composed. "You said you wanted to go away with me for a few days. Are you still interested?"

"That all depends," Alex drawled, dark brows raising in amused pique at her businesslike attitude. "What are you offering me?"

Put that crassly, it wasn't necessary for her to answer. Bored, Alex reached for the notes he'd been scrawling. "Like I said, Kate, your files are a mess."

"We have no regular secretary. Everyone is required to do her own filing. Naturally, we sometimes get a little behind."

"The least they could do is file under the same system!" he snorted.

Kate moved to sit on the edge of her desk. "Look, Alex, it's not as if we don't appreciate what you've offered to do for us here. I'm just not sure what you can do in the space of a week or two."

Shoving back his chair, Alex got up to pace restlessly around the room. "I know. I had the same thought when I first got to look at your files. It would take a bulldozer to dig you out of the disorganization here, Kate."

Music to her ears! "Then you've given up on trying to audit *M.W.*?" Hello Arabian nights, good-bye Alex!

"Not exactly." Alex's dark lashed gaze flickered over the length of her. "I've decided to extend my stay." There was a silence as he watched her reaction to the news. "I called Southwestern Oil today. As of this morning, I am on leave of absence."

Kate sat down, the wind knocked out of her. "How

long?'' The prediction for *M.W.*'s future looked grim.

"Six weeks. Naturally, I'd like to take more." He cast another disparaging look at her cluttered files, the enormous amount of unstructured, unsorted paperwork on her desk. "But I do have a commitment to the regional office where I was assigned. Even this short hiatus was not looked upon favorably."

"Then why take any time at all?" Kate tried to hide the relief lacing her voice. "As you said before the divorce can wait." Forever, if she could just get him away from her magazine. "Business first, right, Alex?" And Southwestern's Riyadh office had beckoned him back.

The corner of Alex's firmly chiseled mouth lifted in a sardonic grin. Wordlessly, he strolled to her side, ran a caressing finger down the pleated slit of her skirt. "You'd like that wouldn't you, Kate?" He prompted, very low. "For me to waltz back out of your life, leave you and *Missouri Woman* alone."

There was no way she could deny it. Running a hand idly through the thick gold layers of her hair, Kate forced herself to meet his glance equably. "I never thought you would exercise your option to publish *Missouri Woman*, Alex."

His stare was grim. "I never thought I'd have to."

"Then why try?" They both knew he was just doing it in an effort to get at her for refusing to follow him to the ends of the earth. "You know your place is with Southwestern Oil."

"Is it?" His voice was silky with challenge. "Months ago you said it was here with you." Desirously, the hand on her thigh traversed higher. Before Kate could stop him, it had trespassed between the revealing slit of skirt, closed seductively around the sheerness of a stockinged leg.

Kate's heart was pounding and where his hand gently cupped her leg a tiny electric jolt had started. She fastened her eyes on the cranberry and silver striped design of his tie, but she could think of nothing but his touch, his kiss, how much she still wanted to make love to him despite their personal differences, how much it would undoubtedly hurt her if she did let things progress swiftly to intimacy. In the whole time Alex had been back, he had not once mentioned love. Yes, he wanted her physically. He did not want a divorce. Yet he was no longer wearing his wedding ring. And as for his attachment to her, he felt the same passionate possessiveness about his favorite fishing rod.

Alex saw the lightning swift refusal in her gold-flecked eyes. "I see," he said coldly. "You won't sleep with me out of wifely duty or even friendship." He distanced himself physically as he spoke. "But you will lay it all on the line for *Missouri Woman*. Interesting, Kate, though hardly admirable."

His harsh words stung. More, they prodded her impulsively into finishing what she'd previously been too fainthearted and honest to really pursue.

"Oh, look, Alex. Couldn't we just forget about the magazine for a moment and settle our marital differences some other way?" Sliding off the desk, she walked over to him, reached up to affectionately and unnecessarily adjust the knot of his tie.

"I know you're angry with me." Kate's voice carried the breathy inflection of the whimsical television blonde. "Sometimes I don't even blame you." That was a lie.

"You don't, do you?" Alex mocked her honeyed tone. The back of his hand came up to touch her cheek, run tenderly down the feminine line of her jaw. Kate schooled herself to remain oblivious to the sensuality of his touch. This was her last trump. It had to work.

"We could let bygones by bygones," Kate whispered, lowering her tawny lashes with a southern belle sweep. "Get back together. Go away. Forget the magazine and the problems here. Isn't that what you wanted, why you came back? So we could spend a little time alone, no business, no interruptions, no phones?" Maybe by the time they returned it would be time for him to leave.

It was a moment before Kate dared meet his gaze. Alex's reception was a thousand times more chilly than she had anticipated. Alex had never been easily fooled. The Mae West come-on had not acted in her favor, not when just seconds before she had genuinely frozen at his touch.

Alex trailed a compromising finger down the neckline of her silk blouse, genially loosened the third, fourth, and fifth buttons. Only because of her pride and the fate of *M.W.* could Kate remain mutely passive. The truth was, knowing his motives she wanted to haul off and slap his implacably handsome face!

A searching hand explored the trembling curves within, lingered possessively on the scented hollows of her flesh, explored the tremulous raising and lowering of her chest with each breath she took. "I take over the magazine first thing tomorrow, Kate," he purred softly. "Of course if you'd like to pave the way for smoother editor-publisher relations..."

"Ooooh!" Kate whirled away with a stomp of her high-heeled foot. "How could you do that to me! Pretend to be—" She floundered, unable to describe the treachery he had just perpetrated upon her.

"Amenable?" Alex supplied rakishly, the only indication of his anger the faint clenching and unclenching of a tiny muscle in his jaw. Icy blue eyes covered her from head to toe as he drawled his final point. "I guess you could say I've had lessons from the best."

Kate had stormed home, more worked up than ever before. How like Alex to play her along, make her think he just might be inclined to work out some sort of business deal concerning the magazine just to see how far she would willingly go, then calmly inform her "No deal." Well, she might have boxed herself into a corner legally at the magazine via that partnership agreement she'd signed, but there was no such entanglement at home. Married or not, there was no written dictate that said they had to share quarters and she didn't intend to anymore.

Kate was in the bedroom throwing everything she owned into a collection of suitcases, trunks, and boxes when Alex walked into the house half an hour later. He called her name twice, and then when she failed to answer, strolled nonchalantly down the hall to find her. His easy demeanor didn't sway in the least when he saw what she was up to. Crossing one leg across the other, he leaned cheerfully against the jamb. He took another moment to survey the amount of belongings she had packed.

"Need a hand? I'm great with damsels in distress."

"I'll bet you are." Kate sent him a glare that would have melted Greenland and continued tossing lingerie into a bag. Undeterred, Alex blithely surveyed the moving preparations. He whistled at a particularly skimpy piece of lace. Kate blushed, but studiously ignored him as she struggled with the reluctant zipper to her tote.

Alex strolled closer. "I hate to be the one to break it to you, Kate, but you're never going to fit all of this into that sporty little RX-7."

He had a point, but there was no reason he should know how unnerved she was by his decidedly sensual, thoroughly disruptive presence. "Actually, Alex, I'd planned to commission you to carry the extra suitcases on your back and run alongside the car."

Alex erupted into laughter. When he'd recovered, he demurred, "I'd be glad to volunteer the services of my jeep."

"No, thanks."

"Can't walk through any hotel lobby with that hanging out of a zippered tote. You'd be labeled a scarlet woman in no time." Skillfully, he extracted in one easy second what she'd been struggling over for two minutes.

Kate snatched the filmy burgundy garment from his hand. When held up to the light, more sunbeams than Kate wanted to count filtered through the skimpy teddy. The fact that Alex knew darn well what she looked like in it did not lessen her flushed reaction.

Light hands on her shoulders, Alex turned her to face him. He let his eyes drift to her trembling mouth.

"I don't want you to go," he murmured softly. "Surely at least that much between us is understood."

Kate tried to fight the sensations flowing through her at his probing gaze, the tempestuous emotion neither seemed able to verbally express.

"When are you going to admit how much you want me, Kate?" Alex whispered, very low. "Call an end to this ridiculous charade and invite me back into your life, into your bed?"

The words were like ice-water on her already battered senses. Ducking his grip, Kate went back to the business of packing. "I wish you'd go back to the desert from which you came!" she snapped.

"No doubt," Alex parried whimsically. "But what would you do without my aid?" He peered into the canvas tote, checking out the contents thrown inside. "Do you really think these shoes ought to be on top of all that lace?"

Exasperation hissing through her teeth, Kate removed the heels and tossed them into the nearest cardboard box. "If you'd stop following me around, I might be able to concentrate on what I'm doing."

He moved closer, capable hands coming up to curve soothingly around her slender waist. Against her protests, his lips trailed down the exposed arch of her perfumed neck, lingered persuasively against her madly beating pulse. "Then you admit I drive you to distraction."

"I admit no such thing!" Kate stalked stiffly past.

Alex traipsed after her, grinning at the flaming blush on her cheeks. "Moving out won't help, you know. You're still going to have to see me at the office every day. Probably will have to work even later than we would have anyway if you insist on distancing yourself this way."

"On the other hand," Kate surmised coldly. "Think of all the things we could get done here. Together, alone, with no distractions or interruptions of any kind. Forget it."

"The sooner we finish our work together, the sooner I'll be able to leave."

"You're just doing this to get close to me," Kate shot back fiendishly. He was using *M.W.* to get back into her bed.

Without warning, Alex looked almost above the argumentative exchange. "Will you get off that? I'm trying to help your organize your magazine!"

Kate wasn't fooled by that look of choirboy innocence. "You're trying to get into my pants!"

Alex laughed. "Would it work?"

Kate counted backwards from one hundred. When she reached fifty-one she felt calm enough to speak. "The answer is no, Alex. To everything."

"Come on, Kate." Alex continued to persuade. "I'll sleep in the guest room. We're both adults, capable of living here as friends. Loosen up."

Kate thought about the money a hotel would cost, money she didn't have. Leasing an apartment was also out of the question. There was no way she could currently afford the required deposits. Nor did she want to commit herself to a year's responsibility rentwise when in all likelihood Alex would be leaving again shortly.

Alex's generosity knew no bounds. "What the heck, Kate," he offered facetiously. "I'll even go you one better and offer you a free nightly massage."

"Peppermint oil and roving hands I can do without, Alex."

Dark brows arched, aiming to please. "Wintergreen? Musk? Seriously, Kate." A gentle masculine hand clamped over her wrist and stopped her headlong flight. "Irreconcilable differences or no, can't we manage to salvage something from the two years we've had? Friendship? Mutual respect? Just a little bit of understanding?"

Kate could not deny she had missed his companionship, the spontaneity and humor of their coexistence. Nor was she able to ignore the tight knot of emotion in her throat his tender words had prompted.

"Oh, all right," she said with a weary sigh. "But only on the condition you behave."

"*Moi?*" Alex crossed both hands to his chest.

"Yes, you!" The sparkle in his eyes confirmed Kate's every suspicion.

For years women had paid homage to the fact that the way to a man's heart was through his stomach. Kate had never really believed that, but under the circumstances it did seem an ideal time to test the theory personally. Although Alex Ryker's appetite in the bedroom may have been wildly imaginative and hedonistic, when it came to the feeding of his six foot plus frame he wanted only the tried and true. Meat, potatoes, plenty of green and yellow vegetables, and occasionally a wedge of hot homemade apple pie or a glass of milk. Kate intended to see he had to go to the local diner to get them, beginning that evening.

"I didn't know you were taking night classes."

Alex strolled languorously into the kitchen two hours later. He paused. "This is a chemistry experiment, isn't it? Biology? Home ec? Consumer advocacy?"

"Try dinner." Kate sliced tofu into diagonal cubes, then turned her attention to deveining the shrimp. "I promised I'd help Fran Wilson test some of the recipes for the February issue."

"Oh." Alex stared dismally down at the stack of peapods on the counter. "Is that it?" A look in the freezer confirmed it also bare, except for the frost-encrusted Stouffer's lasagna.

"For dinner? Yes." Kate sent him a guileless look. "Of course you're welcome to go out."

"And miss this epicurean delight, Kate? Don't be silly." Fastening a speculative glare on her, he folded his arms across his chest. "Now, what can I do to help?"

Kate tossed him a package of peapods. "Try rinsing these off while I make the marinade." With more than her usual concentration, she measured soy sauce and sesame oil into a bowl.

"Well, so much for the formaldehyde." Alex eyed the bean curd suspiciously as he cheerfully went about his assigned chore. "Why don't you test the recipes during normal working hours? Isn't that Fran's job?"

Kate walked over to check the simmering shrimp. "*Missouri Woman* doesn't have a test kitchen there at the magazine. Fran works at home when she can, but a lot of days she has to come into the office to meet with authors and check the layouts and so forth. At night she has to feed two teen-age boys. Needless to say, neither Tim nor Randy is wild about acting as guinea pigs."

"That much I can understand," Alex muttered, checking out the chalk-colored curd. "What did you say this stuff was going to be?"

"Chilled shrimp dish." Kate slid the marinated dish into the refrigerator to cool. "Though if we run it, we'll come up with a more original name."

Alex defected soon after, mumbling something about needing time to get properly psyched-up for the "testing." Kate figured he wanted to get out of the dishes, and went about mopping up the counters and loading the dishwasher. When finished, she removed her apron, smoothed her white silk shirt and trim navy blue skirt. In her effort to keep things as formal as possible between them, she had retained her business attire, her only concession to her time off a pair of fuzzy bright peach house slippers. Scooting across the no-wax powder blue kitchen floor, Kate realized the worn houseshoes were as unsexy as they were comfy.

"I must admit I do prefer those stunning legs in heels."

Kate looked up to see Alex lounging in the doorway. That he'd obviously been watching her for some time brought a scarlet flush across her cheeks.

He, too, had not changed from his suit slacks and pearl gray silk shirt, had simply taken off the tie, rolled up the sleeves and loosened the first several buttons on the clinging gray dress shirt. The result was an even more devastatingly virile, relaxed Alex.

Kate's glance moved eventually to the teal blue and white silk kimonos over his arm. "Where did you get those?"

"The attic." Alex tossed her the smaller of the two

matching garments. "Remember that costume party we went to at Darrel Hendrix's house last winter?"

It would have been hard to forget. "The one where you entertained everyone with your impression of two geisha girls giving Bigfoot a massage and played all three parts yourself?"

Alex gestured sheepishly. "So I had a little too much saki and got carried away."

They both had. And the memories of what they had done later when home before a roaring fire still burned Kate's face.

But he didn't give her much time to recall. "Well, wait until you see what I've got lined up for us now!" Grabbing her wrist, Alex directed her enthusiastically back through the elegant formal dining room, down the hall toward the living room. A miniature blue and white *shojii* screen barricaded the hall. Kate bent to pick up the eight and a half by eleven inch piece of blue construction paper. It had some interestingly bizarre and original chalk scrawls across front and back. Not exactly bona fide Japanese art work, Kate decided, but close enough for Alex's purposes.

"That's a *shojii* screen," Alex announced unnecessarily, replacing the construction paper carefully. "And don't cross that portal until you've taken your shoes off."

Unbidden, passionate memories crowded Kate's mind, sending a warm flush of excitement all the way to her toes. How could she have forgotten what an adventure it was having him home?

"Wouldn't want to spoil the mood, hm?" Kate asked.

"Ah, come on, Kate." Alex walked into the room,

put an old record of *South Pacific* on to play. "As close as I could get to geisha," he explained. "Where's your spirit of adventure?" Evidently, he still had his. He was already unbuttoning his shirt. Kate swallowed. "Alex, I don't think this is such a hot idea!" He wasn't going to stand there and undress entirely, was he? she thought. He was.

Swiftly, she turned her back. As heat crowded her face, the strains of "Some Enchanted Evening" filled the room.

Alex continued to persuade, "How can you possibly hope to give those Japanese recipes a fair shake unless you're in the proper mood to test them?"

Kate knew what he was gunning for, and it wasn't the blue ribbon of the county fair or fair reporting practices. The rasp of the zipper followed, along with the clinking of his pants and belt hitting the floor. Moments later when Kate dared turn back around, Alex was draped seductively along the length of the stone fireplace that occupied one wall of the living room. The silky blue and white kimono clung to every rippling muscle of his tall lean physique. Enjoying her gaze, Alex demurely pretended to adjust the loosely tied belt of the floor length silk robe. Kate wondered what if anything he had left on beneath it. Surely not socks, shirt, or pants as clothing on the floor attested.

"Of course if you're afraid to be here with me under these conditions..." Alex demurred, lifting his shoulders indifferently. He could understand it if she were not of the same hardy strength of character as he.

Kate sighed. There was only one way to handle this tiger and that was to grab him by the tail. "Well, if

you put it that way," she relented with uncharacteris-
tic indolence. "As long as you remember the ground
rules."

Alex raised both hands in surrender. "No trespass-
ing unless invited." His Marx brother gaze made a liar
out of him even as he spoke. But Kate wasn't de-
terred. She knew how to quench those fires. "Wait
right here, darling," she purred kittenishly. "I'll be
back before you know what hit you."

It took Kate awhile to find what she wanted. Fortunately for her immediate purposes, she never threw
much of anything away, and after twenty or thirty minutes, had managed to uncover the necessary items.

Stripping off the routine business clothes and her
usual sexy silky lingerie, Kate donned an old pair of
Alex's thermal underwear and matching long-sleeved
knit shirt. To help support the sagging elastic of the
ankle-length pants, Kate slipped on a pair of bright
red jogging shorts. A hot pink and lavender striped
tank top conveniently took care of the clinging transparency of the material across her breasts. Two pairs
of socks, one green and rust argyle, the other classic
black and orange striped sweat, covered her feet. Kate
pulled the bulk of her hair back into a crooked ponytail on the right side of her head, artistically leaving
several large tufts of tawny hair hanging at odd angles.
A blue and white sweatband was tied around her forehead. Large butterfly earrings she had received as a
joke dangled almost to her shoulders. Belting the silky
teal and white kimono loosely around her waist, Kate
squared her shoulders and started out of the bedroom
towards the living room.

The hall was darkened seductively, as was the rest of the house. Two dim lights glowed in the living room on either side of the sofa. A fire burned softly in the grate. *South Pacific* was still playing, although by now they were on side two. Hearing her approach, Alex moved to switch it back.

Kate was already giggling but the look on his face when he turned around and saw her leaping over the *shojii* screen tore it. He blinked, shook his head as if that would somehow help, and then blinked again. Unfortunately, no matter how hard he tried to mentally adjust his vision, her attire remained the same.

"Are we having dinner or preparing for a nuclear attack?" Alex asked dryly at last.

Kate had to bite her lower lip hard to keep from bursting into gales of self-satisfied laughter. Bowing clumsily, she padded on into the room, Japanese style. "The table looks lovely." She paused to admire the silver and china he had selected from the dining room cabinet.

Having recovered, Alex gestured magnanimously towards the cushion on the other side of the low slung coffee table he'd positioned next to the fire. "Thanks. If you look real hard you can probably see yourself in the dishes. Care for some saki?"

"Thank you, I believe I will." Kate settled herself demurely on the appointed cushion, trying hard to suppress a grin. Whatever his romantic game plan for seduction and or entrapment had been, she had effectively broken the mood. Which suited her purposes just fine.

"I wouldn't have believed it, but after all this time you can still surprise me," Alex sighed, switching off another light. Walking closer, he handed her the small crystal glass of Japanese liquor.

"Well, that makes two of us," Kate agreed languidly. Certainly, she had never expected Alex to come back or to pursue her at the rate he was.

"To better days," Alex tipped his glass in mock salute. His blue eyes said he was amused despite the crushed expectations.

Kate grinned, then added her own salute. "To independent ones."

Alex ignored the gibe. Strolling to the buffet, he returned with the cucumber and shrimp appetizers Kate had made earlier. Nestled in beds of crisp green lettuce, the marinated fish and vegetable dish was perfectly chilled, covered with a sprinkling of sesame seeds.

"Tell me more about *Missouri Woman*, how it's doing," Alex prodded at length. "What kind of audience are you trying to attract now? What has changed there in the months I've been gone?"

Kate speared a tiny forkful of shrimp, paying careful attention to the food's taste and texture, even as she talked. Fran Wilson would expect a complete and detailed appraisal. "Our audience is comprised of women from nine to ninety. We're still not on par with *Redbook* or *Today's Woman*. What sets *Missouri Woman* apart is the devotion to regional affairs. In other words, we're probably not going to run any pieces on California vacations since we make it a point to concentrate on matters, places, and people close to home."

He had served the first course, so Kate got up to retrieve the *suimono*, the clear Japanese soup redolent with thinly sliced mushroom, green onions, and lemon strips. It was hot and perfectly balanced with soy sauce and chicken broth.

"Do any fiction yet?"

Kate shook her head negatively. "No, though I'd like to see something begun. It's so difficult for new writers to get published credits, particularly with short fiction. Eventually I'd like to see *Missouri Woman* sponsor a talent search. And of course the two to four thousand word short stories are the perfect vehicle for translating into print how the women of our region feel about such vital issues as women's rights, the ERA, reduced aid to dependent children, job discrimination, and so forth."

"Would the stories have to feature feminist themes?" Alex asked curiously, pouring them each a little more saki.

"No," Kate shook her head. "That's one thing we do try to do at *M.W.*, Alex. Present both points of view. Naturally, I'm not going to print anything degrading to women. But I will print an editorial or essay regarding the opposition to the ERA as a vehicle towards achieving equality *if* it's articulate and well-written. *Missouri Woman* just tries to be there, present opinions and provide support."

Alex studied Kate intently, gaze made even darker when contrasted with the muted firelight around them. "Do you have any opposition to expanding the format?"

"More articles?" Kate shrugged. Providing they had the staff and the money to print them, she'd love it. "But I doubt we ever get to that place," she said glumly. "At least not in the near future." If she were honest, they'd be lucky to save it from fiscal failure.

Alex got up to retrieve the last and main dish. Chilled shrimp and tofu.

Alex glanced bravely down at the cubed chunks of bean curd. "Lucky for me we had some saki on hand." He poured himself another generous sample. "A health food addict I'm not."

Kate laughed. "Where's your spirit of adventure now?"

"Not bad," Alex pronounced finally when they had finished. Contrary to Kate's expectations, it had been rather good. Kate glanced over at the relaxed form of her estranged husband. The front of his silky kimono had jutted open during the course of their languorous discussions, revealing feathery clouds of dark chest hair. Recalling acutely the sensual touch of his hands, the strength of his arms, desire coursed through her like a fever. Yet her decision to remain platonically aloof stayed. Emotionally, Kate couldn't risk another sexual involvement with Alex Ryker. He demanded too much of her, then gave the same. The end result being that she depended upon and wanted him terribly, and she couldn't survive the hell of another parting, this time probably for good.

Alex finished the last of his saki.

"Do you think it's a little hot in here?" Kate asked abruptly, fanning her suddenly scarlet face. Maybe they were sitting too close to the fire.

"No, but then I'm not dressed for maneuvers with the National Guard," Alex drawled, amused at her swift alcohol-induced discomfort. Before Kate could protest, he was around the side of the low slung coffee

table, efficiently untying the loose knot of her silky
kimono. "Here. Let me help you get this off."

"No, really, I'm fine." Kate moved dizzily to protest.

"You'll be much cooler if we just get the outer layer
of clothing off," Alex soothed, discarding the kimono
conveniently out of reach. "There now, isn't that better?" Without warning, several overstuffed pillows
were cushioning her head.

"I don't—"

In the resulting shifting of positions, his own robe
opened. Kate viewed miniscule black briefs, an ocean
of wiry masculine arm and leg. "Oh, no," she half-
moaned, half-sighed.

"Oh, yes," Alex whispered back. With his free hand
he loosened the wildly positioned ponytail of layered
hair, discarded both covered elastic fastener and
braided sweat band. Tawny gold hair was smoothed
velvetly into place. The tawdry earrings were carefully
removed, tossed aside.

But when Alex reached for the double layer of
clothing either north or south of her waist, Kate rebelled. "No." Beyond that, he had promised to behave!

Alex's mouth slid over onto hers, stilling her protests, wickedly robbing her of breath. Kate's arms
went up to push at his chest but somehow ended up
wound around his neck. Alex laughed deep in his
throat, then slid his lean body more fully over the
length of hers, positioning himself easily between her
long-johned thighs. "And you thought you had everything, including me, so under control," he teased.

Kate knew she'd had at least that much coming for

her earlier mood-spoiling ploy. She gasped as the wet-
ness of his tongue and teeth nibbled experimentally
on the gently sloping shell of her ear, trailed down the
slender column of her neck.

"You're being totally unfair about all this," Kate
whispered haltingly between subsequent kisses. "A—a
villian and a blackguard..." Her arms were weighted
down with the druglike stupor of too much saki, the
recalcitrance towards struggle of a body too long un-
sated. "... A lothario and a rake..." His teeth sank
lightly into the lobe of her ear, making her gasp even
more.

"Keep going," Alex murmured, tracing the trembling lines of her lower lip. Unexpectedly, his gentle
finger caught on the edge of her teeth, pulled testingly
and then slid even further into her mouth. "Call me a
heartless cad, a hellion... the only man you've ever
loved..."

Alex pressed fleeting butterfly kisses over the
corners of her eyes, the line of her cheek and dropped
to tease Kate's softly parted mouth. Never had there
been a gentler invitation to dally. "You don't know
what you do to me," he confessed raggedly against
the velvet of her skin. "Even in those outlandish
clothes." His hands explored the flat plane of her
abdomen, the soft curve of her hips; his thumbs
brushed at the tips of her breasts.

Kate shuddered at the sensations swirling through
her, the sensual core of arousal tugging from shoulder
to thigh. She shifted beneath Alex restively, needing,
wanting, enjoying his kiss, the touch, taste, feel of his
mouth pressing down, then moving lightly against her
own. "I want to see if my memory is as good as I

think," he whispered, holding Kate close, tangling his fingers through the layers of her hair. "If the weave of the kimono is rough when compared to the velvet of your skin, the petal softness here and here and here..."

Two layers of trousers, short and long, were stripped off. Alex removed the last of the interfering garments, between them. The silk of his discarded kimono and hers made a scattered bed of cloth among the pillows.

"I want you," Alex whispered.

Kate trembled under the slow caress of his hands, the determination in his eyes. When he lowered his head lazily to capture her mouth, Kate closed her eyes. Reaching up to entangle one compelling hand in the thick hair at the base of his neck, she drew him even closer.

Alex kissed her lingeringly, the gentle seductiveness of the embrace stealing the breath from her lungs. Shuddering with sensation, Kate whispered his name. Tenderly, she explored the muscled surface of his back, the solid warmth of his shoulders, let her fingertips learn anew the length of his spine, the small of his back, the narrow circumference of his waist, the strength in his taut lean hips. He countered wordlessly with a searching foray from breast to thigh that left Kate breathless and aching with desire.

Arching against him, Kate drew him even closer, her hand sweeping down to explore the pulsing contours of his masculine form.

"You're sure this is what you want?" Alex whispered raggedly against her hair. He elaborated when she'd lifted wide amber eyes to his: "If you're in my bed tonight, you're in it for the next six weeks. No locked doors whenever you're angry. No games.''

The cool objectiveness of his demand dissolved the magic. Kate's ardor fled. While she was trying to discover if there was any love between them, any real hope for a future together, *he* was thinking about his continued physical comfort for the next weeks!

"Boy, you really haven't changed, have you?" Snatching up her kimono, Kate flung it over her shoulders, shrugged into it agitatedly.

Alex got up to help her adjust the belt at her waist, looking even more virile and relaxed, if that were possible, despite his unclothed state, the passionate interlude that had just occurred, and ended, unresolved. When he tucked the gaping fabric demurely across her breasts, Kate noticed he didn't seem all that surprised by the turn of events. Had he sensed she wouldn't be able to comply with his unmitigated demands?

Noticing her gaze, Alex patted her fondly on the shoulder, then leaned forward to give her a swift, chaste peck on the forehead. "Better get some sleep, sweetheart," he murmured gently before departing. "Tomorrow's going to be a very long day and unless I miss my guess, you're going to need all your wits about you." Kate could have sworn he was humming softly beneath his breath as he strode down the hall, toward the guest room.

Chapter Four

Kate awakened to the tantalizing deep woods scent of aftershave, the warmth of a beard-roughened chin nuzzling her shoulder. Glancing down through sleep-blurred eyes, she saw tousled black hair, the bare muscularity of a masculine chest, and an angelically sleeping countenance.

"Alex Ryker, you promised!" So much for his being counted upon to remain in the guest room and bed, Kate thought.

Alex jolted upright at the sound of her voice, initially looking just as startled as she had felt discovering him. Taking in the circumstances, he recovered fast enough. Azure blue eyes drifted down to the sheet draped protectively across her torso, took in the clothing she, too, had neglected to wear. Immediately, Kate regretted her laziness the night before, the impetuous decision to just drop the kimono where she stood and climb into bed, sleep off the disastrous effects of saki and unfinished physical love. But it was too late to rectify her nakedness now. The first order of business was getting him out of her bed, swiftly, before anything else unexpected could happen.

"What are you doing here?" Kate asked. When had he joined her? Had he been there all night?

Disoriented, Alex raked a hand through his precision cut hair. Rearing back even farther, he pulled the sheet to his chin, held it in much the same fashion Kate clutched her end of the daisy print sheet. His firmly chiseled mouth formed an O of mock distress "Who are you and what do you want!"

"Quit clowning around, Alex!"

"Oh, oh! You're after my virtue, I just knew it!" He continued playing the maiden in distress.

Tawny lashes shut. Kate took a deep breath, trying hard to remain unamused. "What are you doing here?"

Alex dropped the pose. "I don't know." He picked up the sheet, wiggled his toes, and glanced downward. "It must have been my feet that carried me here. Actually," he continued at her unblinking glare, "I've been having these nightmares . . ."

"Out!" Kate pointed towards the door, maintaining the draping of modesty with her end of the yellow and white sheet.

"And then there's the sleepwalking. The unbridled fantasizing and—"

Kate reached threateningly for the nearest possible weapon, a fuzzy peach-colored house slipper that had seen better days. "You've got one minute, Ryker."

Alex laughed. Both hands raised in surrender. "You win." He strode across the room in all his naked glory, leaving Kate with quite a mental image to carry with her the rest of the day.

"If you're trying to drive me insane, it is working." Kate stood in the entrance to their kitchen, watching

Alex slide the last of the previous evening's dishes into the dishwasher. He had showered and changed into striking black suit pants, crisp white shirt, coordinating black and silver striped tie. His shirt-sleeves were rolled to elbow length, the jacket off and draped across a nearby chair. A ridiculously frilly powder blue apron was tied around his waist.

He paused to give her a thoroughly appraising look, taking in the dusky rose suit, the white Irish linen blouse, with the scarlet hand embroidery that decorated its cuffs, throat, and pleated button front. The deepening of his blue gaze said Kate looked terrific.

"Insanity is not what I want from you, Kate," he remarked finally in a low voice laced with sybaritic persuasion. "But then I think you know that."

Unhurriedly, he added soap to the dishwasher and started the machine. Kate watched wordlessly as he removed the apron, rolled down the sleeves, and shrugged into the well-fitting suit jacket with the same languid ease. Fastening a solid gold cuff link at his wrist, Alex hazarded a glance at his watch. "We've got time to stop off and have some breakfast before we go into the office."

"Sounds fine to me," Kate agreed. Anything to circumvent the time they spent alone. Because she was falling in love with him again, head over heels, disastrously, in love. And Kate didn't want to risk that kind of emotional blitz, did not want to be left picking up the pieces of a career-shattered relationship when Alex went back to his work, and the Middle East, six short weeks into the future.

But he wasn't making it easy for her to stay uninvolved.

Walking into a crowded coffee shop on Alex's arm at seven A.M. brought back a lot of memories for Kate, most of them excruciatingly good. In the past it had been a capper to a usually glorious night of lovemaking. That morning it was the prerequisite to impending managerial doom for *Missouri Woman* magazine, and the first male authority on the all woman staff.

It wasn't until they were nearly finished with their meal, though, that Alex began specifically cluing her in on his plans for *M.W.* "The books must be done immediately, of course. I also made a list of my own objectives for *M.W.* I'd like to see the implementation of your own computer as well as a new data-entry system. Stronger accounting and justification of expenses, both for individual editors and the set-up as a whole. Paper, typewriters, pens, long-distance phone bills." He arched a reproving black brow. "Yours, Kate, seem to be unusually high."

"Don't start with me, Alex. Not before nine."

Tactfully, he ignored her sarcasm. "On supplies alone you could be saving at least thirty percent of what you are currently paying if you bothered to search aggressively for the best discount. Then comes the question of..."

Teeth gritted in distaste, Kate listened for several more minutes. But when he began to talk about packing up and moving to more spacious, attractive quarters, she interrupted. "Now, wait a minute, Alex. I will admit we do need organization financially— maybe even in regard to our files. But as for the rest of it—"

"Yes?" His glare cut her to the quick, just daring

her to try and refuse him anything he thought would
bolster *Missouri Woman*.

"I think you're going too fast," Kate said finally,
deciding to save the rest of her objections for the
magazine's attorney Darrel Hendrix. Maybe he could
talk some publishing sense into the corporate boy
wonder.

Alex leaned back nonchalantly, studying Kate across
the litter of dishes and discarded napkins. At that second he seemed completely unaware of the clink of
glassware and silver around them, the steady hum of
voices.

"There is always a resistance to change, Kate. We
encounter it every time we audit a management team
or make suggestions and revisions in policy as it
stands. Your staff will undoubtedly feel like they've
been hit by a tidal wave at first. But that will pass."

Alex paused, for the first time seeming to resent
the fact they were still emotionally, personally involved. In any other case, he would simply be able to
pull rank on her, fire the dissenter and move on.

Not this time, Kate thought complacently.

Alex read the penchant for trouble in her guile-free
expression. The corners of his mouth slanted into a
warning frown. "You can make this easy on yourself,
Kate," he counseled. "You can set an example of cooperation and professionalism for your staff. Or you
can fight me.

"Personally, I wouldn't recommend the latter,"
Alex stated silkily at length, reading the mutiny in her
wide gold-flecked eyes. "But it's up to you. And,
Kate?" He paused again as he stood and helped her
with her chair. "Those shoe boxes where you file

your personal business receipts are really going to have to go."

"As you know, *Missouri Woman* has been in financial trouble for some time, always operating just above bankruptcy." Alex Ryker addressed the staff grimly, then went on to explain the scope of their financial and structural difficulties in very detailed yet understandable terms, covering everything from lax administration to nonbudgeting and overspending. "Before we can even begin to recoup our losses, drastic organizational changes will have to be made..."

Kate stood mutely in the background, watching the faces of her loyal but underpaid staff. No one welcomed Alex's interference, yet no one was openly recalcitrant. She wondered how long the calm would last, if they would eventually become so enamored of Alex's personal charm and dazzling business savvy that they would forget to revolt. Would the standards and high ideals *Missouri Woman* had always represented be pitched in favor of crass commercialism and higher salaries?

Alex was routinely handing out mimeographed instruction sheets. Kate studied hers dismally. Certainly no one could accuse Alex of coming unprepared.

With only a cursory glance in her direction, Alex continued quietly. "By the end of the day I expect a detailed accounting of expenditures from each of you, as well as a typed, double-spaced description of your job. Because I am unfamiliar with your duties and preferred types of assignments, this should also contain a brief biography, complete with educational backgrounds, job experience, future aspirations, how you feel efficiency or morale could be improved here at the magazine, where you expect to be career-wise five or ten years from now, where you would like the magazine to be."

"Sounds like a term paper for school," Barb Walsh muttered, tossing her pen onto the battered wooden conference table.

Alex lifted his brow slightly as he turned towards the production editor and took in her truculent scowl. "I agree," he said calmly. "However it is the speediest way to proceed under the circumstances." He paused again. "Anyone who would like to jump ship may do so now."

A stony silence fell. Kate looked down at the paper in her hands, all too aware of the rebellion fast brewing. Myra Benton thumbed unenthusiastically through the new assignments, frowning as she saw the extent of new information Alex was commanding. And as usual, she could be counted upon to argue about it. "What about the rest of our duties here?" the twenty-three-year-old health and beauty editor argued grumpily. "I don't know about everyone else, but I've got appointments scheduled for the rest of the morning."

"Hear, hear," Fran Wilson muttered, also apparently at a loss as to where to begin under the staggering amount of new paperwork.

"Cancel them, and anything else you may have scheduled for the rest of the week." Crossing his arms against his muscular chest, Alex refused to relent. "Take your phones off the hook. As of right now, the magazine is closed and will remain so until we sort through the necessary items."

More grousing coursed through the crowded conference room. Alex turned to his wife. "Kate, I want a detailed accounting of advertisers and revenue expected." He sent her a look when she frowned. "Categorized alphabetically."

Kate was about to tell him what he could do with his lower case *a* when she noticed everyone else was looking at her, waiting to see how she would respond. "Yes, sir." Damn him for ever putting her in that position, she steamed inwardly. Having to act outwardly accepting of something she screamed against with every cell in her body.

"Well, what are you waiting for?" Alex dismissed the staff brusquely. "Unless I'm mistaken, you've got considerably more than a full day's work ahead of you."

"Did you have to be so hard on them?" Kate asked as soon as everyone had scattered to their appropriate offices. The normally clamorous office resembled a tomb—for unknown editors.

"No. I could let them all stand in the unemployment line, which is exactly where they would all be in another month or so if I hadn't taken time off and the energy to thoroughly audit and reorganize this firm."

There was a silence between the two of them that went wider and deeper than their marital separation of seven months. Feeling her resentment, Alex wisely decided not to pursue her objections. "Get busy, Kate. I want those lists of advertisers this afternoon. And unless you want me standing over your shoulder every step of the way, and rummaging through the rest of your disorderly files, you'll see that it is done. Pronto."

Because Alex had commandeered Kate's office for

his temporary headquarters in enemy camp, she was forced to wordlessly grab the necessary files and closet herself in the conference room at the end of the hall. Just making a rough list of advertisers took the better part of two hours, categorizing them by monthly, quarterly, and one-shot deals, another three. She was still working on expected amounts of revenue for the rest of the year when Liz Shaw came stealthily in the door. Aside from the occasional pecking of a typewriter or thumbing of papers, the *Missouri Woman* offices were ominously still.

"How's it going?" Kate glumly took half the chicken salad sandwich Liz handed her. Was it lunch time already?

The pretty redhead rolled her eyes. "I can see why you were so opposed to Alex exercising his publishing option. Is he always this high-handed?"

"When it comes to business? Worse," Kate muttered, adding up some more figures on her pocket calculator. "How's the staff taking it?"

"Three are ready to sign petitions and declare mutiny. The other three plan to spend some time scanning the St. Louis classifieds." Liz laughed. Apparently, she didn't take anyone else's grumbling as seriously as they did.

"I notice you didn't count yourself in that tally," Kate said dryly, jotting down another notation.

"I figured I'd ride out the storm." Liz finished her coffee contemplatively, glancing over at the pile of paperwork and assorted files Kate was still laboring over. "Have you been working on that list of advertisers all this time?"

"Yes." Kate shuffled her papers into the appropriate order. "And it probably isn't as complete and detailed a list as Alex had in mind either." But that was his tough luck.

"When are you going to do the rest of your paperwork?" Liz winked. "Your bio and career goals, the detailed accounting of expenses?" Discarding her used cup into the trash, Liz walked to the door, peered out to see if the coast was still clear.

"As for career goals, I only have one," Kate replied, more serious than her smirk mirrored. "To get rid of the publisher. He knows my personal history, as well as professional. And as for the detailed accounting of expenditures? Well, let's just say I've already turned in my shoe boxes full of receipts."

Five o'clock came and went, then six, and still no one moved from the pile of paperwork inundating their desks. At seven they were all gathered in the conference room for an end-of-day briefing Alex had called. Since Kate had not spoken to Alex once since their last icy confrontation, she hadn't the slightest idea what it was about. Nor, she admitted, did she really care.

Alex didn't waste any time with amenities. "As of right now, overtime will be required of those wishing to remain on staff." Alex stated, resolutely handing each editor another set of forms and tasks to be completed. "These in particular, are due at nine tomorrow morning." There was a groan around the table, but Alex remained implacable. Shirt-sleeves rolled to his elbows, tie lowered several notches, there was no question Alex had been working every bit as diligently as his newly acquired staff. That did not necessarily lessen the rebellion brewing at his inordinate demands.

"Naturally, those who comply will be compensated financially." Casually, Alex revealed the bonuses. Kate saw several editors perk up immediately, which wasn't surprising considering the hefty amounts. "We'll also see about immediate cost-of-living raises," Alex finished, raking a restless hand through thick dark hair. "There is no question that every staff member here is grossly underpaid."

The staff waited, more biddable now. Alex went on to detail specifically how he planned to finance his actions, the drastic increase in advertising he wanted implemented immediately, how necessary it was for everyone to cooperate every step of the way, how grateful he was for every courtesy shown him thus far. Kate frowned, waiting for someone to jerk out their hanky and tell Alex they loved him too.

"Naturally, we'll be raising the cover price fifty cents an issue," Alex went on, ignoring Kate's open cringe of dismay. Fifty cents! Was he mad?

"Don't you think readers are going to resent the increase in price?" Liz interjected bluntly, tapping her pencil on the edge of the conference table.

"Not if we give them the full color, expanded format I have planned," Alex replied, obviously pleased someone had the foresight to challenge his quick, allegedly unstudied decision. "Naturally, I'll be open to suggestions from everyone on the staff as to where and how we might go about this, any specific editorial areas you feel are insufficiently covered now."

A murmur of pleasure rumbled around the conference table.

"Still, I doubt the increased cover price pays for much more than mailing, distribution, and production costs," Kate said calmly. "Even if you run more ads—"

Alex looked at Kate. One hand against his waist, he rubbed at the back of his neck wearily. "We're talking a minimum of fifty additional pages of ads for the February issue, Kate. And you're right, it will take at least that much to finance the expanded format."

"Fifty!"

"Right." He ignored the shrill displeasure in her voice. "Roughly one cent per page in terms of cost to the reader. And eventually I'd like to see even that number increased. For the record, Darrel Hendrix agrees with me. As do the other independent stockholders."

"You talked to them?" Kate was enraged.

"All forty percent of them this morning." His icy gaze seemed to say further: *Fight me on this, Kate, and you'll only be hurting yourself.* He had taken over *M.W.* now, and inch by inch he was shutting her out, subjugating her every authority in the magazine she had founded and supervised since infancy.

"As for work assignments turned in today"—gesturing behind him, Alex indicated two string-wrapped shoe boxes crammed full of paper— "whoever turned in these in lieu of expense vouchers is going to have to do them over." Alex tossed an ominously thick sheaf of the appropriate forms onto the center of the conference table, then hazarded a telling look at Kate as the *M.W.* staff grinned ear to ear. "I expect a signed completed voucher for every expense made during the past fiscal year." And on that note, the staff meeting was adjourned.

"Cute, Alex." Kate walked into her private office as soon as they were all dismissed. He followed, looking no happier about the current professional tension between them than she.

"I didn't think so." The door shut, giving way to a sudden uneasy silence. Kate swallowed and wondered abruptly if she might have pushed him too far by openly defying his instructions in front of the staff.

Her contrition faded as she noticed the newly organized appearance of her office. Alex had totally usurped her private quarters. Gone were the helter-skelter stacks of correspondence and articles to be edited that usually covered at least half of Kate's desk. Plants, belongings, handbag, suit jacket, had all been relegated to a small folding table in the corner of the room. *His* suit jacket was hanging over the back of *her* desk. His paper, pens, notes, and masculine scrawl were everywhere she looked. Even the room had the faint woodsy tang of his aftershave. For all the managerial authority he had left her he might just as well have kicked her out onto the street.

Noticing her scowl, Alex walked over to return the shoe boxes full of receipts. Dark brows raked up in mock repentance. "I had to work somewhere."

"How about somewhere west of the Pecos?" The suggestion slipped out before Kate could censure herself.

The easy grin faded. Kate knew the smartest thing was to extricate herself from the situation swiftly. But when she tried to move past him towards the door, he stopped her. One hand pressed lightly against the closed door he leaned over her warningly, enjoying the proximity the position allowed.

"I meant what I said this morning, Kate." His tone underlined every word. "I want a detailed accounting of expenditures for the entire year from every member of the staff. That includes you."

Kate ducked out from under the veil of his outstretched arm, uncomfortably aware of the tingling response his closeness had prompted. "I was busy," she defended herself cavalierly.

"So do it tonight."

Kate was so exhausted she could hardly see much less add. At some level she knew the fatigue was at least in part emotional, the stressful result of having him right across the hall from her all day long, fencing with him at night, waking up unexpectedly in the same bed, then wondering at his motives, and/or lame excuses. Yet she knew she had to maintain their physical and emotional distance. To do otherwise would be to court disaster.

"I'll do them tomorrow," Kate announced loftily as she dumped the boxes onto the small table he had assigned her belongings. Grabbing her coat and handbag, Kate headed for the door.

Alex did not move to let her pass. When she tried to brush by anyway, he reached insouciantly out and shifted her so she was standing right in front of him. "Tomorrow you'll be busy with other things. Do them tonight. Here or at home, I don't much care." His touch may have been gentle, but the firmly chiseled mouth was taut with resolution.

The building was suddenly much too quiet. Kate

became aware of the sounds of the other staff members leaving: doors shutting, lights being switched off, the laughter of a shared departure after a wearying day.

"Really enjoy playing Hitler to the underlings, don't you, Alex?" Kate used sarcasm to cover her unease, the fact that the working day had abruptly come to an end. And it was all too apparent by the change in Alex's gaze that he was quite prepared to take up at home where he had left off that morning.... "It must be a real trip juggling us around," Kate continued. "Especially when compared to the five million dollar budgets and extensive staffs you're used to managing."

Alex refused to be sidetracked from his gentle regard. "I'm trying to help you, Kate," he said softly. Pensively, he trailed a finger from her cheek to her chin, then gently tilted her face up to his. "Can't you at least trust me that much?"

Not when she knew he was planning to leave again in just a few short weeks, probably as heartlessly as he had before. "I don't want you running my life, Alex," Kate said stonily. "I don't want you publishing my magazine."

Wordlessly, Kate broke free of his light grip, turned and walked out the door, very well aware that the designated string-wrapped shoe boxes of receipts were still far behind.

Anger propelled her home. Fatigue and lingering depression directed her to the living-room sofa. Kate awoke what seemed years later.

"Come on, sleepyhead," Alex nudged her gently awake. "Sit up and have something to eat. Then you

can go on back and climb into bed if you want." He
grinned. "Alone."

From out of the fog came the blissful aroma of
steaming pepperoni pizza, the sensation of an ice-cold
drink being pressed into her hand. Kate took a sip of
Pepsi, and with a great deal of effort, blinked herself
entirely awake. The wall clock revealed it to be ten
o'clock.

"That late?" She stifled another yawn.

Alex handed her a plate of thick, crusty pizza, inundated with meat and cheese. "That late." His features
softened affectionately as he took in the rumpled
length of her trim suit. "You really were tired,
weren't you?"

Kate put aside her plate long enough to smooth
down her blouse and run a hand through her tawny
hair. "Evidently." She tucked a stockinged foot beneath her, settled the plate back onto her lap. "I never
meant to fall asleep, though." She yawned again.

Alex grinned. "Don't worry about a thing. I brought
your shoe boxes home for you."

Kate's bad mood returned. Alex laughed and victo-
riously got up to turn on the news. While they ate, he
revealed to her the findings of his initial audit.
"Frankly, Kate, I don't think you're in as bad trouble
as Darrel Hendrix first thought—just extremely unor-
ganized, lax about enforcing policy. Once an efficient
way of doing business is established, costs cut, as well
as a full-time business manager or publisher in my
stead appointed to ride herd on day-to-day operations
and make certain things never get this unbalanced
again, I imagine you'll be fine. In fact, you may be
able to give everyone a much deserved raise even

without the revenue from the additional advertising."

Kate heaved a big sigh of relief, silently blessed Alex for being able to tunnel down to the facts. "You're not staying more than six weeks then?" Kate didn't think she could deal with him on such an intense 24-hour level for very much longer.

"You know I have to go back." The admission tautened his jaw. Kate was silent, realizing the news of his departure didn't bring the relief she had expected.

"Now, about those receipts," Alex started again as soon as they had finished their meal. He ignored Kate's grimace of distaste. "I went over most of them for you at the office. But there are still some I just can't figure out, and like it or not you're going to have to help decipher."

"How are things on the home front?" Liz Shaw walked into Kate's office shortly after seven the next morning. "Or is it even safe to ask?"

"Sheer drudgery." Kate stretched, remembering the three additional hours she and Alex had spent going over and categorizing her list of personal and business expenditures. "Needless to say, no more shoe boxes," she finished dryly, pointing to the new multi-indexed filing system Alex had set up.

"That wasn't what I meant," Liz reproached.

"Good morning, ladies!" A youthful masculine voice interrupted. Kate and Liz looked at the intruder, exchanged a glance. Whoever the young blond interloper was, they didn't know him. He looked more like a California lifeguard fresh from a summer on the beach than any of their clients. "Which one of you beautiful ladies is Kate Ryker?"

Now they *knew* he didn't belong. Kate stood from behind her desk and extended a reluctantly welcoming hand. "I'm Kate Ryker," she said quietly. "What can I do for you, Mr. — ?"

"Andrew Brenner." The surfer pumped Kate's hand vigorously, giving her time to take in the sharkskin suit, elevator shoes, and too slick grin. "Pleased to make your acquaintance, ma'am."

"Likewise, I'm sure," Kate said dryly, shooting Liz another amused woman-to-woman glance. "What can I do for you, Mr. Brenner?" *Missouri Woman* was supposed to be closed, the phones off, the front door locked. She wondered how he had gotten in.

"Actually, I'm here to represent my boss." Extracting a printed card from his inner suit pocket, the young salesman placed a business address of the Hayes Heaven Used Car lot in her hands.

Kate sighed. Hayes had tried to arrange to see her personally again at least ten times the past week, but this was really too much.

"Mr. Hayes told me the two of you have a little trouble getting along." The salesman read her reaction accurately. "But I'm sure between the two of us we can work that out, pretty lady." His lascivious wink left no doubt as to how he thought he'd be able to manage the coup. Not about to miss the fireworks, Liz seated herself casually behind the file in the corner and propped her trousered legs up along the old-fashioned steam radiator.

Kate withdrew the hand he still held firmly in his puppylike grasp, and hesitated curiously. "Tell me, Mr. Brenner. Does you boss always send you out to conduct business for him? I assume of course you're here about his desire to advertise Hayes Heaven Used Cars in our magazine."

"That's right," Andy Brenner nodded, shaking his fluff of blond hair vigorously as he did so. "And no, as a mater of fact, Mr. Hayes doesn't go to this much trouble for anyone else."

"Then why me?"

The salesman shrugged. "I don't know."

"Does Mr. Hayes read *Missouri Woman?*"

"No."

"His wife then? Girlfriend? Daughter?"

"Hayes doesn't have any children,"Brenner replied. "And as for ex-wives or girlfriends, I don't think any of them can read." Brenner grinned, mentally recalling the entourage.

"Then why is he so determined to advertise in *Missouri Woman?*" Kate probed. "Particularly when I've told him time and time again I don't run ads on used cars." Sexist, discriminating, every approach he had sent Kate was extremely unpalatable.

"I don't know." Again, Andy Brenner shrugged his athletic shoulders. "Maybe he doesn't like to be turned down. All I know is he gave me strict instructions to see that you signed the ads he wants as soon as possible, and the longer the contract runs the better."

"Naturally, there's a hefty bonus in it for you if you succeed."

Brenner grinned, struck by Kate's insight. "Lady, I like the way you think!" Before Kate could recoup, he had both her hands, was pressing them towards his lips in what he obviously considered a suave, decidedly European manner. "Now, couldn't we discuss this in more intimate surroundings? Say lunch? Better yet, dinner, dancing...?''

"Sure. Any time you say." Alex Ryker lounged in the doorway startling them all. "Entertaining again, Kate?" His dark brows raked upward in mock reproach.

Brenner blushed as he turned to encounter Alex's disapproving stare. He gulped when Alex straightened the six-foot-plus form and sauntered languidly forward.

The sun-kissed salesman turned back towards Kate, hazarded a look at the suddenly wary Liz. "I thought the staff here was all women."

"Was." Alex clamped an intimidating hand over the young man's shoulder, then paused to identify himself as publisher and chief of all business affairs, including advertising.

"I see." Andy Brenner stammered and blushed his way back towards the door. "Well, since I only have authorization to deal with Ms. Ryker, I think I'll be going."

"Good idea." Alex made no attempt to dissuade. "Do you always do business with rakes?" Alex asked as soon as the surfer had departed. "The kid was hardly old enough to wipe his own nose!"

Kate grinned at the unusual display of jealously, shot Liz an arch look, deciding impetuously to pay her estranged husband back for a little of the grief he'd recently inflicted on her magazine. "Oh, I don't know. Andy Brenner's kind of cute. Of course the fitness club salesmen are the best." Kate winked at Liz, then finished with a low lecherous whistle meant to provoke.

"If you'll excuse us," Alex calmly escorted Liz to the door.

Tossing down her pencil, Kate waited until they were alone. "Did you need something, Alex?" she asked sweetly, still stinging over the way he had organized her office, usurping all control. "Perhaps a little more room at my desk? Like to commandeer my files again? Borrow my pencil sharpener? Ruin any respect or authority I might formerly have commanded at this magazine?"

"Upset because I kept you up half the night doing paperwork that should have been completed months ago?" Alex teased, seating himself on a corner of the desk they now reluctantly shared.

"I don't need you managing my time so closely." She fixed her gaze on a stack of unedited articles on the corner of her desk. If he wanted to organize the financial side of *Missouri Woman*, fine. She did not want him telling her or her staff what to do otherwise.

Alex waited patiently for her to run down her lengthy list of additional grievances. "And just how do you think audits are conducted?" he asked when she had finished complaining about what he had done to her office as well as day-to-day running of the magazine.

"I don't care how things are conducted at other companies!" Kate grated against his reasonable tone. Standing, she placed both palms flatly on the desk. "This is my company, Alex! A magazine I started and nurtured from infancy!"

"And no longer control," Alex interjected resolutely. "We can do this through the courts if you pre-

fer, Kate," he continued quietly. "I can sue you for-
mally for mismanagement, fraudulent accounting,
and whatever else I can get a lawyer to dig up. And
you can bet if it comes to that, I won't choose someone as kindhearted as Darrel Hendrix!"

Kate stared at him wordlessly, too upset to talk.
There was no doubt Alex meant every word. Vaulting
to her feet, she tried to move past. He slid around the
corner of the desk just as easily, placed a detaining
hand on her arm when she persisted in escape. After a
moment, Kate lifted her gaze to his.

"I won't tolerate anything less than your full cooperation from this point forward, Kate," Alex spoke
through clenched teeth. "I mean it. I've invested fifty
thousand dollars of my own savings into this. I'm not
going to see it go down the drain just so you can retain
some of your regrettably foolish pride!"

"Do you want me to quit?" Kate's rejoinder was
stormy. Although Alex wasn't hurting her in the
slightest, she knew she couldn't break his grip if she
tried.

"I want you to cooperate!" Moving slightly to the
left, he grasped her by the shoulders, forcing her head
up to his. "Damn it, Kate! Set a positive example for
your staff!"

"And if I don't?" Kate knew the moment the
words were out it was the wrong thing to ask. It
seemed her only defense against the powerful masculinity of his sinewy frame, the desire their proximity
and exasperated anger generated.

Alex released her, walked resolutely towards the
window behind her desk. A moment passed, and then
another. With one swift, compelling jerk of the cord,

the venetian blinds were raised. Alex stared out into another perfect autumn day.

"I gave you one day for open resistance, Kate. That's it. Any more and I'll fire you. It's just that simple."

The rest of the day brought even more havoc. Alex officially broke ties with the company that had been doing their billing and arranged to lease their own computer, as well as hire a systems programmer to work exclusively for *Missouri Woman*. New offices and furniture were arranged for, based on a bank loan that would be paid for in part by the raised cover price. Detailed, harsher expense tallying and temporary limit on all long-distance calls and business lunches finished up the afternoon. Kate was so frustrated and powerless she wanted to scream, at the very least send Alex scuttling towards the next transatlantic jet.

Kate left *M.W.* at an unprecedented four o'clock, drove straight home and fixed herself a cup of jasmine tea. Kicking off her shoes, she curled up on the sofa with a stack of local newspapers she'd been too busy to read. When Alex arrived home an hour later, she was still there, her tea untouched and cold, the papers yet unread.

He walked slowly into the darkened living room. His gaze roved casually over the length of her. Something flickered in his eyes before they became unfathomable. "We missed you at the afternoon staff meeting."

Remembering his threat, Kate wondered if he were going to fire her. Considering what was happening to *Missouri Woman*, she wished he would. "Under the circumstances I didn't feel I had much to contribute."

A muscle clenched in Alex's jaw, but his stance remained coolly relaxed. "The purpose of those twice a day meetings is so we can keep tabs on what every member of the *M.W.* team is doing during the transition, Kate."

For that much Kate was truly ashamed. Her intention had never been to make things harder on her staff. Heaven knew they'd stuck with her through thick and thin. "I'm sorry." Kate swallowed her pride with effort. "I didn't think." Again, she looked away.

Alex let out a heavy sigh, raked a hand through his hair and moved closer. He perched on the edge of the sofa, eyes straying to the line of her calves curled up neatly beneath her skirt. Reactions spread through Kate in a warm drift of awareness, tempering her anger, making it so much easier to forgive.

Alex reached over to curl his hands around her palm. Without warning, she realized the solid gold band was back on the third finger of his left hand. Catching the direction of her gaze, he tightened his grasp, letting the action say so much more than his words. Kate swallowed the emotion in her throat, while the intimacy of past love, shared moments together, and tender happiness drew her closer still. Gently, Alex lifted her chin to his. His mouth moved over hers tenderly, cementing the apology with a soft, meaningful kiss.

"What do you say we call a truce, Kate? Have at least one night, just you and me?" he murmured against the pliant contours of her mouth.

By mutual agreement they dined in the pleasant old English atmosphere of the Golden Lion Restaurant on state route 65. Kate wore a black crepe jumpsuit that hugged her slender frame and emphasized the trim shapeliness of her legs, the subtle curve of her hips. The straight neckline demurely covered the swell of her breasts. A sequined glitter black over-blouse, long-sleeved and high collared, covered the bareness of her shoulders. Thin strapped silver mules completed the outfit. A platinum chain adorned her neck, matching silver hearts her ears.

"You look lovely tonight," Alex murmured as he seated Kate in a velvet-backed chair. His gaze lingered on the glorious disarray of her tawny gold hair.

Kate murmured appreciatively and glanced down at the menu placed before her, fighting her own reaction to her husband's virile presence. In crisp black evening suit, he was even more potently attractive. "It's been a long time since I've enjoyed a night on the town."

"A long time since we've been out together," he agreed gently, watching the wary play of expressions across her face.

Taking a deep breath, she launched into the subject she'd been wanting to approach since his arrival home. "You're wearing your wedding ring again."

His gaze met hers levelly. "I never should have taken it off."

"You say that like part of a business agreement," Kate joked to cover her hurt at the pragmatic tone of his voice.

Alex's jaw jutted out uncompromisingly as he thought of the tumultuous months past, her efforts to obtain a swift, no-fault divorce. "Maybe to me it is. You're my wife, Kate. Whatever happens between us, either in our personal lives or at the magazine, *that* will never change.

And now he had the most powerful insurance policy of all, Kate thought, the publishing rights to *Missouri Woman* magazine.

Kate said little on the drive home. Alex watched her covertly as he drove, studying her beneath half-shuttered lids at every traffic light. Kate's amber eyes were circled with the shadows of exhaustion. She seemed sad, wary, ill at ease. Alex felt responsible. For leaving her, returning to the States and contributing to her sleepless nights, even for wanting her as much as he did. Capable hands gripping the wheel, he directed her sporty Mazda to their house in the hills.

"How about a nightcap? We could build a fire, have a brandy, put some old records on to play." Alex suggested amiably as he fitted his key into the lock.

Kate skirted past him, into the front door, up the stairs. She'd forfeited managerial control of her cherished magazine to him. That was enough for any one day or even week.

"No thanks, Alex. As you mentioned earlier this evening we do have a full day at *M.W.* tomorrow. And I am exhausted."

Her cool detached tone infuriated him. "The magazine first as always, hm, Kate?" Alex's tone may have been light but his tone was increasingly resentful. "Before us, before even something as simple as a shared brandy before the fire. How much longer are you going to punish me for trying to help?"

Forgiveness wasn't all he wanted from her and Kate knew it. "Interesting, Alex! Particularly since you're using *M. W.* to try and get back at me for refusing to follow you to the ends of the earth!''

Alex arched a brow. Kate cursed herself inwardly for allowing fatigue to goad her into the beginnings of a fight. She strode to the living room. To her fury, Alex refused to relinquish the easy grip he had held upon her arm since leaving the car and the action, instead of freeing her, merely towed him along beside her. Palm still encircling her silk-covered arm, he reached over to switch on a light. Obviously he was willing to continue the discussion until dawn if he thought it would settle the complicated dispute between them. But Kate knew it would take more than a simple long talk to end the fiery stalemate. It would mean one of them would have to give up a career.

Fiercely, Kate retained her composure. "I agreed you could sleep here, Alex, but only by default. Please don't put me in the position of having to refuse you physically or kick you out." *By court order,* Kate almost added, then stopped.

The masculine arm dropped. Alex opened his mouth as if to retaliate in kind, then thought better of it and strode directly to the bar. Breath suspended in her chest, Kate watched as he uncapped the brandy.

Abruptly feeling she had to say something, anything, to placate him and maintain the peace at least for that one evening, Kate said, "Look, I'm sorry if I've been upset. But you know how much *Missouri Woman* means to me and—"

Alex's face blazed with contempt. "Evidently a hell of a lot more than our marriage! Or me!" Frustration, hers and his, permeated the room as he sloshed brandy into a tumbler.

Kate's temper flared at the unjustness of the accusation. "Oh, come off it, Alex! Stop playing the masculine martyr! You know the only reason you're still here in Springfield is because of the challenge I present! If I'd gone to bed with you that first day you'd already be back in the Middle East carrying on for Southwestern Oil!"

Alex capped the brandy with more than usual care, but Kate was too distraught to notice the additional tautness beneath the lean, strong lines of his cheekbones. Dark brows arched above glittering ocean-blue eyes. "In other words, I'm just here for a little sexual R and R. Once I make love to you again, I'll be long gone."

"You said it!" Kate agreed.

There was a silence. Alex put the bottle of brandy back on the polished wooden surface of the bar, but made no effort to retrieve his drink. "Well, that ought to be one misconception easy enough to correct." The oak coffee table was moved close to the heavily draped picture windows, satiny throw pillows tossed to the carpeted floor. He knelt to light the prebuilt fire.

"What are you doing now?" Kate asked as he leisurely flicked off the lamps.

Alex did not pause until the room was bathed only in the dusky blue-yellow lights of the fire. Slinging off jacket, vest, tie, he moved to within inches of her, studied the sudden irregular rise and fall of her chest. Smoky blue eyes desirously raked the lines of her black crepe jumpsuit, lingered on the exposed slope of her neck, the swell of her breasts above the square-cut bodice. Trailing light fingertips down the length of her arms, he captured her wrists lightly, drew her even closer.

"I'm going to love you, Kate," he said, voice velvety rough. "And then contrary to your low opinion of me, hang around for more."

Kate got as far as the sofa before he caught her arm lightly and swung her around to face him. Before she could even begin to do more than mouth the protest crowding her throat, his other hand was circling her waist. Kate was drawn up against the sinewy determined length of him, the warm firm pressure of his palm splayed across the middle of her spine.

Kate tried to fight, breathe, turn her head away. Molding his free hand around her jawline, Alex lifted her chin to his, held it there until the kiss was perfectly executed and amorously returned, replayed. Kate shattered under the onslaught of his desire, felt without warning the moisture burning at her eyelids. She had wanted him for so long, but not like this, not just to prove a point, that she loved and desired him still.

The saltiness of a lone tear made its way down to the juncture of their mouths. Alex paused, lifted his head slightly to gaze tenderly down at her as his index finger traced the moisture's origin. She saw then that his intention had not been to wound, as she had first thought. Only to love.

"Damn it, Kate," Alex whispered, holding her close. "Don't cry. I can take anything but that."

A moment passed, and then another. Just a breath away from fulfillment, Kate teetered on the edge of indecision. It would be so easy just to give in to his warmth, his masculinity, the tantalizing musk and deep woods scent of his skin.

"I don't want to be hurt," she whispered finally. "I don't want to get emotionally and sexually involved with you again." Especially knowing he still planned to leave.

"I don't want to hurt you, Kate," Alex said gently. Framing her face tenderly with both palms, Alex turned her gaze back, forced her to look up into the smoky depths of his eyes. "Can't you see that's the farthest thing from my mind?"

The warmth of his gaze and fingertips caressing first her face, then shoulders, transmitted itself all the way down to her toes. Kate swayed dizzily, weakening. And in that instant his posture changed, grew tauter, more determined.

"I want you, Kate," he said softly. "I'm not going to lie about it. But I'm not going to take you against your will, either."

Breathless seconds passed. Kate could not bring herself to find the impetus to flee, but she would not initiate the embrace, either. Firelight flickered in the grate.

Wordlessly, Alex walked over to turn on the stereo. Soft, seductive music filled the room, furthering the invitation. Again, Alex took her into his arms. Kate's lashes fluttered slowly shut. His mouth lowered to hers again and when she still held back slightly, trailed to the nape of her neck, traced feather-light patterns, above, below, around her ear, then dipped lower to the neckline of her dress. Alex pushed the slinky black crepe aside with his thumbs, noticed she was wearing no undergarment beneath.

"God, Kate," he murmured, brushing the rosy crest with the edge of his tongue, then tasting it with his mouth. "What you do to me—"

Winding both hands through his hair, Kate held him to her, gasped as the swirling sensations rippled through, tore down the defenses she had built. His hands slid down to her waist, moved across her bare back and spine, lingered on the slender length of her arms, captured her wrists. Kate pressed herself more fully against him. The tautness of his arms slid around her back, caging her in once more. Restlessly Kate undid the buttons of his shirt and drew it impatiently off. He countered with the zipper against her waist, helped her discard the black overblouse, sheer black pantyhose and tiny bikini panties of translucent lace. Kate was lowered to the sofa. All other considerations faded. Kate loved Alex, needed him, wanted him. For the moment that was enough.

Standing next to her, he began to undress. Every nerve ending aching to be touched, Kate leaned up on her elbows, watching, savoring the ease of his movements, the flexing of muscle under slightly tanned skin. When naked, he settled himself down alongside the length of her, rolling sideways on the broad width of the custom couch. His hands made gentle prompting forays over the length of her, his gaze lingering on the attractive dip of her lissome thigh. His fingertips grew to know the curving muscles of her calves, the slenderness of her ankle, the silken texture and scent of every inch of her skin. Kate moved to kiss him languidly, knowing she had waited too long for that moment, wanted it too much to rush, but when he deepened the kiss unexpectedly, tongue searching out

every corner of her mouth only to withdraw and
lightly tease, and explore, she knew a different kind
of tension.

Alex pulled her down to the floor, wrapped his
hands in the length of her hair, and moved so that she
was beneath him. The close demanding fit of their
bodies coupled with the ever deepening intimacy of
their kiss, made Kate arch against him in impatience.
But Alex was calling the shots by then and he would
not be rushed. He stroked her with his hands, then
followed the excruciatingly gentle sensations with his
tongue, lips, mouth. When his teeth carefully closed
over the hardened tips of her breasts, Kate softly cried
her need, pressing the beard-roughened surface of his
face to her skin, reveling in the pleasurable sensations
the chafing created. Alex trailed downward with his
lips across the flat plane of her abdomen to the petal
soft juncture of her thighs. Kate gave herself up to the
mastery of his moves, then at length when she could
endure no more, initiated the same caressing, arous-
ing rite of love across the length of his pulsing frame,
lingering, loving, seducing.

"Kate," Alex whispered her name, and then once
again. His hands were slightly rough as he pulled her
upwards, then moved so that again she was beneath
him.

"I want you," Kate murmured helplessly against
his mouth, reveling in the crushing weight, the demands of the caressing hands upon her.

"And I want you," Alex whispered. "Have for
months. You'll never know how much." Kate trembled with the heat and the pressure of his entry, the
maelstrom of pleasure soon engulfing them both.

Arms wrapped tight around his neck, she felt the burgeoning response, shivered when the spasms of total pleasure arched her even tighter against him. They drifted back slowly, sated, then clung together long minutes afterward, studying the fire, blocking out the questions and problems the future held.

Chapter Five

Kate awakened to scarlet memories of the previous night, and an empty but thoroughly rumpled king-sized bed. In the distance, she could hear Alex puttering about the kitchen. A cozy domestic scene, yes, but had it been wise to encourage it? The intimacy would only complicate their already difficult working relationship, to say nothing of how Kate would feel when he left for the Middle East again.

Still wondering at the wisdom of her actions, Kate staggered sleepily to the shower. Twenty minutes later, she was dressed and headed for the sounds of activity.

Alex was in the kitchen, efficiently sorting through a myriad half-empty and never-opened spice bottles. Kate lounged in the doorway watching the interesting play of expressions across his face.

"I realize you've never been wild about my cooking," she said at last. "But don't you think this is a little drastic?"

A low chuckle rose from his throat. "Don't be silly," Alex chided, swinging around to face her. "I'm sorting your peppers."

That explained it.

Kate passed on the opportunity to help him decide what to do with the cayenne and headed somnolently for the coffee.

Alex sorted through another group of spices, replacing two on the bottom shelf of the cabinet next to the stove. Frowning, he pitched half a bottle of outdated sage.

Kate poured herself a cup of the extremely black brew, nearly choked on the first gulp. That wasn't coffee, it was motor oil with a touch of bark.

"What are you doing to the cabinets?" He had dressed casually in brown gabardine slacks, and, impossibly, looked more handsome and all-American than ever, muscles rippling beneath the thin snug-fitting contours of the expensive cotton shirt.

"Alphabetizing your spices." Alex paused to take a quaff of his own coffee. "How do you like it?" he said, raising the enamel cup and indicating the unusual brew.

"Rivals Mrs. Olsen's best," Kate breezed. "What'd you put in it?"

Alex grinned at the wariness in her tone. "Cinnamon. There are a lot of Europeans at the Southwestern Oil headquarters in Riyadh. Plain coffee seems to be a thing of the past, at least over there."

So was lovemaking if his extraordinarily uninhibited moves the night before had been any indication. Kate blushed despite her thoughts, found she had to lower her gaze from his assessing study.

Alex went routinely back to organizing his *C*'s. "Do you realize it took me nearly half an hour to locate the cinnamon this morning?"

Kate watched supple fingers curve lingeringly around a container of basil. "I knew where it was."

"You were also asleep. I didn't want to wake you."

Kate nodded her appreciation. If he was trying to convince her to return with him to Saudi Arabia, it was working, at least on an emotional level.

Alex added a lone container of dill weed to the shelf, skipped the *E*'s and *F*'s when he found no appropriate herbs, then added four containers of ginger, frowning profusely all the while. Kate could imagine the direction of his thoughts as it would appear on one of his consulting reports. Disorganization, overspending, inefficient use of existing materials.

"It's the same thing at the office," Alex said, moving on to the marjoram. "Everyone has their own filing system, completely unique and unfathomable to the average person."

"I suppose you intend to remedy that." Kate got up from her stool at the counter to pour herself some more of the cinnamon laced brew. She shuddered as the first bitter swallow went down.

"Sure do." Finished, Alex dusted off his hands, closed the cabinet, and helped himself to another cup of coffee. He, too, grimaced at the first acidic taste. "Tell me the truth. Do you think I put too much cinnamon in this?"

Kate cleared her throat, and the flakes of bark-derived spice clinging to it. "It's a possibility, Alex."

"First of all, I want to thank everyone for their outstanding cooperation thus far." Alex stood at the head of the conference table, passing out sample boxes of files and master instruction sheets.

Kate sat at the back of the conference room, note-pad, and individual instruction sheet in hand. Although it was only his third day as acting publisher, Alex had turned an enemy camp into an adoring female harem of workers. Kate was unable to decide if it were his looks, the charm he could exert when he so desired, or simply the fact that he had been working as hard as the rest of the staff, all for the betterment of *Missouri Woman*, and higher salaries for them all.

"The most crucial and difficult endeavor still lies ahead of us though. And this is the organization of our master files." He looked up and sighed, then relented with a devilishly engaging grin and offhand gesture. "Not that your methods up until now haven't been *innovative*." The stress on the last word brought a round of laughter from the staffers at the table. "But I think it's become clear we need a highly organized system to streamline our operations here at *Missouri Woman*.

The staffers were all nodding agreeably, looking with interest at the guidelines he'd prepared for them to work by. Alex continued pragmatically, now that everyone's attention and cooperation had been caught.

"Most difficult will be the creation of a master-file, a place or room where all articles, contracts, letters of agreement or dissent are filed. These are to be in alphabetical order, by name of author or party involved. Later, we might switch to cross-filing, indexing by both article title, subject, and author, but for now to simplify matters and greatly speed things up..."

Kate drifted, making idle notations on her legal pad as she pretended attention. She wondered if Alex

knew how long any of this was going to take, if it
would even be worth it once he left. Surely then,
everyone would go back to her own system.

"Isn't that right, Kate?" The cool masculine drawl
jerked her from her disjointed reverie. "Ah, yes."
Clearly caught daydreaming, Kate blushed, then settled obediently back to the business at hand, all too
aware of the staff's generally disapproving reproach.
Darn him, she thought, resentment crushing her
again.

"You know it occurs to me you could make more of
an effort towards turning things around here." Alex
stated matter-of-factly as soon as the meeting had adjourned and he had escorted her to a private corner
down the hall.

"Give me back my office and maybe I will." Kate
countered in exactly the same tone.

There was a pause. It was clear from the aggravated
look, the muscles clenching slightly along his jaw,
Alex wanted to shake her, or kiss her, or whatever
would do the trick. Finally, he said simply, very low,
"Our new quarters will be ready in a couple of days,
Kate."

Confused both by their passionate lovemaking the
night before and the abrupt return to business as
usual over her protests that morning, Kate used the
only defense she had, anger. "Maybe then I'll be able
to get something accomplished. Until then, I'll leave
you to your admiring entourage!" Kate could have
shot herself for expressing the jealous reaction aloud,
the moment the words were out. But it only served to
soften his response all the more.

"I know it's difficult for you," Alex said gently.

"But because of the time element, my short stay in the States, we have to proceed swiftly."

Another thing Kate objected to. His love-her-and-leave-her attitude. "Why don't you go back to Riyadh now then? *I'm* certainly not stopping you!"

Alex frowned, resisting her goad. "I don't have time to argue with you now, Kate," he said calmly at last, one eye on an interested staffer lingering at the other end of the crowded narrow hall. "But we will discuss this later."

Not if Kate had anything to say about it. Mouth set recalcitrantly, she watched him retire to the conference room.

"I'm taking the rest of the day off." Kate stuffed her briefcase full of unedited material for the January issue.

Liz Shaw's eyebrows raked upwards in dismay. Everyone else was still enjoying a leisurely catered lunch before tackling the migraine-inducing job ahead— one their publisher had announced he would personally oversee. "Did you clear this with Alex?"

"I don't have to," Kate said tightly, stuffing another sheaf of typed papers into her leather case.

Liz clearly thought it would be wise to do so, if only for sake of decorum. "You know Alex wants those files sorted today—all of them, so they'll be ready to move into the new offices next week. And it will help us get acclimated over there more swiftly if it is already done."

"Then let him do it." Kate grabbed her coat and headed swiftly down the corridor for the stairs before Alex could discover her flight. She had to get away, had to think, sort things out, before he played any more havoc with her senses, or her will. Much more passionate lovemaking and she would temporarily lose her will for an independent life, depend on him as shortsightedly as any fifties woman. And then where would she be the next time he decided to jaunt off to another part of the world and work sixteen and eighteen hour days, seven days a week, resolving a managerial crisis for Southwestern Oil?

Once home, though, Kate was still unable to concentrate. Deciding not to waste the pretty day, Kate went back to the bedroom and stripped off her business attire, donned an old pair of faded jeans and a heavy flannel work shirt, and a matching paint-splattered gray sweatshirt jacket, complete with front zipper, pockets, hood.

Going down to the basement, she discovered the unopened cans of paint Alex had purchased for the cedar trim at the back of the house. Later, paintbrush and tray by her side, Kate was propping an eight foot extension ladder next to the lowest part of the overhang. In the bright autumn sunlight, it was easy to see the spots Alex had alluded to. Kate figured it wouldn't take very long to patch those light spots up and she could work off some tension in the process.

Half an hour later, she was beginning to think she had overestimated herself. Her right arm hurt from wrist to shoulder blade and socket, and her neck was definitely beginning to hurt from craning it too far upwards.

"Need a hand?"

Kate turned to see Max Collins standing at the bottom of the ladder. "Hi, Max." Kate carefully balanced the aluminum tray of paint on the ladder's back shelf, then carefully set down the brush. "What are you doing here?"

"I came by to beg your forgiveness." Max gestured helplessly as Kate extracted a paint-covered wet rag from the pocket of her sweatshirt and tried to remove most of the mahogany stain from her hands. "You know that article I said I'd do? Well, it doesn't look as if I'll be able to get to it for another month."

Thinking of the way things were currently at the magazine, Kate couldn't see much was lost. "That's all right, Max. Whenever you're done, just let me know and I'll run it." Though sometimes pressed for time, Max was always dependable about eventually coming through.

"Thanks, Kate. I was hoping you'd understand."

"The bit about the aid to dependent children increase you're pushing for will still run." Kate read accurately the worry still clouding the senator's face. Carefully, she stuffed the wet rag back into her pocket and began a one step at a time journey down.

"You're a real pal, Katie," Max grinned, still craning his neck upwards to see her face.

"Don't I know it!" Kate quipped dryly, squinting against the glare of the sun. "What's got you so busy over at the Senate?"

"Oh, just another routine fraud investigation," Max expounded, putting out a hand to steady her suddenly shaky descent. "We've been after this guy for—Kate! Watch out!"

Too late, she was tripping, the whole of her weight falling forward, off the ladder. Max jumped forward, holding out both arms despite the unusually immaculate condition of his suit. Her arms reached for and

clung helplessly to his neck. Saved, Kate slid weakly
down the length of his secure stance, her face and
body pressed intimately against her childhood friend's
chest. Kate gasped as his belt buckle caught her in the
abdomen, then relaxed and fell slightly back as her
feet touched the ground.

"Kate?" Max hurriedly smoothed the tangle of
hair from across her forehad. "Kate, are you all
right?"

"Senator, you do have a way of popping up at the
most inopportune times." The lazy drawl floated
warningly around the corner of the house. Kate immediately disengaged herself from Max's comforting
embrace. She was blushing furiously as her back
grazed the aluminum ladder.

Max also moved back another step, face reddening
furiously despite the innocence of his rescue. "Ryker."

"One and the same."

"This was all—" Kate blushed even more when
her husband's dark brows arched her way. Playing
hooky from the office had been bad enough. But
this...

"Perfectly innocent, I know," Alex finished dryly.
He turned towards Max, his charming best. "Senator,
if you'll excuse us Kate and I have a few things to
discuss. As you can see she left the office a bit early
today."

Too early, evidently.

Realizing Kate wasn't in any trouble except what he
had obviously little to do with, Max offered his apolo-
gies, and departed.

"Did you have to run him off so quickly?" Kate

asked, starting haughtily back up her ladder. After all, the only defense was a good offense, she thought.

For the second time that day her painting was interrupted. Alex twirled her around and hands clamped firmly around her waist and brought her resolutely to the ground. Kate swallowed as she looked up into the genuinely angry contours of his face.

"Under the circumstances," Alex said, 'I thought I was more than polite." His dark glance flickered over her disapprovingly, lingering on the open zipper of her scruffy gray sweatshirt and the view of softly rounded skin visible from his height. Deliberately, he forced his regard to her flashing amber eyes. "What are you doing home this time of day? And painting for heaven's sake! It must be forty degrees out here!"

"I didn't feel the slightest chill," Kate answered honestly. In fact, as steamed as she was by his constant intervention at *Missouri Woman*, she doubted she'd be cold all winter no matter how frigid it got.

"Obviously not." Hands on her waist, Alex shifted Kate even closer, as if to share the warmth of his tall lean frame. "And that didn't answer my question," he said softly. "What are you doing home this time of day?" One thirty, she really had no excuse not to be working, particularly when the rest of the *Missouri Woman* staff was on constant overtime.

"I thought I'd paint the trim," Kate said icily, pushing away from his affectionate hold. "You mentioned I'd been a little lax in outdoor upkeep."

He twirled her back even more firmly than before. "You're needed at the office, Kate."

Kate disregarded the icy-blue glare, the taut unyielding line of his jaw. More than ever, she needed some time to herself, time away from him. "Tough."

The next thing she knew she was backed against the house, the shadow of paint tray and ladder above them. Realizing she couldn't push past or even attempt to make any sudden moves without the danger of mahogany stain cascading over them both, Kate stayed put. Alex braced a hand on either side of the brick behind her. He leaned closer, as if in the lowest position of a vertical sit-up, the warmth of his breath stirring her hair.

"If you have a grievance, state it, Kate."

"I want you out of *Missouri Woman*," Kate said through gritted teeth. "Out of my office. Off my back!"

"This isn't about the magazine, Kate. Haven't you figured that out yet?"

Kate kept a lid tightly on her turbulent emotions, hid her unease from his assessing study. "Precisely why we should not be working together at all, Alex. If you must interfere at *M.W.* can't you at least do it through a third party? I know Darrel Hendrix offered to act as intermediary."

"I didn't come halfway across the world and take a six-week absence to let someone else publish *Missouri Woman* in my stead."

"I don't want your charity or your advice," Kate's stubborn streak made her insist. More to the point, she didn't want to fall hopelessly in love with him again only to have him leave. And that danger heightened with every subsequent moment they spent together.

Silence fell between them as Alex's patience wore thin. "I see." Moving back from the wall, Alex regarded her paint-splattered state with critical, entirely impersonal eyes. "Go in and get dressed," he directed quietly. "What you had on earlier today will do fine."

Kate smiled through clenched teeth. If he thought he could order her around by virtue of being either publisher or husband, he had another think coming. "In case you'd forgotten, I've got some painting to do."

The dark brows raised another fraction of an inch. As the seconds clicked off, he fought to control the muscle working volatilely in his cheek. "I'll take care of the painting at an appropriate time."

Kate had been subjugated beyond endurance. "Oh, really? You're making those kinds of decisions for me now too, hm?"

Alex took another deep breath, looked away a breath-stealing moment. When he finally swung back to her, he looked capable of just about anything. "Don't provoke me, Kate. I'm operating on a very tight schedule and short supply of patience as it is. Though for the record, our assignation has to do with magazine business, nothing else."

Kate swallowed the rest of her objections, tossed her paint-smeared rag onto the grass knoll between them. "I'm only doing this for the sake of the magazine, Alex."

"I know." His gaze raked the length of her exasperatedly. "Believe me, Kate, I know."

Kate took her time about getting ready to go. When she emerged from the bedroom half an hour later, Alex had his feet propped up on a footstool and was cheerfully making notes on her legal pad of information.

"Is there nothing of mine off-limits to you?" Kate snatched the pad from his hands. Was there nothing he wouldn't invade and claim as his own?

"I was utilizing the time efficiently, a lesson you'd be wise to take to heart. And if you don't mind, I'd like my notes back." His tone was as remote as that of a stranger's. Rising lazily, Alex retrieved the pad long enough to remove his sheets of notes and fold them in quarters. Sliding the small bundle of notes into the inner pocket of his doeskin blazer, he asked her politely, "Ready to go?"

Kate had changed into a sleek jade pantsuit and casual silk shirt. The masculine inspection of her from head to toe left no doubt he approved. *Foiled again*, Kate thought with a sigh, recalling his instructions to dress as before.

The drive to downtown Springfield was swift and pleasant. "I thought you'd want to see where *Missouri Woman* is going to be housed," Alex said quietly as he turned onto a small sidestreet near Durst Park. He parked in front of a seven-story office building, complete with tinted glass and sleek black steel. Kate glanced at the prestigious structure, the immaculately landscaped property, the quality of the automobiles parked outside. Mercedeses, Cadillac Sevilles, not a Chevy or a Ford in sight.

"We can't possibly afford this place," she said.

"Correction, sweetheart. You're already paying for it." Alex hopped down from the jeep and walked around to help her out. "I signed the lease this morning."

"Without even consulting me?" Kate exclaimed.

"Funny, you were nowhere to be found."

"You could have waited!" Kate shot back combatively. The audacity of the man!

Alex sighed heavily, looking as if he'd explode if she questioned or argued about even one more decision. When he spoke however, his voice was low and perfectly controlled. "Read the partnership agreement, Kate." He escorted her towards the building entrance civilly. "Anything that has to do with the business arrangements—and that includes building rents, equipment, leases, and contracts, just to name a few—I can preside over."

"But I never thought you'd actually use any of those powers when I signed them over to you last year!"

"That's your problem." Alex held open the smoky hued glass door. "Mine is saving *Missouri Woman* from bankruptcy. Frankly, Kate, I'll do or go after anything I have to in order to accomplish that goal."

Including sleeping with her? Kate wondered.

"What happened between us last night has nothing to do with this." Alex paused, just inside the door, accurately reading the direction of her thoughts.

But to Kate the two were intertwined hopelessly. How could she hate him for what he was doing to both her and the magazine, yet yield to him pliantly every night?

"I don't agree to this," Kate said stiffly as they took the elevator up to the thickly carpeted seventh floor. She would go see Darrel Hendrix, fight to have the decision overturned.

"You don't have a choice. That partnership agreement is ironclad, in my favor." Alex strolled down to the end of the hall. Using his keys, he opened up a luxuriously appointed but empty suite of fifteen rooms. Done in colors of soft pearly gray, white, and gentle beige, the understated beauty and elegance of the offices made their current uncarpeted head-quarters almost laughable.

"This will be our new computer room." Alex indicated the spacious room at the end of the hall. "This room for filing. A reception area will be here, a reading room here. Everyone will have his own offices, including me."

Kate's heart seemed to stop. Was it possible? Would he change his mind and come back to reside in the States on a permanent basis? "I thought you were only going to be here six weeks."

"Even a figurehead needs a place to come when he is in town." Alex stepped into the largest office, the one he had decorously decided to make his own. "I like *Missouri Woman*, Kate. I like the spirit of the pub-lication, which admittedly is due largely to your keen editorial sense and high standards. I like the staff. They work well with me and for me. Plus I enjoy the aspect of running a smaller operation by myself, for my own profit. So, no, I have no intention of giving away my hold as publisher, even if we do eventually decide to go our separate ways once more. Of course because of my own career interests and obligations I won't be able to be here full time. But I imagine I'll be able to pop in and out enough to keep things well in order."

Alex tossed her a spare set of keys. "I'm going out of town, Kate. Some advertisers I have to see.

Try and keep things running in the black until I return."

Alex spent the next ten days dividing his time between Springfield, St. Louis, and Kansas City. He called occasionally to check in or leave word where he was staying, but that was the extent of his communication with Kate. In an effort to forget their new estrangement, Kate worked fiendishly, arranging her own files in the prescribed new order, overseeing the move from their current quarters to the elegant new Durst Street address. That Alex was personally financing at least part of the costs according to Darrel Hendrix was never far from her mind. No longer could Kate accuse Alex of publishing *M.W.* strictly for revenge. He truly wanted *Missouri Woman* both to survive and flourish.

As could have been predicted, it didn't take long for word to get out. Newly interested advertisers and writers were flowing through the new office, asking for Alex, crowding the reception desk, booking them solid with back to back commitments and appointments. Unfortunately, in the crush of confusion, Gavin Hayes was one of the first to get in to see Kate.

Wearing a wine-colored suit of polyester, pale pink shirt, and flashy white tie, the used-car king walked into her office shortly after lunch.

"Well now, Mrs. Ryker," he drawled ingratiatingly. "I had heard things had changed around here with the appearance of your husband. But I had no idea." His glance bounced appreciatively off her new chrome and glass desk, the white sling-style chairs. "Just goes to show you what a good man could do."

"How can I help you, Mr. Hayes?" Kate asked wearily, having given up on trying to get rid of him without an audience.

"I heard you're looking for more advertisers, aggressively looking." Hayes prowled the room, pausing to inspect three potential cover shots for the February issue.

Kate fought the urge to run. Successful businessman or not, Hayes gave her the creeps. "My husband handles all the advertising now," Kate lied, feeling in this instant a little embellishment wouldn't hurt.

Hayes turned to give her a glittering smile. "I would imagine you've got quite a bit of influence with him." His dark eyes raked her form ingratiatingly.

"Yes, she does." Unannounced, Alex Ryker strolled lazily into the office. Hayes straightened immediately at the younger man's powerful presence. "Mr. Hayes, of Heavenly Used Cars?" Alex presumed.

"As a matter of fact, you're just the person I was loking for." Introductions were quickly made. Hayes stuck out his hand amiably. Alex returned the gesture with less than enthusiastic fervor, then listened patiently to Gavin Hayes's whole spiel.

"Unfortunately for you, Kate was right," Alex decided firmly at last. "We have no opening in our magazine for your ads. However, if you'd like me to refer you to—"

"Turning us down is hardly good business," Hayes countered, the blaze of anger leaping into his dark eyes.

Alex lounged negligently against Kate's desk. "Perhaps not, but the decision stands.'' And on that note, Alex showed him out.

"Thanks," Kate sank down into her new charcoal contoured chair as soon as Alex had escorted the surly car dealer to the elevators and returned.

"Does Hayes always give you that rough a time?" Alex did not seem pleased by the prospect.

Kate wondered why Alex didn't move to greet her at least a little more personally now that he'd shut the door to her office and they were at least temporarily alone. Did that mean he was still angry with her for the fights they'd had regarding *M.W.*? Or just no longer interested in her as a woman, his wife?

"Just lately." Kate ran a hand wearily through the layers of her hair, spilling them recklessly about her shoulders. Until that moment, seeing Alex again, she hadn't realized how much she had missed him.

"Ten to one, Hayes imagines all women easy targets for his kind of fraudulent dealings." Alex glanced around. "The office is really beginning to shape up now that all the furniture has been delivered and put in place," he remarked, pleased.

"Quite a change from the old quarters, I'll agree with you there. I just hope we can pay for it," Kate remarked. And that the magazine's copy wouldn't suffer because of the exorbitant expense.

"If you want to attract the best accounts, you have to look worthwhile, Kate. And as for finances, I've already signed up seventeen new accounts. Enough to keep you here for the next three months without owing me a cent."

"Already?" Kate was astonished.

Alex gestured offhandedly. "*Missouri Woman*'s got

a good reputation, Kate. Now that advertisers know
it's being handled with the express purpose of doubling circulation—"

"You told potential customers that?" Kate hoped
they could live up to the claim.

"That's the least of my goals," Alex commented,
amused by her shortsightedness in that regard. The
moment lengthened. He gazed down at her fondly,
then reached out to lightly trace her cheek. Kate was
so aware of him she could barely breathe, knew he
must be able to hear the thunderous pounding of her
heart, but again he appeared not to notice or particularly want her positive response to his presence.

"I've called an impromptu staff meeting." Alex
pivoted away crisply, already heading for the door.
"They should all be in there now. And, Kate, I'd appreciate it if you not only attend this time, but paid
attention as well."

Chapter Six

Kate followed Alex into the spacious new conference room, acutely aware of the interested gazes of the *Missouri Woman* staff. She knew some of the editors were speculating as to the real reason behind Alex's extended absence the past week and a half and wished she knew at least a little more than they did about it.

Kate took the seat to Alex's right. He preferred to remain standing. The other editors and employees relaxed in the comfortable tweed chairs around the large, informal oak table.

Kate studied Alex silently as the routine pleasantries were exchanged between publisher and staff. Even wan with fatigue Alex was exceedingly handsome. Kate knew that whether they remained married in any real sense or not, she would never get over him, never stop loving him.

"As indicated earlier, *Missouri Woman*'s format will be expanding," Alex continued routinely, one hand thrust casually in the pocket of his trousers. His suit jacket hung open, revealing a trim waist, lean taut hips. "The February issue will feature seventy-five more pages, fifty of which will be geared toward advertising.''

Kate froze. She knew about the fifty ad pages—but what did he have in mind for editorial? That decision alone could completely alter the scope and appearance of *Missouri Woman*. But Alex was already going on, disregarding her thinly veiled dismay.

"Those twenty-five pages of additional format will eventually be expanded to fifty. At the moment, I would like to see them reflected in three additional columns monthly—the material to be decided upon by our editor-in-chief." He sent Kate a cursory glance of acknowledgment. "I also want three works of fiction per month. Eventually, this should be increased to include a serialized or condensed novel. Again, the material to be decided by Kate, though naturally I would suggest in keeping with the tradition of *M.W.* that the fiction reflect an extremely positive view of women, their capabilities. The problems of the business world can be shown, but the woman should always emerge the victor, and not the victim of archaic thinking, practices, and so forth.''

Alex sent Kate a questioning lift of his brows.

"Sounds fine," she managed evenly, but beneath the table her fists were clenching and unclenching in the soft wool of her dusky blue skirt. How dare he make decisions of that scope without consulting her first!

"I want to commend you all on the fine job you did organizing and implementing the master file system. Undoubtedly, it will make things swifter and simpler for everyone. Now, are there any questions? Any problems I can assist anyone with before I leave?"

Fifteen minutes later, the impromptu staff meeting was dismissed. Kate stalked out into the hall.

"I'd like a word with you, Kate." Alex strode by, motioning Kate down the thickly carpeted hall to his masculinely furnished office. "See about getting some art work onto the walls. And some plants for the individual offices and the hall would also be nice."

"Yes, sir," Kate answered snippily.

"I don't have time to argue with you, Kate." Alex riffled the mail on his desk.

"Nor to inform me of your plans for format changes," she spat back.

Alex paused. "The editorial content of those additional twenty-five pages are your domain, Kate. I thought I had made that clear. I simply made a few suggestions as to which direction you might go based on what I've been able to discover thus far about consumer interests and needs. Possibly I would have been able to do more had your previous reader mail been better organized and tallied."

Kate shut her mouth firmly. There was no way she was going to give him the incentive to start in on that again. "Alex, we simply do not have the staff to—"

"I agree. Get someone to edit fiction. A few more lucrative accounts and we'll be able to swing another full-time salary."

"I can handle the fiction." Kate sighed. It was their headstrong publisher she was worried about.

"You're busy enough as it is." Alex seemed to zero in on the faint smudges of fatigue beneath her eyes. "In fact—" Gaze narrowing, he started closer.

"What kind of ads are you placing?" The implacableness of Kate's unexpected query stopped him cold.

Alex gestured loosely. "All kinds. Clothes, vacation resorts, I'm hoping to get a few more household products. Which is why I'm going to Cincinnati. Procter and Gamble—"

"I'm really not interested in your itinerary," Kate said, still infuriated beyond words. Nor could she complain about his travel expenses, since for the moment they were all coming directly from his personal bank account.

"Have it your own way." Alex slid a sheaf of neatly typed figures into his engraved leather briefcase and started for the door.

"Now where are you going?" Kate followed him exasperatedly.

He turned so briskly she ran into his chest. Swinging the briefcase up around her waist, he held her there against him. Katie drank in the heady scent of his masculine cologne, the clean fragrance of his skin and clothes. "I thought you weren't interested."

His free hand came up to gently lift her chin. Kate willed herself to move away, but her body didn't move. Alex shifted his weight slightly, drawing her nearer. Through the softness of her cashmere sweater and silky bra, her nipples tautened with responsiveness, aching towards the gentleness of his touch. Once again she realized how much she had missed him, how much she still wanted him, despite their personal and professional differences.

Sensing surrender, Alex leaned forward slightly to drop his briefcase onto the carpet. "This isn't what I had intended, Kate," he whispered, drawing her near.

Despite the presence of a very busy staff just on the other side of the door, his mouth descended slowly, inevitably to hers. Kate gave in to the desire, using her lips and tongue and teeth to take the kiss deeper still. She molded herself against his warmth and his heat, reveling in the satiation only he could give her. Passion coursed over her in waves as his tongue probed her lips, searching, invading, demanding. When the rough caress had ended, Kate knew a physical frustration more potent than ever before.

"Ask me to come home with you tonight," Alex directed challengingly, lips poised seductively above her mouth. "Tell me nothing else matters. Not what goes on here, not our professional differences, or our careers, only us."

Kate froze. "You're asking me to return to Riyadh when you go, aren't you?" Though the possibility had been phrased hundreds of different ways, Alex's male expectations had never changed. He wanted a wife by his side, a dutiful, loving corporate wife.

Tension snaked back into his frame. But he didn't deny her assertion. "I'm doing everything possible here to at least give you the option. I want you with me again, if only intermittently."

Or in other words, Kate thought bitterly, only at the convenience of his work schedule, assignments, and career demands would they ever have anything remotely resembling a full-time marriage. Unless of course, she gave up her career completely.

"I want a future together, Alex. Not just an occasional passionate tryst between your Southwestern Oil assignments."

"Always have to have things your own way, don't you, Kate?" Only by the slight hurt glint in the electric blue eyes, the sudden clenching of a muscle in his jaw could Kate tell Alex had been similarly affected, disappointed. "I'll be at the Hilton." Alex walked past her to retrieve his briefcase. "Try not to miss me too much." And then he was gone.

Kate spent the next several days editing articles, meeting with authors, and checking possible covers and photo layouts for the February issue. By the end of the week she was exhausted, but Darrel Hendrix insisted they meet for cocktails anyway.

"You look worn out, Kate," Darrel observed as he seated himself across from her in the plush leather booth. "Sure you can't stay and have dinner with Sally and me later? A lot of the old crowd is going to be here"

"No thanks." Kate shook ink into the tip of the pen and signed the papers Darrell handed her. Briefly they discussed magazine business. "Expecting Alex back any time soon?" Darrel asked.

"I don't know." Kate watched the singles crowd jockey for position at the bar. "He didn't say."

"Do you know if he's been buying up any additional stock in the magazine?" Darrel calmly sipped his bourbon and branch.

Kate froze, stirred her Virgin Mary with a green plastic swizzel stick and stalk of celery. "What do you mean?" Surely Alex would have mentioned something to her, or told Darrel. Unless he didn't want them, and especially Kate, to know about it.

Darrel frowned, perplexed. "As you know, you and Alex jointly hold sixty percent of the *M.W.* stock. Because of the changes he's been making, your new offices and expanded format, the price of the stock has been shooting up quickly. No one can buy in blocks larger than five percent without filing with the SEC. This insures your continued control of the magazine. Even if an outside party did manage to get all forty remaining shares, which is doubtful because Sally and I hold ten, your employees another ten, they couldn't hope to win a fight for control of *M.W.* or buy you out as long as you and Alex agreed on how *Missouri Woman* should be run. Which is why it doesn't make sense—"

"What doesn't make sense?" Kate cut his rambling short.

Darrel glanced over at her thoughtfully. "Kate, I got word today that someone from out of town is offering outlandish prices for *Missouri Woman* stock. They're only buying in one to two per cent shares at the moment, generally in the names of their attorneys or brokerage firms. But the methodical way it is occurring, the fact that they came after my shares, too, suggests someone is trying to get a large chunk of the *Missouri Woman* interests. If it's an unfriendly person, Kate, it could mean trouble."

Darrel had given Kate a lot to think about. And although eventually he'd insisted the interest in *Missouri Woman* stock was probably just coincidental, due to their beefed-up image, Kate wasn't so sure. It wouldn't be unprecedented for Alex to want that share within his voting reach, or even to try quietly to get it. Certainly, it would be one way to insure that Kate at least listened to whatever he had to say. If necessary, it would be then even easier to overrule her business-wise.

Kate drifted off to sleep thinking about a partnership agreement she never should have signed and the remote possibility of trying to issue new preferred stock, or covertly buy up some more shares of her own. She woke to the shadow of a man drifting quietly across the master bedroom. Kate sat up with a start as Alex neared, the print sheet falling back to reveal a lacy lavender silk teddy.

"Relax, Kate, it's just me. I finished up a little sooner than I thought." Alex yawned and tossed both suitcase and jacket aside. He grinned, revealing a flash of white teeth. "Miss me?"

More than he needed to know. "Was I supposed to?" Kate countered lightly, running a hand through the tousled length of her silky gold hair.

"I don't know," he said, very low. "I sure missed you."

Recalling what Darrel Hendrix had surmised might be happening to the additional forty percent shares of *Missouri Woman* stock, Kate studied her husband warily. Would Alex go to such lengths to control her? She knew how single-minded he could be when it came to getting what he wanted, and that went double where business was concerned.

Alex seemed to take the mute indecision of her gaze in stride. Sitting down on the edge of the kingsized bed, he kicked off his shoes and began removing his socks. The pants slid to the floor, soon followed by his shirt. Alex slid onto his own side of the bed, settled down onto his back, one strong arm slung behind his head. Seconds later, he was asleep, the only sound in the room the metered sounds of his breath and the wild pounding of Kate Ryker's heart.

Sometime during the night, Kate turned to find

herself covered by a heavy masculine arm. When she tried to lift the confining weight from her breasts, Alex snuggled closer.

"Mmmmmm." He brushed her shoulder with his mouth.

"Alex." Kate blinked herself awake, then placed both hands on the protectively curving weight. "You're crushing me."

"Well, I certainly don't want to do that." The lazy amused drawl indicated Alex was in full wakeful command of his faculties and his muscular limbs as he swung himself lithely over the length of her. Propping the bulk of his weight on his elbows, he peered sensually down at her, sighed again, and then began exploring her forehead, earlobes, the corners of her eyes, the soft curving line of her cheek with his soft, warm lips. His mouth moved slowly down to capture hers, part and probe. "If you want the truth, Kate," Alex murmured against her skin, "I had to get home. I couldn't stand being away from you one more second. The emotional distance between us is killing me."

Warm hands slid around the slender circumference of her waist, rolled her slightly onto her side, cupped and molded her against him. The thin silk of her lavender teddy was no defense against the raw masculine strength of his desire. Kate tenderly smoothed the muscular surface of his chest, ran her fingers through the crisp dark mat of curls laying against his suntanned skin.

"Love me, Kate," Alex murmured persuasively. "Let me love you."

"Oh, Alex," Kate sighed, snuggling closer. "That's all I've ever really wanted."

Tangling his fingers in Kate's unruly gold mane, Alex tilted her head even further back, used the pressure to reinitiate the kiss. Kate gave him full access to her mouth, let him taste the sweetness of her parted lips as she explored his. Roughness alternated with tender promises. Gently, Alex eased the slender straps of her lavender silk teddy down across her arms, used his free hand to caress the gentle slope of her breast, his thumb and forefinger to circle and tauten the silken, pink circle. Kate felt the wild passion only he could evoke. Tenderly, she whispered his name.

Lazily, his other palm traveled upward to her breasts, neck, lifted the mass of her hair from her throat and ear. His tongue pressed light, teasing kisses down the arch of her neck, lingered at the juncture of her collarbone, then traveled back up to nip playfully at the lobe of her other ear.

"So many nights were spent thinking of you, of being together again, like this," he confided, both hands moving deliberately down to span the slenderness of her waist.

Alex tumbled Kate back against the fluff of pillows, the soft dark cloud of hair on his chest brushing the sensitive tips of her breasts. Wordlessly, he divested her of the lacy lingerie, dropped his own briefs to the floor. Possessively, he slid his body back over the length of hers.

"Whatever else happens, Kate, we'll always have this," he whispered. "This part of our relationship will never change." And for the moment, for Kate, his passion was enough.

He lay beside her, one hair-roughened thigh resting

between hers as he sensually explored every silken inch of her skin. When his kisses trailed lower across her abdomen to her thighs, Kate had to bite her lip to keep from crying out with the pleasure, then gave in to it until she could experience no more.

Still tingling with the need Alex had only partially satisfied, Kate swung herself lithely over her husband, lavished upon him the same slow, loving worship. She reveled in the masculine texture of his skin, the clean scent of his aftershave and soap, the hardness of his muscles beneath the satin of his skin. Then his hands reached down to span her waist and lift her upwards.

Control was rapidly lost for both of them, their joining was wild and passionate, a searing explosion of heat. Arms and legs entangled hopelessly, they were content to drift languidly. Kate had never felt so complete, so much a part of him, so needed or loved. She fell asleep to the slowing, strong beat of his heart, conscious of the scents and textures of his skin, the fierce protective, sensual need in the arms drawn around her back.

Sunlight slatted in through the sheer white drapes, falling brightly across the kingsized bed. Cheerful off-key whistling filled the room. Kate ignored the breathy rendition of "Some Enchanted Evening" and tumbled lazily over onto her stomach, but when Alex broke into full, badly vibrating chorus it was too much. Peering out from underneath the pillow she gave him a baleful look.

"Must you do that so early?" she demanded huskily. Had he no mercy whatsoever?

"Sorry." Alex held up both palms in a gesture of

surrender and went routinely back to his shaving. Whistling soon permeated the air again. This time "Younger Than Springtime."

Kate came out from beneath the pillows again. "Don't tell me you're going to do the whole musical." They'd seen *South Pacific* twice during the early days of their marriage—at his insistence.

Alex paused, removing shaving cream from his upper lips with a twin blade razor. "Well, I know a little bit of *Oklahoma.* If you—"

"Forget it." Kate snuggled back beneath the pillows, listening as the whistling and humming trailed back off into the shower. She supposed she should be grateful it wasn't his usual post-ecstasy tune, "The Star Spangled Banner."

Pressing her lashes tightly shut, Kate amused herself with instant replays of their passion the night before. Anything to forget momentarily the responsibilities and complications awaiting them in the outside world. But the velvet tongue against her shoulder several minutes later was more than her imagination, no matter how vivid.

"Alex!" Kate rolled over with a start. Instantly, she was tingling from head to toe.

"I thought that would get your attention." Alex nuzzled the creaminess of one rounded shoulder, nibbled his way enticingly up towards the madly beating pulse in the hollow of her throat.

The rub of the sheet against her naked skin heightened the pleasurable sensations. "What time is it?"

"Time for us to be at work, sweetheart." Alex grinned again. "What's the staff going to say?"

Kate frowned, thinking of all she had ahead of her.

"Are you coming in today?" He had been remarkably absent the past weeks, always off on some outside appointment or meeting with potential clients and advertisers.

"Nope." Alex got reluctantly up from the bed and continued knotting his tie. "I'm catching the first flight out. I've got a few people to see in Dallas."

"What kind of account is this one?" Kate asked, wishing he'd slow down long enough to at least let her look at the ads he was lining up.

"Clothing. Several of their department stores there have expressed an interest in the terms I set. Most have stores in malls here as well. The major ones, anyway." He frowned, examining a slightly razor-chafed place on his chin. "The ones that don't have mail-order services, which sometimes prove more lucrative. Were there any important messages for me at *M.W.*?"

Kate knew he usually checked in with the new receptionist at the office daily. "No, why?"

Shrugging, Alex turned away so she could no longer see his face. "I just thought Darrel Hendrix might have called, that's all. He said something about getting together socially while I'm in the States."

Kate recalled the conversation with Darrel about *M.W.* stocks. She shrugged it off. It couldn't be. Alex wouldn't try to control her in such an underhanded fashion, no matter how much of his own time and money he had invested in *Missouri Woman*, or how uncooperative she had been.

"Something wrong?" Alex was watching her closely.

Kate got up from the bed, reached for the silk robe

beside the bed. "It's nothing. I'll make us some coffee before you leave."

Alex followed her into the kitchen a few moments later, looking professionally capable in a light tan suit. Wood-scented after-shave clung to the rugged planes of his face, the fresh scent of shampoo and soap on his clothes and skin. Kate had the sudden urge to take him by the hand, lead him back into the bedroom, and make love more passionately than ever.

"You look tired, Kate." Alex accepted the ceramic mug she proferred, his blue eyes darkening as they trailed searchingly over her face.

Kate's ardor faded as swiftly as it had appeared. "Thanks a lot," she turned away wryly.

"Notice I said *tired*." Alex moved behind her to rumple her hair affectionately. "As in overworked. Not anything else." Without warning, he set his mug down and turned her around, pulled her more completely into his arms. The minty warmth of his breath stirred her hair. "You're still the most beautiful woman I've ever met in my life."

Kate clung to the warmth of his chest, burying her face in the crook of his shoulder, taking comfort in the steady reassuring beat of his heart. With his approaching departure, both their moods had fallen. The remembrance of times past? Kate wondered unhappily. Or an unwanted glimpse into the future?

"I wish you didn't have to go," she murmured against his coat.

"Well, in that case I'll try and make it back early." Alex laughed softly at her reticence, then released her. Swiftly, he picked up his briefcase and headed for the door. He turned in the portal, once again all busi-

ness, her boss. "Oh, and Kate? See that you hire a
full-time fiction editor no later than the end of this
week." And on that commanding note, he was gone.

Kate was so furious she could have screamed. How
like Alex to be exquisitely tender one moment, then
throw out orders right and left the next—orders in
Kate's opinion he had no real right to make. However, there was no use stewing over what could not be
changed, Kate admitted, rushing to get ready for
work.

Kate spent the next few days editing articles for
the February issue of *Missouri Woman*. "Moving
Day Blues" detailed one homemaker's thoughts on
company-initiated transfers, the effect it had on the
whole family, particularly the children, tips on making
the process easier. Wielding her red pencil wryly, Kate
wondered how much of the article would have per-
tained to her life had she followed Alex and his job to
the ends of the earth. Would she have bounced back
as positively and enthusiastically as the author of the
article?

"Is this a private work session or can anyone come
in?" Alex Ryker stuck his head in Kate's door. Three
days since she had seen or heard from the rake, and
her heart still thumped wildly against her ribs.

"Hello, Alex." Feminine pride kept Kate's voice
cool.

Whatever he'd expected, a blasé welcome was not
on the list, despite his laxness in calling or checking in
with her personally. Mouth flattening slightly, Alex
strolled in, shutting the door behind him. Again, he
seemed to take her wariness deliberately in stride.
"You know I think I'm not the only one in need of a

little rest and recreation," he observed softly, studying her with an achingly tender look. "When was the last time you had a vacation?"

Kate shrugged, fighting the passionate pull she felt whenever in his dynamic, persuasive presence. "Maybe a year or two ago." Kate frowned, trying to recall. "Our honeymoon?"

"The offer to go away with me still stands."

Kate was able to read no emotion on his face. If he had said he loved her, wanted her, needed her. "There's a lot to do here at the magazine," she finally hedged.

Alex grimaced, glanced away impatiently. "Is there ever not? Damn it, Kate—" With effort, he cut short his reproach. After a moment, he moved closer, let his gaze drop to the open neckline of her silk blouse, the thin gold chain around her neck. Desire, swift and searing, immersed them both, but he did not repeat the invitation again.

Unconsciously, Kate's hand fidgeted with the tailored lapel of her blazer. "When did you get in?" she murmured, fighting down her nervousness at his presence.

"A little while ago." Completely composed once again, Alex sauntered closer, fists in the pockets of his trousers. "I would have come in sooner but Marge, our new but very efficient receptionist, told me not to interrupt."

Kate cringed. "I meant that for other members of the staff."

Alex fitted one lean hip onto the edge of her cluttered desk. "Well, apparently Marge isn't versed in the publisher/editor etiquette yet. Which reminds me.

How's that new computer programmer I hired working out?"

Kate frowned, flipping her red pencil down onto the stack of as yet unedited copy. "Why didn't you tell me you'd hired a man?"

Alex shrugged, hands palm up. "Was it necessary?"

"I would have hired a woman."

Alex grinned, shoving back off the desk top. "Reverse discrimination, Kate? The man is perfectly capable."

"Still—" Kate began.

But Alex didn't want to hear her view on equal-opportunity-above-and-beyond-the-call-of-duty. "Meet me in my office in five minutes, Kate. We've got some business to go over and I'd rather we did it there."

Kate was tempted not to show up, on principle, but realizing Alex would only come looking for her if she did not react as ordered, she picked up a pen and pad of paper and followed him there. He was seated behind his massive oak desk, hands folded behind his head when she entered. Kate noticed he had taken off his suit jacket and loosened his tie. Which meant only one thing. A long session in store for both of them.

Obediently, Kate shut the door and took a chair opposite him.

"Okay, Mr. Publisher," she said with a sigh. "What's so important?"

"Have you hired a fiction editor yet?" He got straight to the point, leaning forward, Kate imagined, to examine the circles beneath her wide amber eyes.

"Give me a break!" Kate settled back even farther into her chair, sensing this was going to be a long meeting. "You just issued the dictum three days ago."

"As I recall, I issued the *first* 'dictum' even farther back than that. Would you prefer I hired someone to do the job? I'm aware you're busy."

"Alex, that's my domain." Kate had to fight to keep her voice level.

"I've promised the premiere of our new fiction for the February issue," Alex said quietly. "Do you know how many days we have before that issue goes to press?"

"Seven!" Kate snapped. "And we're never going to make it."

"Which is precisely why you should have hired someone three days ago," he shot back in a hard businesslike tone.

Kate sighed and folded her arms across her chest. With effort, she reminded herself that she was a professional. "Look, Alex, finding quality fiction takes time. You don't just send out a few feelers and get inundated with a hundred letter-perfect short stories."

"Don't you think I'm aware of that?" he asked bluntly.

"No." Kate mocked his disapproving glare. "Maybe by the May or June issue we might be able to—"

"No dice, Kate," Alex directed flatly. "I want three short stories in the February issue. A short excerpt from a new novel or as yet unpublished work would also be nice."

"You're asking the impossible," Kate said.

"I am doing the impossible trying to turn this magazine around. Three days, Kate. Either present the material necessary or hire someone who can." And on that note she was summarily dismissed.

"Don't you think you're carrying this midnight oil bit a little too far?" Liz Shaw paused in the doorway to Kate's private office an hour after quitting time.

Kate was elbow deep in fiction, most of which had come from the University of Missouri's lit department and was highly unusable for what she had in mind. "How many of those manuscripts have you been through today?"

Kate rubbed tired eyes. "I don't know. One hundred. One hundred and fifty."

"Nothing?" Liz asked.

"I want something upbeat, light," Kate said, stretching wearily. "Something to reflect the life situation today, but not get bogged down in no-real-solution/ suicide endings. Most of the pieces in that stack deal with parent/child conflicts, wife-beating, kidnap, and rape. They might earn a C+ in some frosh lit class on the drudgery of the human experience but little else."

"Thought about calling New York literary agents?" Liz shut the door quietly and took a seat next to Kate's desk, coat and handbag still over her arm.

Kate frowned, raising a blind to look out over the darkening November landscape beyond. "I wanted Missouri writers for the fiction debut."

"Given Alex's deadline, I sincerely doubt that's possible," Liz said gently.

"Most agents don't place short stories," Kate argued dispiritedly. But Liz was right. She didn't have a hope in the world of finding much publishable in the stack she was currently perusing. The writers, talented as some obviously were, were just not familiar with the commercially oriented prose Kate wanted.

"Still, some might have authors who were willing to give it a shot, or better yet, have something already written, something we might be able to use or adapt. Kate, it's worth a try."

Kate turned around, letting the thin-slatted fashion blind fall with a snap. "You're right, of course. I should have thought of that myself."

"You would have if you weren't so overworked," Liz comforted. Shaking her head wearily, she added, "We're going to have to do something about expanding the staff, though. Alex is right. The seven of us currently working can't begin to handle the amount of material he wants on such short notice."

Kate took the hint. "I'll see what I can do."

"Well, don't wait too long." The amiable redhead trudged slowly towards the door. "Or your charming husband is going to have a mutiny on his hands. And you can include me in that tally."

Kate spent the rest of the evening ringing up literary agents and sorting through the rest of her files, ones Alex had not yet managed to uncover and organize for her. From that, she found seven letters from local novelists. Thirty-nine phone calls later, she had located all but one—who apparently had moved, and gotten them to promise to bring their as yet unpublished works into the *M.W.* offices in the morning. Dawn found her asleep on the sofa in Alex's office, curled up around a pile of neatly edited articles.

"Kate? Kate..." Someone was shaking her shoulder rudely.

"Go 'way!" Kate mumbled, throwing the bulk of her coat back over her head. She only wanted a few more minutes of sleep. Just fifteen... maybe twenty... twenty-five...

The next thing she knew the tempting aroma of freshly brewed coffee was being shoved under her nose. The warmth of a strong masculine hand slid underneath her shoulder. Kate was carted up to a sitting position. When she finally managed to open her eyes, a freshly shaven and showered Alex Ryker was staring kindly down into her face.

"What are you still doing here?" he reprimanded bluntly, concern lighting his vivid blue eyes.

"Working." Now that Kate was awake her bad mood returned full blast. Why pretend he didn't know she'd been slaving away all night? She certainly hadn't been home.

Alex handed her the coffee, then correctly assuming she wanted a moment to collect herself, walked over to open the blinds. Dusky light poured through, illuminating the elegant new *Missouri Woman* offices unbearably for anyone as weary as Kate.

Alex shook his head, then hands folded behind him, leaned back against the wall, still perusing her with that thinly veiled sensuality she knew so well. Even as disheveled as she was, it was clear he still found her terribly attractive. *To each his own,* Kate thought, drowning herself in yet another jolting dose of caffeine.

"Do you know what a scare you gave me when I got up this morning and found your bed hadn't been slept in?'' he said. Clearly, he thought she would have shown up eventually. Kate was slightly pleased to know she had proved his second guess wrong, if only accidentally.

"I entertained out of town clients last night," he finished drily. "Came in late and took the bed in the guest room because I didn't want to wake you."

"How thoughtful," Kate said acidly. She brought the mug to her lips, still muttering to herself, and burned her mouth on the scalding brew. "It's reassuring to know even slave drivers need their sleep."

"What did you say?" Alex frowned.

"Never mind." Kate sighed. Glancing at her watch, she started. "I've got to get home and get cleaned up," she said.

"Good idea," Alex agreed. "It'll do you good to take a few hours off." Thoroughly disgusted with both his high-handedness and his disinterest, Kate didn't bother to correct the misconception.

"What are you doing back here?" Alex asked a scant hour later as Kate strolled crisply past the still-empty reception desk. Only seven forty-five, most of the staff wouldn't be in for another hour.

"I've got appointments starting at eight," Kate said, closing the door to her office with a resounding thud.

The morning passed with a maze of activity. Liz and Marge took calls from literary agents sending manuscripts air express. The price for published works had been upped roughly three hundred percent since Kate and Alex had last talked, but she figured that was just one bill he was going to have to foot since he was the one so insistent on an immediate fiction debut.

Six of the appointments with would-be novelists had proved fruitless. But one work, *Shattered Dreams,* had real possibilities for condensation in *Missouri Woman.* Dealing with the author's own remarkably clear-sighted journey from teenager to lover to wife to motherhood and finally independence, Kate wouldn't be surprised to find it on the next list of a New York publisher, once the word was out and *Missouri Woman* had the rights. But that was the least of her worries.

"Ms. Shambaugh is perfectly willing to work on revisions," Kate informed Alex as quitting time of that day approached. "And I'll do the cutting myself, since we've got a max here of ten thousand words. But we're still going to need typist fees and copying charges and so forth, all of which I assured her we would pick up."

Alex's eyebrows raised. "That's a little unusual, isn't it?"

"Asking for a revised condensed first novel in seven days is unusual. But I think we can do it if we all work together."

Alex gestured agreeably. "All right. Whatever you say."

Kate paused. Now for the real stinger. "There's also the matter of the fee we owe her."

Alex frowned. Although as publisher he had been rounding up and then delegating money like mad, he strictly forbade any of the staff, even Kate, to dish it out or okay it at the moment without his express approval first. "How much?"

"Seventy-five hundred dollars," Kate said. "Take it or leave it."

"Seventy-five hundred dollars!" Alex righted the

contoured swivel chair swiftly. "Are you out of your mind?" They had agreed on three thousand.

"So you have to hustle a few more advertisers," Kate said coolly, putting the pressure on him as he had done to her. "You're the one who promised the new clients an excerpted novel."

The panther looked about to spring, but his immediate reaction was crisply amenable. "You're right, of course." He placed his fingers together temple fashion over the surface of his desk. "And if the novel's as good as you say it is, I'm sure it will be worth it. But I want to see the excerpting done first."

Kate had to work night and day for the rest of the week and well into the weekend to get *Shattered Dreams* ready to go to press with the rest of the February issue. But by the time Alex returned from New York, and his latest ad gathering jaunt, the herculean task was completed. Now all that was left was the sorting out of short stories Liz Shaw and their drafted-into-service receptionist Marge had selected.

"Darrel Hendrix called." Alex strolled into Kate's office shortly after five on Monday. "He and Sally want us to go over there and have dinner."

Kate was still staring blindly at the stack of stories in front of her, so blitzed from the effort on *Shattered Dreams* she couldn't even begin to read the collection of stories with a clear mind. "Can't," she mumbled wearily at length, rubbing her eyes. "I've got tons of work yet."

"The stories can wait until tomorrow," Alex decided, walking around to stand behind her chair.

"They're due tomorrow," Kate sighed.

"So read them in the morning." The fingers kneading the back of her neck were doing wonders towards dissipating the tension, but Kate pulled away anyway. After all, it was mostly his fault she was having to work so hard.

"You go." Hand covering her eyes, Kate switched on her reading lamp and leaned over the typewritten pages. Much as she liked both Darrel Hendrix and his wife Sally, Kate wasn't up to any cozy hearth-and-home scenes. And that's exactly what the Hendrixes had, the perfect family of five.

The light above her eyes was deliberately switched off. Alex pulled Kate gently out of her chair. Before she could protest, he'd twirled her towards the coat rack. "We'll both go. We need the break, Kate." He paused, silently imploring.

"All right," Kate said finally. "But just for a while."

Chapter Seven

Dinner at the Hendrixes' was always informal and early, never later than seven. Kate and Alex stopped by the house to change into jeans and shirts, and then headed across the posh north Springfield subdivision to their attorney's immaculately kept home.

Sally was in the kitchen, one eye on the dinner, the other watching their active eighteen-month-old daughter Kristin. Alex rounded up Darrel, seven-year-old Ty, and fifteen-year-old Angie for a game of touch football on the lawn. Watching them from the picture window in the dining room, Kate felt a brief stab of envy.

"You know you could go out and join them," Sally Hendrix said softly behind her, handing Kate a glass of chilled white wine.

Kate watched Alex plotting strategy with a madly giggling Ty, dark heads bent together, both in jeans and hooded navy blue sweatshirts. The football games had become a predinner ritual. Now, as always, seeing her ruggedly handsome husband interacting affectionately and generously with someone else's son, Kate wondered if he missed having children of their

own, if it were one of the reasons he was so determined to get their marriage back on track or if it
would inevitably be one of the reasons he would
leave her—because she wasn't ready yet, and he apparently was—or at least leaning heavily in the direction of parenthood.

Kate thanked Sally for the wine. "To tell you the
truth, they're a little rough for me, Sal." As if to prove
Kate's point, Angie shot forward, intercepted Ty's
pass, adeptly blocked both opponents and hopped,
skipped, and jumped over the bumpy back lawn for a
touchdown. Ty stomped his foot in chagrin but broke
into giggles again when Alex initiated their "Mean
Machine" chant. Spirits renewed, Alex and Ty leaned
down into another huddle while Darrel and Angie
conferred.

"He's probably telling her to let Ty take the next
one," Sally predicted, amused. "Ty can only handle
so much loss at a time."

"Ditto for Alex." Kate turned away from the window and walked back over to the corner of the dining
room where Kristin sat banging pots and pans together. Kate knelt down to touch the toddler's silky
blond hair and take a pretend bite from the proferred
wooden spoon. Kristin was Sally's last child, and the
image of her flaxen-haired mother.

"She's getting so beautiful," Kate murmured. "And
so big! The last time I was here she was barely walking."

"I know, stranger." Sally gave her friend a look of
mild reproach as she settled down into the rocking
chair in the corner of the big homey kitchen. The
center of the Hendrix home, it was always filled with a

tempting array of food and smells, warmth, light, love. Sally couldn't have feasted on much of what she cooked, though, because her figure was still as trim and youthful as ever, despite her forty-two years. "It's good to see you and Alex back together. How long is he staying?"

Kate let out her breath in one long shaky sigh. "Don't waste much time getting to the heart of the matter, do you?"

The attractive blonde shrugged. "I didn't think I had to. You know how fond both Darrel and I are of you and Alex. Neither of us was pleased when you split."

"Well, we weren't exactly jumping for joy, either. Sorry, I'm a little touchy." Kate sat down on a straight-backed chair opposite Sally and wisely changed the subject. "Have you seen the new format of *Missouri Woman*?"

Sally nodded. "Alex sent over some galleys of the three new columns and a couple of the articles. Darrel said you had signed a terrific new novel just last week, that advertisers were literally beating down your doors."

Which reminded Kate she still hadn't seen a detailed listing of the new ads set to run. "Well, it is better. Lots. And we have Alex to thank for it." She took another sip of the dry, aromatic wine. "You'll have to come down to the new offices someday soon and have the grand tour."

"Hey! Mom! We won! Alex and I won!" Ty came screaming in the door a few seconds later, narrowly missing his baby sister as he scrambled for his mother's lap. Kate scooped up the blue-eyed Kristin, and kept her safely out of harm's way. Angie stomped in next, rolling her eyes as if to let her mother know she had deliberately thrown the game. Darrel's sly grin confirmed it.

Alex bent to give Kristin a kiss, then bestowed another more meaningful one across Kate's mouth. When he lifted his head and gazed down at her tenderly, his blue eyes seemed to say. *This is what I want for us. One big happy family. The breadwinner, devoted homemaker, and rambunctious group of children.* But Kate wasn't sure she was ready for that. Blushing, she turned away.

"Come on, sport," Alex ruffled the back of Ty's unruly brown hair, interrupting a breathless blow-by-blow description of the entire game. "Let's go wash up. You can show me where the bathroom is."

"Aw, Alex, you know where the bathroom is," Ty complained cheerily as they set off.

"Then we'll see who can use the *least* amount of soap and still get clean...."

Darrel grinned, watching the two of them depart, then peered into several of the pots simmering on the stove. "Dinner about ready, hon?"

"Mm-hm," Sally shot a fond look at her husband's expanding waistline. "Just give me a minute."

Kate was put in charge of Kristin as Sally put the dinner on the table. There was a huge platter of tender, braised pork chops, bowls of scalloped potatoes laced with cream, sweet green peas studded with tiny pearl onions.

"Angie prepared the salad," Darrel announced proudly after grace. His daughter blushed to the roots.

"Aw, Dad..."

"Getting to be quite a cook!" Darrel continued to boast.

At the other end of the table, Alex and Ty were sparring wordlessly over the rolls. Alex glanced up as he passed the cloth-covered basket on, focused on the beautifully prepared fruit and cabbage salad gracing the center of the table. Complete with fresh-cut oranges, apples, seedless grapes and whipped cream, it was a culinary delight.

"Hey, that is a work of art," Alex decided, visibly impressed. "Angie did this all by herself?"

Angie blushed again. "It wasn't that hard, Alex. Honestly, anyone can follow a recipe."

"Where did you get the recipe?" Kate inquired, slipping a generous scoop of the appetizing mixture into the salad bowl next to her plate.

"Out of a cookbook," Angie lowered her gaze shyly.

"She's been taking Home Ec this semester," Sally interjected, saving her daughter from further embarrassed explanations.

"Well, it must have been better than the version I took," Kate grinned. "Because we sure didn't make anything like this."

"Oh, we're still stuck on cream puffs and muffins and biscuit dough in there," Angie became more talkative as the meal progressed. "But I like to experiment. To do that you really have to scour the papers and cookbooks, figure out what works and what doesn't. Right now I'm saving tuition money so I can take a special gourmet cooking seminar at U. of M. next summer. It's part of a special program they offer high school students. I'll get college credit for it, too, if I pass."

From across the table, Kate and Alex exchanged a glance. "Are you thinking what I'm thinking?" Kate asked.

"Must be," Alex retorted. Darrel and Sally looked baffled. "We might be able to help supply that tuition money," Alex continued pragmatically. "If Angie's amenable to a little hard culinary work, and you're willing to take on the responsibilities and paperwork necessary for her to have a part-time job."

"We've arranged for a test kitchen at *Missouri Woman* but it's still being built," Kate explained. "In the past, most of our recipes were tested out at staff member's homes after office hours. With the expansion of the format, though, it's started to become a real problem. No one has time to purchase the ingredients, much less cook or get a valid, documented reaction. Sal, you were an English major. Would you be willing to type up the reports?"

"Kate, you know we'd be glad to help *M.W.*," Sally retorted. "Plus this would be such good experience for Angie. And I'd be here to supervise, of course."

"Well, Angie?" Kate looked at the teenager seriously. "What do you think? Do you want to work for *Missouri Woman*? We could start on a part-time trial basis, see how it works out, and go from there."

"I'd love it!" Angie's eyes were shining. "I promise you, Kate, you won't be disappointed in me."

"That's my girl," Darrel said proudly. "Never any lack of enthusiasm, either."

"Which is exactly what we need," Alex added in mock sincerity. "Believe me, if you'd tasted Kate's shrimp and bean curd efforts the other night—"

"Oh, Alex!" Kate blushed as everyone laughed, including herself. In the middle of the free-for-all, the baby spilled her cup of milk and threw her dinner roll to the floor. Standing up in her high chair, Kristin took a flying leap for her Daddy's lap, smearing jelly and butter on his shirt as she went. Sally got up to get a washcloth and fresh bottle of milk.

"Bedtime for you darling," she crooned, taking her young charge in her arms for a round of good night hugs and kisses.

By the time Sally had returned, they had settled on salary, hours, and the way it was to be done. Sally enthusiastically agreed to help supervise and decide the fate of the recipes, as well as document any problems. Alex insisted she also be paid for her efforts.

Monday Night Football followed, along with a pecan pie, also made by Angie, and coffee. Rich with butter and sugar, and chock full of nuts, the southern dessert was topped with generous dabs of whipped cream. Kate and Alex helped with the dishes, then headed home at halftime, arriving at their house just in time to see the second half begin.

Kate made a fresh pot of coffee, and after pouring Alex a cup disappeared with the thermal insulated carafe into the den. There, she buried herself in the pile of short stories she had taken from the office. It was nearly midnight when Alex came in to check on her.

"Still working?" He was still dressed in the grass-stained jeans, madras work shirt, and blue-hooded sweatshirt.

Kate stifled a yawn. Now that he mentioned it, she was exhausted. "I've still got a few more of these to wade through. Tomorrow morning, I'll reread the best six and select from there. The others will probably be scheduled for later issues of *Missouri Woman*, because they're all pretty good.''

Alex didn't argue the fact that she needed to get the job finished. ''When do you think you'll be coming to bed?''

Was that an invitation to dally? His innocent expression gave no clue. ''I don't know,'' Kate said wearily. ''A little while.''

''By the way''—Alex stopped just as he was ready to walk out the door and leaned idly against the jamb—''I meant to mention it the other night, but the reason I slept in the master bedroom with you is that there's some sort of problem with the bed in the guest room.''

''Too lonely?'' The assessing words were out before Kate could prevent it. She blushed a deep rose red at the reminding look he gave her. Their last night together in the king-sized bed had been a very passionate one, by mutual consent.

''Whatever the reason,'' Alex continued, grinning, ''there *is* a problem with that bed in the guest room. It seems a bit unsteady. So until I get the chance to crawl under it and check it out more thoroughly, I suggest you sack out with me in the master bedroom. And don't worry about waking me up. Whatever time you come in is fine with me.''

''Thanks, but it looks like a late night,'' Kate said primly. She needed time to sort out her feelings and his before they were together again.

Abruptly, Alex's patience wore thin. Nor did he seem inclined to devote the time for an in-depth discussion of their future or lack of one, either. ''Suit yourself.'' He shrugged as he straightened and turned

to walk out of the room. He got as far as the doorway
before he pivoted back. Swearing eloquently, he
pinned her with a stormy azure blue gaze. "Why are
you avoiding me, Kate?" His voice was low, compelling. "Falling asleep at the office simply so you
won't have to come home—"

"You haven't been exactly available yourself,"
Kate countered defensively. "Always out of town, on
overnight jaunts." She knew he wanted her physically, at least when he was home nights. He had yet to
tell her he loved her, try and work out a future they
could reasonably share.

"If I'm gone it's only because—" Alex stuck his
hands in the pockets of his jeans. "Forget it." A deep
sigh of resignation rippled his tall, lean frame. "Do
what you want, Kate. But I'm going to bed in the
master bedroom. You know where to find me if you
want me. And, Kate? The bed in the guest room *is*
wobbly."

Kate sat there long moments after Alex had departed. How dare he try to tell her where she could
and could not sleep! And as for the guest bed being
unsafe, he must be a fool to think she would go for
that one even if it were a nineteenth-century antique.

Kate banished his warning from her mind. Alex
was just trying to wangle her into another erotic sleepless night, keep her awake with stirring visions of how
it could be between them if she'd agree to follow him
back to his job in Riyadh. Well, it wouldn't work. Not
only would Kate go to sleep on the "forbidden" mattress, she'd keep him out of her dreams, too!

Carrying out that determination, however, did not
prove as easy as it seemed. Among other things there

was the problem of suitable nighttime attire. After a quick but necessary ice-cold shower, Kate recalled Alex was asleep next to the bureau containing her clothes. Not wanting to wake him, she finally selected a shirt from the collection of his clothes in the guest room closet. Sleepily, Kate rolled up the sleeves, buttoned the front, and crawled into bed.

The cool percale sheets were scented with the tang of his aftershave. Swearing her fate, Kate tossed and turned in the darkened room. If there was anything she didn't need was a reminder of how virile and masculine a cologne Alex wore, nor how much she would be bound to miss the very same scent when he was gone again. Upon reflection, Kate noted, the guest bed did seem a bit wobbly. Pride kept her from admitting the same to Alex by crawling into his bed. Pounding her pillow with her fist, Kate tried one last time to get comfortable. Once to her right, then over again on her left side. On her stomach, her back....

Crash!

The mattress and box springs dropped heavily to the floor, landing with a thud that left Kate breathless and shaky. Alex was in the room ten seconds later, rumpled black hair falling across his forehead into his eyes.

"Kate! What in the—!" What started as a mild exclamation erupted into a roar of laughter. When he could speak again, Alex limped over to her. One hand still clutching his side, he wiped the tears from his eyes. "So you didn't believe me, hm! Are you all right?"

"Yes, I'm all right!" Kate snapped, embarrassed. "Do me a favor and help me out of here." The bedclothes had gotten trapped between the mattress and the floor, leaving her pinned helplessly beneath the sheets.

Alex dropped his lean frame lithely across the top of her. His hands came up to gently frame her face. "I think I kind of like you this way," he teased softly.

"Alex, come on, this isn't funny." Kate's hands were trapped against the hard bareness of his chest. Crisp hair curled beneath her fingertips. "When did you start wearing pajama pants?" Kate's eyes trailed down to the loosely tied blue trousers around his waist.

"I bought them my first day back when it became clear I was going to need something if I was going to stay here." His lips lowered to brush the nape of her neck. "What are you doing in my shirt?"

"I didn't want to wake you coming in to get one of my gowns," Kate admitted.

Alex's fingers agilely worked open the top few buttons on the borrowed shirt. It came to Kate then how much he took for granted, how much he still demanded from her, at work, at home. Some inner part of her went very cold. "Well, now that I'm up," Alex began confidently.

"Alex, please." With her hand, Kate stopped the assuming gesture. "Help me up." She didn't want to begin anything she couldn't finish. The past few weeks had provided frustration enough as it was.

Alex sighed, and got obediently to his feet. "All right. But roll over to the other side so I can free this edge of the sheet." Kate did as directed. Alex lifted the mattress. But instead of giving her a boost out of the blanketed trap, he slid in beside her.

"I've missed sleeping with you, Kate," he retorted quietly, blue eyes raking longingly over the length of her. "Missed holding you at night, smelling your perfume, feeling the silk of your hair brushing against my skin."

The tips of his fingers brushed down the half parted length of her shirt, slid into the velvet bare skin beneath. Kate shivered as he lightly caressed her breasts, slid his hand contemplatively lower towards the lacy edge of her bikini panties.

"Let me make love to you, Kate," he whispered persuasively.

Kate wanted to. But the thought that he still intended to leave in another few weeks time stopped her cold. She didn't want to be hurt again, loved and left all in one simple step. How could it be so painless and easy for him? Did he love her that little?

"I can't," she admitted finally, lowering her eyes to hide the pain she knew would be revealed in them.

"You mean you won't."

Kate knew to Alex one refusal was the same as the next, regardless of the reason. Wordlessly, she watched him get up from the collapsed bed. He offered a hand down resolutely. After a moment, Kate took it.

"It's not as if you're the vestal virgin and I'm the rampaging warrior." Alex stated bluntly as Kate started down the hall for the linen closet and some extra blankets and pillows. "I have seen women before. I do have some control over my primitive urges."

Kate turned to face him, stuffing a pillow into his chest. "Maybe, just maybe, it's not you I'm worried about, Alex Ryker."

He paused. Both hands coming up to brace the wall unexpectedly, Alex held her captive against the linen closet. If he'd been devastatingly attractive before, dark hair rumpled, blue eyes hot with desire, clad only in the sexily thin pajama bottoms, standing so close to her, in so physically superior and suggestive a position, he was enthralling now. Kate felt her senses swim as he yanked the pillow lightly from her grasp and tossed it aside. Palms flat against the wall, he slanted down until his bare chest touched her breasts. His mouth moved lightly across the madly beating pulse in her neck.

"Kate, you're torturing me," he murmured, trailing his mouth languidly up to capture the lobe of her ear. "You're torturing us both. If you'd just return with me to Riyadh," he began.

Abruptly, they were back where they had begun. Nothing had changed. Slowly, Kate shook her head. "Alex, I can't." Silence fell. Alex pushed away from the wall, stood staring at her for a long moment more before he trekked back towards the master bedroom. "Sleep tight, Kate," he murmured.

Not surprisingly, she did anything but.

Kate awakened to find Alex had already left for the office. Wisely, she spent the first half of the morning working at home. It was nearly eleven by the time she arrived at *M.W.*

Kate reported to Alex first thing. "Marge said you wanted to see me."

"I thought you might want to go over the list of new advertising accounts I've signed." Walking over to his desk, he flipped out a typewritten list, then several additional color layouts. Kate perused them all carefully. Liquor, cigarettes—most notably the Virginia Slims ads—dog food, and apple juice. "So far so good?" Alex asked.

"I don't care for the amount of cigarette and liquor ads you've picked up, but otherwise no objections."

Alex didn't seem surprised by Kate's lukewarm reaction. Wordlessly, he handed her some more. These were less in keeping with the standard view of *Missouri Woman*. First there was a dancing cat with a silly expression, then a bar of soap containing bath oil that promised to make a woman soft and smooth all over. "Where are these ads going to be located?" Kate asked.

"Near the front."

Her original assessment had been correct, then. With Alex choosing the ads and padding *Missouri Woman* with commercial hype, the look of the small regional press would change. It would resemble all other national women's magazines.

"Those will be midsection in the magazine," Alex handed her another group of ads. "From the March issue on, Liz will be handling the layouts. But basically we are charging advertisers not only for the size of the ad, but also for position or placement. Those who want theirs towards the front or middle sections pay more."

Kate started to argue with Alex about craftsmanship, the artistic way *Missouri Woman* had been layed out before, then stopped herself. She could change things as soon as he left. One issue wouldn't make or break them, particularly if they labeled it later as a publishing experiment.

"Mini-pads, maxi-pads, tampons, and feminine hygiene spray." Kate glanced up at her "silent" partner with very little patience. "This may surprise you, Alex, but the burning quest of most women is not to discover which menstrual product works best. Or even how many different kinds there are on the market." Which, judging from the sheer number of ads he'd placed, he'd done his best to discover.

"I didn't say it was." Alex looked slightly peeved she hadn't respected the number of new accounts he'd placed. "But this will pay your expenses this month, including that novel you bought at two and a half times what I was prepared to offer."

Kate went silently back to her ads. "Strawberry shortcake, strawberry refrigerator pie. You can sure tell spring is coming, at least as far as the presses are concerned."

"You agree with those?" Alex was watching her carefully.

Kate nodded. "Nice photos, vibrant colors." She flipped through more food ads. "Where are all these located?"

"Near the back."

Kate flipped through corn oil, housepaint, and dishwasher soap that didn't leave spots. "Fifty more pages of this stuff, hm?"

"More, if I could get it," Alex agreed.

Kate made no comment. But when she got to the internationally marketed face cream she stopped. "'Does your husband mistake you for his mother?'" she quoted part of the out-dated copy aloud, unable to believe Alex had actually signed the account. "'Is he interested in younger women? Introducing the new moisturizing lotion that will eradicate your wrinkles and put a new lift into your life!' Alex, tell me you're kidding!" Kate implored.

"I'm not kidding."

"Not in my magazine!" Kate tore the offensive copy in two and flipped it across his desk. Dancing cats and corn oil maybe. But not that.

Alex sighed and shook his head. Reaching into his drawer he pulled out another, then held it carefully out of her reach when she tried to do an instant replay. "Kate, this ad is in every woman's magazine in the country."

"It's a put-down to women!"

Alex chose not to address that point. "The account is a lucrative one, Kate. One of the best. In fact, their face cream is one of the most popular moisturizers in this country."

"And we can't get the ERA passed."

"Now, Kate—"

"I won't be a party to such blatant discrimination, such Dark Ages thinking!"

"Well, I will be," Alex said quietly. "And since I am publisher and legally able to make all such decisions, it stays. We need the money, Kate," he continued quietly when it looked as if she were still going to explode. "Your entire staff needs hefty raises, and cost-of-living increases." Kate was silent. She knew in that regard *Missouri Woman* had not kept pace the past few years. "Sit down and look over the rest of the ads," Alex directed. "I'd like to get a feel as to what you like and what you don't, so at least in the future I will know."

Kate noticed he hadn't said he would avoid them.

He just wanted to know which ones would be liable to bring trouble. "How about the sexy lingerie ads?" Alex asked. "The designer jeans? Do those offend your sense of what's right for *Missouri Woman*?"

Kate saw he was serious. "The jeans ads could sometimes use a little more...upright positioning." Kate shrugged finally. "But I guess if you really want to see how they fit..." She left the thought hanging. "As far as the lingerie ads go, I probably would have run them before had I been approached."

"Then you don't object to a woman being presented sexily in the ads?"

"As long as it's not demeaning, or an insult to our intelligence, no. *Missouri Woman* is working to dismantle the myth of the woman who lives only for her man. We are determined to show that all women can lead happy, fulfilled lives, with or without men, Alex."

"I noticed," he said dryly.

"Women have varying needs, Alex. They also have a right to expect more out of life than just seventy or eighty years of being someone else's helpmate and appendage. Some want careers outside the home. Some make a career inside the home. It's whatever the woman wants. Regardless, the crucial question is no longer can she or can she not stave off more wrinkles, and if she doesn't, will her husband leave her?"

Alex took the opportunity presented, fortifying himself first with another deep breath. "About this face cream, Kate—"

"No."

He sighed, tried again. "Kate, I agree their approach is a little less than ideal. But they're not an American firm—"

"I don't care who puts out the moisturizer." Kate stood resolutely and headed for the door. "If any advertiser comes in here promoting women who live only for their men or the hour at which their hubbies come home at night, they're out. That goes for editorials, articles, and ads. I won't represent that archaic view, not in *Missouri Woman.*" The door slammed behind her as she left, echoing the finality of her words.

Chapter Eight

Alex strolled into Kate's office an hour later, the tailored business suit and white silk shirt accentuating his dark good looks, the tan he had acquired his months in the Mid-East. Deliberately, he left the outer door open, ignored Kate's still vaguely peeved glare.

"I gave the staff the rest of the day off."

Kate tossed down her pencil. "Good idea." She only wished she had thought of it. "Everyone's in need of a hiatus, however brief."

Alex sauntered closer, eyes still fixed fondly on her upturned features. "You're included in the tally."

Kate glanced back down at the story she had just finished editing. Although it was not scheduled to run until March, she hated to leave anything undone. "You go ahead, Alex. Have fun. I'll be along later."

Gently, he leaned forward to cover the typewritten pages. The brisk masculine scent of his cologne drifted down, inundating Kate in memories, most of them excruciatingly passionate. "No one will be able to leave in good conscience unless you do too, Kate."

Kate paused, more irritated than she would let on.

Because he had signed the blatantly sexist moisturizer account? she wondered. Or because he had swiftly acquired so many ads, most of which she could find no real objection to? "Good point, Alex. I'll just take these few things home..."

Liz Shaw stuck her head in the door, chiding, "We saw that! No homework allowed, Kate! For anyone! So you can just put that briefcase away!"

Alex raised strong gentle hands helplessly. "You heard the managing editor." The rest of the staff thundered in, surrounding Kate at her chrome and glass desk. Talk turned excitedly to the new February issue which had just made its way over to production and the printer's. Leaning back in her swivel chair, Kate put her anger aside, realizing they really did have reason to celebrate.

Talk turned to the various ways to whoop it up. Alex crossed quietly around behind Kate's swivel chair. Grabbing her coat from the nearby rack, he tossed it over her shoulders, his hand lingering warmly and possessively across the width of her back.

"Lock up for us, Liz. And, editors, don't do anything we wouldn't do. We bid you good day..."

"Nice idea, Alex. But what makes you think I'd want to go hiking with you after that ad you placed?" Kate walked briskly towards the elevators at the rear of the seventh floor, Alex by her side.

Alex pushed the down button to the left of the elevator doors, then paused to help Kate into her coat. "Look, I know the past few weeks have been difficult. You have every right to resent the way I've taken over as publisher. And as for the moisturizer ad, in the fu-

ture I'll take what you said into heartfelt considera-
tion. But the bottom line is, it had to be done. You've
needed a tough, good business manager or publisher
for some time now." Kate made no reply and he went
on, more softly. "This may be the last chance we have
to enjoy the fall leaves, Kate. Think of it. Crisp cool
air, bright autumn sunshine."

He watched her for any signs of weakening. The
minute he saw temptation flicker in her eyes, he ca-
joled, "I'll even bring the lunch. You won't have to
do a thing."

Kate thought about the lonely months she'd en-
dured while Alex had been working in the Middle
East, half a world away, times when she would have
killed for an invitation such as this from the handsome Alex Ryker. Did she really want to keep denying herself no matter what the future held? Was her
pride worth it?

"All right," Kate conceded finally. "You win."

They'd taken separate cars to the office, so they
took separate cars home. Kate was first to arrive, and
after depositing coat and handbag across living room
sofa, went back to change. She selected snug-fitting
Levi's, turtleneck sweater, and plaid flannel shirt. For
added warmth, she was taking along a hiking coat,
gloves, and knitted wool cap. Western-style boots
adorned her feet. Alex was in the kitchen, securing
the latch on his backpack when she sauntered in.

"Oh, no, you don't!" he exclaimed, when she tried
to investigate the contents of their lunch. "It's a surprise."

"Hadn't you better change?" Kate leaned idly
against the counter.

"I'll just take this with me." Alex grinned, back-pack slung loosely over his arm. "And speaking of changing." He glanced down at the business suit he still wore, then over at her feet. "Hadn't you better switch to real hiking boots?"

"Those twenty-pound monstrosities you bought me the first week we were married?"

"It's pretty muddy out there." He frowned thought-fully, but made no other attempt to persuade.

"These will do fine."

"Okay," Alex called over his shoulder as he disap-peared down the hall. "But don't say I didn't warn you!" The door slammed. Kate recalled the guest bed incident, vacillated, then decided why not. Just think-ing about those marine shoes made her legs ache. Besides, they really weren't all that broken in. Her western boots would do fine, wouldn't they?

Three minutes later, Alex was ready to go. Kate surveyed the sensible jeans, as warm and snug-fitting as hers, the turtleneck sweater and plaid shirt, the open yellow down vest. His black hair lay in tousled disarray across his forehead. His blue eyes were made even deeper by the midnight shading of his sweater.

They strolled out to the jeep. Alex stowed his back-pack in the rear section, then opened the door for Kate, walked around and slid behind the wheel.

"I didn't ask you to go along with me today just for the break in routine," Alex informed Kate unexpect-edly as they whizzed out of the city limits and into the rolling autumn-colored countryside beyond. "I have a luncheon meeting scheduled in St. Louis tomorrow around noon. I'm taking a commuter flight out and I want you to come with me." Before she could protest, he added seriously, "If it goes through, it's going to be the largest account *Missouri Woman* has ever had. It could carry the magazine financially the next couple of years."

"Who's it with?" Kate turned slightly to face him. She was surprised Alex hadn't mentioned it that morning when they'd discussed the rest of the ads.

"The Beautiful You Cosmetics Company," Alex replied, glancing in his rearview mirror as he prepared to switch lanes. "They've proposed an eight to ten page spread featuring their make-ups and so forth. If you agree, it could bring some very nice revenue to the magazine."

Why did Kate have the feeling he was hiding something? Beautiful You Cosmetics Company was a nationally prominent firm, known for its quality product. "Is there anything objectionable in the copy?"

Alex glanced in the rearview mirror again. "Not that I could see, no. But with the amount of money and importance of sums involved, your approval was desired both by the company and myself. And since you're going to have to be working with their sales representative the next few years, it made sense for you to meet him now, while I'm still here. Which reminds me, have you seen or heard from Gavin Hayes lately? Has he sent any more surfer boys around to drum up business?"

Kate grinned. "No, sorry to say, he hasn't."

They drove into the forested hills south of Springfield, past the turn off for Wilson's Creek National Battlefield Park. "Where are we going to be hiking?" Kate asked.

"Mark Twain National Forest, unless you know of

some place better." Alex sent her a probing glance beneath arched brows.

"Sounds good to me." It wouldn't be hard to escape the demands of the magazine in such an area of undeveloped splendor, Kate mused. Though by the same token, knowing how many thousands of acres the Ozark park contained...

"I brought my compass, just in case," Alex said as though reading her mind. The Jeep tumbled abruptly off the road, slid to a halt next to a graveled lane about a quarter of a mile from a desolate concrete bridge.

"Here?" Kate asked. She'd hoped they would stop at a ranger station and take a well-market path.

"Still like to play it safe, hm, Kate?" Alex grinned. Hopping down out of the jeep, he yanked open her door genially, gave her a steadying lift down. "Relax. I've been here before."

Kate hadn't. "Where's the path?" She glanced at the dense thicket of trees and underbrush crowding the slope.

Alex lifted the backpack and fitted it onto his back. "Don't tell me you forgot to pack the breadcrumbs, Gretel! We're not going to get lost," he soothed, pointing past them to the bridge. "And if we do get a little turned around, we can always follow the stream back."

"What happens if I insist on a slightly safer trek?" Kate asked.

"I've got the lunch."

He also had the keys to the Jeep—Kate realized, scrambling down the slope after him. Leave it to Alex to turn their afternoon off into some sort of survival test for magazine editors. Alex leaned up against the base of a nearby tree, thumbs hooked casually in his pockets.

"You're going to love the view," he promised as she swiftly caught up.

"How much farther do we have to go?"

"Not far."

The next question was did she still believe in Santa Claus? Alex started off again, Kate in hot pursuit.

"At least tell me what's for lunch." Kate wanted to know if it was worth it.

"You'll find out when we get there." Alex proceeded with infuriatingly long, but languid strides. Talk about bossy and autocratic!

"And I thought you were bad at the magazine," Kate swore, ducking another tree branch. She paused to catch her breath and pick the burrs off her jeans. "Ow! Blast!"

"What'd you do this time?" With effort, Alex pried the bleeding index finger from her lips. Whipping a handkerchief from his pocket, he carefully checked for splinters, applied pressure to stop the bleeding. "You know there is one thing I forgot," he murmured, ripping the cloth apart to form a small bandage. "Band-Aids and disinfectant. With you around, Kate, we should never be far from either." He tied the bandage with a square knot. *Boy scout!* Kate thought.

They proceeded down the roughly sloping terrain. Their breath was so frosty they could see it in the air, the afternoon completely still except for the noise they made and the faint sounds of an occasional bird or rustle of the leaves in the wind.

"What happens if we come across a snake?" Kate

asked eventually, keeping an eye out for any coiled critters that might be laying in wait.

"I don't know." Alex shrugged broad shoulders indolently. "Run? Give me a break, woman! It wasn't covered in the business management handbook."

"You're a great comfort in my time of need," Kate rejoined, still keeping close to his side. It made her feel more secure when her thigh brushed his as they walked. "Are you sure you know where we're going?" Kate asked eventually. The blue sky above was gradually changing to gray. The air grew damper, more distinctly chilly. On the other side of the slow moving water was a sloping ridge of carved red-orange rock, at the top of which, another fifty feet straight up, was another stand of towering oak, pine and walnut trees.

"Mm-hm," Alex nodded, pointing to the towering ledge above. "Up there."

Kate craned her neck back as far as it would go. "Nice view," she said dryly. "Now how do we get up there? Helicopter? Perhaps Batmobile?"

"Keep walking." Alex gave her a friendly but necessary shove in the appropriate direction. With effort, Kate kept subsequent comments to herself and they traveled wordlessly along the creekbed for a while, slipping and sliding in the slick surface of moss and mud. Kate had to remind herself he was the one carrying the pack with the lunch.

"When we finish with this tromp..." she muttered cantankerously.

"Now, darling, cool down." Taking her arm gallantly, Alex slowed his pace a little as they skated past the bareness of unleaved trees and headed even deeper into the woods. "You know I only have your best interests at heart!"

"That's what Patton said to his troops! How much farther?" Kate breathed wearily at last when the towering ledge of rock above them had ended, melding nicely into a steep expanse of more fallen leaves, muck, and ridiculously slanted trees, growing at forty-five degree angles from the ground.

Alex squinted up towards the top. Though the incline had lessened it was still treacherously steep, and slick as well. "We're there. At least as soon as we cross the creek and climb the ridge."

"But there's no bridge!"

"No ski lift, either," Alex pronounced drolly. "Come on." And then when she hesitated, "The water's only about a foot and a half deep." He gestured towards the rocks and driftwood scattered across the shallow pool. "I'll help you."

Kate saw he was serious when he said he meant to climb that cliff and picnic there. She didn't doubt the view was gorgeous, but there was no way she was going to get killed hiking up there. "Actually, Alex, I kind of like it down here," she decided enthusiastically.

Alex caught the acclaim for the cop-out it was. "Uh-huh, sweetheart. Those that eat, eat up there. Ready?"

"As I'll ever be," Kate muttered. Two slippery steps across the river, Kate changed her mind. Skipping back to shore, she decided breathlessly. "You go. I'll just stay here and watch."

"Now, Kate." Identifying her panic, Alex marched purposefully back over towards her. "You know I can't go anywhere without you."

"You went to Saudi Arabia once."

"My mistake." And before Kate could do anything more than gasp her protest, she was hauled up and over his shoulder like a fifty pound sack of potatoes.

"Alex Ryker put me down!" Kate shouted, the ground swimming crazily past her eyes. Frantically, she grasped his belt loops and held on tight.

"Here?" Alex stopped innocently in the very center of the creek. "Or here?" He stepped even deeper into the icy water, glancing unconcernedly down as it sloshed against the tops of his waterproof hiking boots.

"How about the other side?" Kate answered meekly, calculating it to be only about five or six good strides to shore. She could kick his shins there.

"Only if you promise to be nice." Alex waded nonchalantly across the creek. When he finally put her down, it was not to chastise her for her bad sportsmanship, as she had half-expected, but to capture her mouth and cover it with his own. Kate's hands went up automatically, curved possessively over the width of his shoulders. His tongue gently parted her lips, but once within did only a cursory search for surrender. Alex traced the trembling outline of her lips with soft, gentle strokes of his thumb. "I missed you while I was away, Kate," he confided.

The trek up the slippery, leaf-covered slope was not as difficult as Kate had expected. With Alex directly behind her every step of the way, she only slid once. Leather gloves covering her hands, she reached the top relatively unscathed. Once there they strolled silently towards the uppermost portion of the ledge.

Open to their view were miles and miles of the Ozark hills, the fall colors of the changing leaves, the starkness of bare trees against the light wintery gray of the sky. Not even the faint rushing noise of the stream below was discernible from the height of the lookout. It seemed, for a time at least, that the world had finally narrowed to just the two of them. No distractions, no interruptions, no running.

"I knew you'd like it up here." Alex's arm slid companionably across her slender shoulders as he pulled her in close to his side. In the far distance, Kate could see the metallic blue of his canvas-topped jeep, the desolation of the paved road beyond.

"When did you find this place?" Kate asked, resting against the solid warmth of his chest, the down of his vest acting as a soft cushion between their two forms.

"Last year, before I left for Riyadh. I started thinking about hiking up here again during that last trip to New York. I knew I wouldn't have much time left once I got everything settled with the account executive from Beautiful You Cosmetics. I thought it was something we could share without the past or the future interfering."

His return to Riyadh. "Then you are going back?" Kate asked, swallowing the knot of emotion welling up in her throat.

"I have to." Alex's mouth formed a grim line. "I thought I had made that clear."

"Why don't you quit?" Kate searched his eyes for the hope only he could give. "Why don't you come back here, to me, our home?" They'd once had so much.

"Because the stint in the Mid-East is part of my job," Alex said roughly, recapturing his grip on the backpack containing their lunch. "It's what I do, Kate. More than that, it's a challenge and an experience I don't want to give up."

Silently, they selected a picnic site at the uppermost part of the cliff. Together they spread the Indian blanket he had brought over the leaf-strewn ground. Kate was not disappointed by the lunch. Crisp, tender, fried chicken that had been picked up at a local restaurant, potato salad, and a bottle of Kate's favorite white wine, which had been wrapped in foil to prevent it from losing most of its chill. Black Forest cake, dripping with brandied cherries and cream, and a thermos of steaming hot coffee completed the impromptu feast. "You're spoiling me," Kate sighed, leaning back against a nearby tree after they'd companionably completed the meal.

"You could get used to it," Alex stated softly. "Why do you run from me, Kate? Why do you run from the stability I offer?"

Kate took another sip of her coffee, the burning draught nothing compared to the searching intensity of his gaze. "I've seen too many women build their whole lives around the men they marry, Alex, including my own mother. When things go awry, they're the ones who suffer most. The men go back to their work and the satisfaction a successful career brings."

"Just because your father left your mother—" Alex began approaching a subject he knew had always been difficult for Kate to discuss.

"He deserted us," Kate corrected bitterly. "And she had no career or college degree to fall back on.

Fortunately, she was able to get a grant and go to school during the day, waitress for a living at night. But it was such a struggle, Alex. And I was old enough to understand what was going on. I decided then and there that I would never place my entire future in the hands of a husband or a lover or anyone else, no matter how much I cared for him."

"Isn't that what you've done with *Missouri Woman*?" Alex prompted. "Investing everything, including yourself, our marriage, and the inheritance from your mother?"

"*Missouri Woman* is my future, Alex. It's my security." Even her marriage to Alex hadn't stifled Kate's need to succeed and operate independently of everyone else.

"I could be your future, Kate."

"That's what my father said to my mother." She lowered her gaze from his icy blue stare, knowing she was not being fair in making that comparison. The two men obviously had very little in common. "I care about you, Alex," Kate said finally. "Perhaps more deeply than you'll ever know. But you're asking me to give up too much."

"Don't be silly, Alex. If I got up the slope without any problem, I can certainly get down." Kate stood at the top of the slippery cliff, speaking with a great deal more confidence than she felt. The surface of her western boots were slicker than his cleated hiking footwear, but she refused to let him help her after what he had just asked—no, what he had *expected* of her. Despite their growing closeness the past weeks, nothing had really changed. Alex still expected her to follow him to the ends of the earth simply because she was his wife. Kate had no intention of giving up her career to do so.

Alex adjusted the pack on his back. "I still think it would be better if I went first, Kate."

"Beast before beauty?" The comment slipped out before Kate could censor herself.

But Alex merely laughed. "Well put, sweetheart. Now let me go first so I can catch you if you start to fall."

"I might knock us both down," Kate theorized solemnly.

"Don't worry," Alex replied confidently, already stomping lower down the slope. "I'm strong enough for both of us."

That was precisely the kind of remark that rankled Kate the most. No doubt, Alex didn't even realize he was being sexist. Obediently, Kate let him start down the mud and leaf strewn slope. She followed at an infuriatingly slow pace. Fall indeed...!

When Alex reached the bottom, he turned to find her a good thirty yards behind him. "You see?" Kate parried with a lofty sweep of her arms. "I am quite capable of managing this myself."

"Do me a favor," Alex frowned, "and watch what you're doing. Kate! Quit showing off!"

"Afraid I'll fall because I'm a member of the *weaker* sex? You know, Alex, statistics show..." Still spitting out theories right and left, Kate dramatically stormed down. As she neared the bottom she assumed the high-stepping stride of a high school majorette, bowed, pirouetted, and bowed again.

"I think I get the message, sweetheart," Alex announced dryly at last, still gazing contemplatively at the last fifteen feet of slope between them. "Now do me a favor and come on down before you hurt yourself."

He'd done it again, this time deliberately. Kate stared at the teasingly superior gleam in his eyes. "Why don't I just jump? Better yet—climb up and start the whole thing all over again, even faster!"

'Kate—!" Alex paled visibly.

"Some people are such sissies." Kate pranced down the remaining slope, was nearly at the end when the toe of her boot caught on a partially exposed root. Kate landed in Alex's arms, as predicted, nearly knocking them both into the frigid stream behind him. When she could breathe normally again, she demonstrated her blithe attitude. "Scared you, didn't I?"

Darkness was beginning to descend, inundating the woods in a dusky gray cloud. A faint mist permeated the air. But the invigorating thrill of the afternoon hike, the danger just surpassed, and the wine recklessly imbibed during lunch made Kate oblivious to the need to hurry. She didn't want to rush home. She wanted the afternoon to last and last.

"You scared someone," Alex rejoined wryly. "Now come on," he ordered imperiously. "If we don't hurry we're going to get stuck out here for the night." Crossing the stream with swift, sure steps, he slung his backpack onto the opposite shore, and then started back to assist her.

"Oh, no!" Kate wagged a finger towards him. "This time I'm crossing it all by myself!" And to prove it, she leapfrogged to the first rock.

"Kate—" Alarm rioted across his handsome features.

"Something wrong, darling?" Kate called cheerily as she pirouetted completely around and then somehow, miraculously made it to the next piece of driftwood without falling.

Alex took another step forward bent on rescuing her whether she wanted him to or not. Kate took another step back. Wills clashed. But the middle of a frigid stream was no place to have a confrontation that had been brewing for weeks and weeks.

"Have it your own way then." A muscle clenching in his jaw, Alex turned and walked resolutely back to the opposite shore. Hands crossed implacably across his chest, he said, "Go ahead."

Kate's mouth dried up without warning. Her legs felt shaky, the beginnings of a very bad wine headache about to start. Alex glanced up at the sky. All too aware of the darkness, Kate continued. One step, two. The third leap was a bit tricky. Kate slid across the slick wet stone, started to fall back, then caught herself. Alex started forward. Pride intervened.

"I can do this without any help from the chauvinists, thank you," Kate announced haughtily. After all, there were only two more leaps to go.

Muffling an oath, Alex turned and glanced back towards the bridge. Kate leaped, missed, and fell, one foot twisting down beneath her. The water was cold.

"Stop screaming!" Alex rushed forward to help her, then dissolved into fits of laughter as he saw her soggy jeans. By the time they got up once, Kate was soaked nearly to shoulders. The fact that she fell a second time specifically because of her husband's hysterical mirth did not increase Kate's.

"You jerk!" Kate swore, shoving him aside as she stalked the last two feet towards the bank. Since she was already soaked it was no longer imperative she be careful. Alex followed, still doubled up with laughter.

"I'm sorry." Coughing, he bent to wipe the tears from his eyes. "It's just that the seat of your pants..."

"Spare me the details," Kate said icily. She knew full well she had absorbed and mostly held an additional two gallons of water, all of which seemed to be concentrated in the ballooning swatch of denim across her lower spine.

As she stomped back in the direction of the road she felt the liquid disperse, bit by trickling bit. Alex was behind her every slosh of the way, still roaring. And when he wasn't doing that, his effort not to was almost worse.

"Oh, shut up!" Kate said the moment she slammed in the jeep.

Alex circled around to the front and climbed into the driver's seat. Kate dumped the water from her boots out the door, slammed it shut, and removed her soggy socks.

Alex started the jeep and turned on the heater. Chilly air assaulted them both, worse than the frigidness of the encroaching nightfall. Kate's teeth began to chatter. Her fingers seemed appallingly numb. "Let me help you." Alex was no longer amused as he reached for the zipper to her pants.

"I can't undress here! Are you crazy!" Kate pulled back, would have bolted given the opportunity. "Anyone could come by!"

Ignoring her protests, Alex began unbuttoning her coat. "You can't keep those wet clothes on, either."

"I'll change when I get home." Teeth still chattering uncontrollably, Kate pushed his hands away. He pulled her to him and held her still. "Sweetheart, listen to me. One way or another, we're getting you out of those clothes."

"I don't have anything to wear."

Alex whipped off his down vest, then his wool shirt. "Be glad I'm in a generous frame of mind."

Reluctantly, Kate tried to remove her jeans. She got the soggy pants only as far as her hips when the strength in her numb arms gave out. Straddling the gear shift, cursing steadily, Alex managed the rest, including the damp bikini underwear. Up on the road, a car drove by, headlights sweeping the cramped confines of the Jeep.

"Duck!" Kate yelled, really regretting the transparency of the Jeep's doors.

Alex stayed right where he was. "Keep that up and they'll hear you," he remarked facetiously. "Now come on." His fingers crept up to the buttons on her jacket.

"That's only half wet!" Kate clutched the material to her chest. Honestly, sometimes the man carried gallantry too far.

"Half too much." Tall frame stooping over her, he pushed past her trembling hands, pulled the coat off, and flung it briskly into the seat behind her. With a lot of swearing about bucket seats and stick shifts, the table cloth was retrieved from the backpack and wrapped around Kate's waist. "I think there's a little coffee left." Alex rummaged around, then handed

Kate the wide-mouth thermos. She gulped lukewarm liquid straight from the mouth, passing the rest to Alex. He shook his head and passed it back. "I'm not the one who got soaked. All of it, Kate—now. Whatever warmth that has will help."

Kate watched him recap and toss the thermos aside. "Now the shirt and sweater." Swiftly his fingers worked down the buttons of her flannel shirt, divested Kate of both that and the turtleneck sweater beneath. Still working quickly, he helped Kate into his shirt, then fastened the buttons, slid on the warmth of the down vest over that.

"Crazy idiot," he murmured, leaning forward to kiss her lips.

The electricity that accompanied the chaste embrace stunned them both. Alex leaned back slightly, eyes fastened on her face. "Kate, I—" Alex began, running his thumb and forefinger contemplatively across her lower lip. And then his mouth was covering hers.

He did not ask permission, he took, and when she had surrendered all she had to give, he coaxed her into yielding even further. Kate's lips parted, allowing him further access into the honeyed sweetness of her mouth. Her hands lifted to the back of his head, drawing him closer, her fingertips curled in the thick layers of his hair.

Alex groaned at the revelation of her spiraling desire and moved even closer, swearing as he encountered the stick shift still between them. Shifting uncomfortably, he moved a leg over the cumbersome object, pulled Kate half onto his lap. Before she could protest he was administering another series of long

drugging kisses, reaching for the buttons on her borrowed shirt.

He took his own sweet time working them apart.
When he finally freed the material and slid his hand
onto the warm flesh inside, Kate shivered with delight, then gasped as he teased the pink satin of her
breast into responsiveness, cupped the fullness with
his hand.

The roughness of his slightly bearded chin chafing
her skin, Kate pulled Alex even nearer. His hand
drifted lower, past her waist, was soon tugging at the
blanket despite Kate's muffled protests that it wasn't
the time or the place.

Alex mumbled something Kate didn't understand,
then jerked free the Indian style blanket to capture the
slender line of her hip, drop across to the other, settled exploringly between. Kate arched against his
hand, then clutched his shoulders again as he sent her
into another paroxysm of delight.

Alex swore again as another car whizzed past them
on the bridge fifty yards to their left. Wearily, he released Kate and leaned back against the seat. "I guess
we'd better get out of here before someone decides to
play Good Samaritan and come down here to see
what's wrong," he said, then thrust the rumbling jeep
into drive.

It was raining steadily by the time they arrived home.
Kate giggled as she recalled some of the weird looks
they had gotten at a few stop lights along the way from
the passengers in other cars. Kate had to admit she had
been a sight, wrapped only in Alex's oversized shirt,
vest, trailing Indian blanket wrapped sarong style
around her legs, and soaked western boots.

"Yeah, real funny," Alex remarked, sliding the Jeep into the garage. "What would you have said if we'd been stopped on a traffic violation, or God knows, pulled in to some hospital emergency room because of an accident?"

"I'm with Greyhound," Kate quipped as he lifted her down from the high riding vehicle. "I would have left the explanations to you."

Alex grinned, shaking his head in mock consternation, then started to reach for her. Kate deliberately held him at arm's length. "I think I'd better get cleaned up first." She was all too aware she smelled more like the creek than any feminine perfume.

"You do that," Alex advised softly. "I'll take care of things down here, including your clothes."

Kate affected a mock sigh. "Lunch and laundry, too."

"Move it, lady."

Kate sauntered on into the house, humming softly as she went. All things considered, the afternoon had been nice. The evening promised even more of a truce if she'd read Alex's last glance correctly. Now if she could just get him to change his mind about returning to his job in the Middle East....

Kate bathed leisurely in Chanel No. 5 bubble bath, shampooed her hair, and scrubbed the woodsy grit from every inch of her body. Only when the water reached a tepid stage did she get out, dry her hair, and wrap herself in a thick wine-red robe on top of a completely translucent Victorian gown, one Alex had always liked.

Alex was already in the living room by the time Kate padded out. He was stretched out on the rug before the blazing fire, studying a legal pad of notes. As she drew closer, Kate noticed the hair at the back of his neck was still damp, as if he'd been too impatient to blow dry it thoroughly after he showered, then froze as she noticed the business he had been working on was not *M.W.* but Southwestern Oil. "It came in the afternoon mail," Alex said roughly when he noticed the direction of her stunned gaze.

Kate fought the emotional reaction simmering just below the surface. After all, she had known this was coming, known in a few short weeks he would be going back.

Alex surveyed her lingeringly. "You look nice."

"Thanks." Kate had already appreciated his white lambswool sweater and tight jeans, but she bit back a similar compliment. There seemed no sense in encouraging a liaison between them now, hoping he would change his mind after all and stay in the States. "Are you hungry?" Kate forced normalcy into her tone. Since he had fixed lunch, it seemed only fair she see about their supper.

"Well, now that you asked," Alex drawled, reviving their earlier sexier mood as he reached out lazily to slide a hand beneath the hem of her burgundy robe and caress the shapely lines of her calf.

Kate reached down to gently unhand her leg. "I meant food, Alex."

Alex sighed his disappointment, then moved to sit Indian style on the rug. "Well, now that you mention it, I have heard a few rumblings in the direction of my stomach."

"Soup and a sandwich?"

"I imagine that would calm the troops." Alex followed her out to the kitchen. Hips against the counter, he crossed his arms against his chest and watched her rummage purposefully through the pantry and the refrigerator.

"Any preferences?" Since Alex had been back, the refrigerator and freezer had taken on a more crowded appearance.

"Split pea and ham, if you've got it."

They did. All too aware of him, Kate layered thin slices of baked ham and swiss cheese onto freshly baked rye bread. Sliding the sandwiches into the microwave, Kate set the timer, then rinsed crisp green leaf lettuce and sliced tomatoes under Alex's unerring eye. On the stove, the split pea soup simmered aromatically.

"About this meeting in St. Louis tomorrow," Alex began, pulling portable dinner trays from the uppermost pantry shelf.

"I'd really rather not go," Kate decided. Now that he was leaving, she felt it better to maintain the emotional and physical distance she had originally vowed to keep.

"About that, I'm afraid you *don't* have a choice." Alex's voice was unusually firm. Kate looked up and he continued, "You know I don't have much time left in the States, Kate. And this is my vacation, after all, or what little I'm going to get for the next year or so."

Kate knew all too well he had sacrificed nearly a month's pay, as well as a good deal of time and effort to save *Missouri Woman* from fiscal failure. "If you're thinking of going away," she said finally, sensing what was coming next, "I think it's a wonderful idea." It would probably be better for both of them, in fact, now that they knew where they stood.

"Then you'll come with me?" Alex apparently saw no reason why she shouldn't, particularly given her pliant physical reaction to him in the jeep.

"No, Alex, I won't." Carefully, Kate poured boiling soup into thick ceramic mugs, then arranged the sandwiches on plates. Alex added glasses of ice water, napkins, and silver. He didn't speak again until they were comfortably ensconced before the fire, Kate on one side of the couch, he in an easy chair perpendicular to her.

"Kate, you said before it was years since you had a vacation."

"So?"

"So nothing." His voice cut incisively across hers, then lowered imploringly, "You need a break. We both do."

"Maybe from each other."

The rugged features set unpleasantly. Alex's patience with her was depleted. The meal was finished in utter silence. "The plane leaves at seven tomorrow morning," Alex said as he carried his tray to the kitchen and then strode down the hall. "Be sure you're ready to leave for the airport by six."

Chapter Nine

The temperature dropped overnight to a startlingly cold twenty-two degrees. Springfield was blanketed in an icy, gray gloom, the drive to the airport treacherous and harsh despite the four-wheel-drive vehicle transporting them.

Kate had mentioned nothing more about Alex's plans to take a few days off. She knew he needed the rest and assumed from the amount of luggage he had packed that he planned to be gone several weeks. He knew she had no intention of being persuaded into accompanying him.

"Where are you going after the meeting?" Kate asked curiously as soon as they had boarded the DC-9. Only the amount of business clothing still left in the guest room closet made her think he was not returning to Riyadh sooner than he'd planned.

"I rented a condominium in Corpus Christi," Alex replied, glancing down at the airline itinerary cursorily before stowing both passes in his pocket. It had always been customary for him to hold both passes when they traveled together. Kate had resisted the urge to ask for her own, deciding to wait until after the *Missouri Woman* business had been concluded.

Kate's thoughts drifted to the miles of National Sea Shore on Padre Island, the sandy white beaches, shimmering blue Gulf of Mexico, sunshine, warmth. "I envy you the time off," she said quietly, imagining the relaxing days he would have.

"You could still go with me," Alex pointed out gently. Blue eyes lifted to hers, imploring her to make the most of what little time they had left together before he departed for another part of the world. But Kate shook her head sadly. It hurt too much already. She wouldn't deliberately make the parting more difficult than it was at that time.

Alex concentrated on Southwestern Oil documents for the rest of the flight. Kate leafed through article proposals prepared by her staff, the list of possible candidates still vying for fiction editor. All were qualified in some way or another, but no one had yet captured the spirit of *Missouri Woman* as it was then being read, nor brought with them adequate sparks for the future. She supposed she would just have to keep doubling up on both, until she found someone to fill the position.

Their lunchtime meeting was to take place in one of St. Louis's poshest riverfront restaurants. Kate and Alex arrived straight from the airport with little time to spare due to the back-up of incoming flights. The maitre d' seated them in the rear of the spacious top floor dining room. While waiting for their client, Kate gazed at the winterscape beyond. The cold weather might have been frigid enough for snow, but the Mississippi River was still operating in all its industrial glory. Barges and tugboats crowded the murky gray-brown waters for space; old-fashioned paddleboats and tankers filled up the rest.

At Alex's direction, the maitre d' brought a full magnum of champagne. "If this meeting goes as planned, we're all going to have something to celebrate," Alex confided intrepidly, his hand moving possessively to the back of her chair.

When he leaned towards her to pour a bit more champagne into her already brimming glass his blue eyes repeated the earlier invitation to join him in South Texas. Kate had to turn away to hide her reaction to the bold caress of his dark-lashed gaze. After everything that had happened between them in the past, the fact she knew he was leaving her shortly, he still had the power to take her breath away with just a look. Knowing the often pleasurable, passionate results, why did she continue to resist? Was it any fairer to ask him to give up his job than it was to give up hers?

Alex's hands snaked across the table to touch hers. "Remember, Kate. This is a half million dollar account."

"Alex!" The immaculately dressed accountant executive walked over to join them. Alex stood as the two men shook hands. "And this must be Kate Ryker, the dynamic editor in chief."

Kate blushed as they exchanged formal greetings. Had Alex really built her up as much as Nick Santini's respectful gaze indicated? "Mr. Santini, how nice to meet you."

"Believe me, the pleasure is all mine," Santini said, pulling up a chair. "As you know, Alex and I have been working on the initiation of an account. We're aware that *Missouri Woman*'s got one of the fastest growing, most loyal readerships in the Midwest. Your partner here seems to think you are solely responsible for that."

Kate nodded. "We pay strict attention editorially to both the article and advertising sections of *M.W.*" Though Kate supposed that was changing considering the amount and type of ads Alex had placed, beginning with the February issue. "What specific product did you want us to advertise?" Though the Beautiful You Cosmetics Company was well known, not all their products carried up-to-date advertising. Still, Kate had decided to keep an open mind, at least until after she had talked to Nick. Her staff needed pay raises. This might be the only way to get them.

"You're familiar of course with our exciting new line of Firebrand perfume?" Nick accepted a glass of champagne from Alex.

Kate froze. No wonder Alex had been so vague when he'd approached her about the meeting. He had to realize the new fragrance carried one of the most chauvinistically outdated ad campaigns in recent perfume history!

Sensing her reaction, Alex nudged her lightly beneath the table. The unsmiling expression in dark blue eyes said, *Cool it, Kate.*

"Of course I'm familiar with Firebrand," Kate turned back to the account executive sweetly. Maybe there was still some way they could work this out. Maybe Alex knew something she didn't in way of a revised campaign. "You've had billboards and commercials in every major city in the country."

"And we're off to a good start, too, I might add," Nick continued enthusiastically. "However, since the initiation of the perfume, our sales have slacked off slightly. Naturally, we expected this to happen—"

Kate knew why, recalling the gist of their ads. Free samples and product newness would only carry one so far.

"—and are doing everything we can to build up the image, including actively looking for new sources of advertising. Places we can advertise on a long-term basis. Frankly, Ms. Ryker, Beautiful You Cosmetics would like to establish the same rapport with our clientele as you've managed with your readership. And of course, you've got to admit our ten page color spreads of both perfume and cosmetics would liven up your magazine."

The implication being that it was rather dull as was. Kate let that one pass only because Alex had gone to so much trouble to arrange the contract and meeting. "I assume you brought the layout with you?"

"Sure did." Reaching down into the briefcase beside him, Nick Santini pulled out a variety of potential ads. All had the same multifaceted approach. Professional, severe-looking career women; overwrought housewives fed up with the dog, the doorbell, the phone, and the children; and Firebrand perfume rushing in to save the day, and allegedly lure hubby home. Which wouldn't have been so bad had the other images not been such a blatant put-down for women. Male cologne ads never showed men falling apart because of a little pressure or work.

"Well, what do you think?" Nick asked enthusiastically as their plates of chicken and shrimp curry arrived. Kate dug into the jasmine and orange spiced rice. "No offense, Nick," she began carefully, ignoring Alex's quelling look, "but what would your company think about developing an exclusive approach for *Missouri Woman* readers?" A way that would sell perfume without offending them.

Up until that point, Alex had been silent, letting Kate carry the bulk of the business discussion. But at her suggestion, he put down his fork. "Kate, Nick has gone to a lot of trouble here."

"Gavin Hayes went to a lot of trouble, too." In Kate's mind, one put-down to women was the same as the next, despite the dollar signs attached to the account.

"Let her go on, Alex," Nick Santini intervened. "I'd like to hear what Kate has to say."

"Look, Nick, I like your perfume. The fragrance is sensational. I'm only saying that to do really well in *Missouri Woman*, you're probably going to have to go with a different approach."

Nick frowned. "We've spent millions of dollars researching and developing this campaign, Kate. On a national level."

"I know my readers, Nick." Kate ignored Alex's prodding foot. "There's no way on earth you're going to sell your perfume if you stay with that sexist pitch."

"We are talking about the whole Firebrand image!" Nick reminded.

"A *national* account," Alex added.

"Right." Kate lost her temper and saccharinely described some of their ads. "The lady fries up the bacon with one hand and sprays on perfume with the other. In between, she agonizes continuously over the simplest demands of life, usually while uncouthly spitting the limp hair out of her face.''

"You have just decimated a million dollars worth of marketing research," Nick observed tensely.

"I also think you have gone a little overboard," Alex rejoined tightly.

Kate noticed the muscle twitching in his jaw, but felt for the magazine's sake she had to go on regardless. "Look, Nick, I know you have a job to do. But I can't in good conscience sell you ad space that will only alienate my readers."

Alex's white-lipped expression said he wished she would. Kate ignored him and went on, "Our readers are all very enlightened women. Frankly, Nick, they're going to resent any attempt to put something over on them. And that's what the current line of Firebrand advertising does. It promotes the myth of the woman who lives only for her man—something we at *M.W.* have been trying for years to eradicate."

Alex reached for the magnum of champagne, apparently having given up on trying to intervene between Kate and the Firebrand representative. Kate shot him an irritated look, then turned back to Nick. "Look." She pointed to a four-sectioned ad, used mostly in magazine's and television. "The first frame shows a woman cooking breakfast—"

"Bacon," Nick interrupted.

"Bacon for her family. Look at how she's dressed, Nick. In a housecoat and electric curlers. Look at her family. While she's slaving away they're all just sitting there, waiting. No one's even offering to make the toast! Is that a situation you would like to promote?"

"According to research, it seems typical," Nick stressed, tugging at his collar.

"Maybe twenty years ago," Kate countered. "But not anymore. And if it is, we at *Missouri Woman* certainly don't want to reinforce it. The second frame depicts a woman in jeans pushing a child on a swing. That one's okay—casual, happy, realistic. The third frame is a woman in a business suit with her hair pulled back in an extremely tight bun, no makeup. She's wearing eyeglasses that would run interference for the Jets! What do you call that? Is she supposed to look scholarly, capable, or just all dried up?"

"Kate!" Alex choked on his champagne.

Nick turned a slight shade of lilac. "That's supposed to be a dedicated career woman."

"Where does it say a woman can't be pretty and smart too?" Kate countered. "Does anyone ask a man to forgo looking *his* attractive best to be taken seriously in the business world?"

"Anything more than that"—Nick tapped the picture resolutely—"is considered a blatant come-on."

"By whom?" Kate wanted to know. How could these ideas exist in such a modern world? Why were they permitted to?

"Unfortunately, more men than you can count." Alex sighed heavily and poured himself another consoling glass of champagne.

"Look, Nick, my point is only in the last frame where the woman is actually spraying on the Firebrand perfume and her husband or lover is waltzing in the door does the woman look complete. In this last frame, she is incredibly beautiful, exotic, happy. In the other frames, she is only half madeup. Now you tell me, what does that do for the image of women in general? Does it help them gain any more self-respect or heighten their images and or expectations of themselves? Or does it simply reinforce the old saw that a woman without a man is half a woman!''

"Ms. Ryker, I did not write this ad, I just sell it,'' Nick Santini said very tiredly at last. Alex seemed to agree. Kate could have strangled him for not backing her up.

"Then you're both missing the point,'' Kate accused.

"And you're too idealistic,'' Alex muttered censoriously, pouring the last bit of champagne into their long-stemmed Waterford glasses. No one had even touched their curry, but the waiter was discreetly keeping his distance, afraid to interfere in the melee in any way.

"How could we fix it?'' Nick Santini inquired. It went without saying that aspect of company policy was beyond his scope. He could, however, report back on it. And Kate thought, would.

"Change the copy to a complete, pulled-together woman in every frame. Delete the reference to and or possibility of a man, at least to the point where he makes her day perfection. Women wear perfume for themselves, Nick. Or they should.''

Nick was silent. "You realize I can't offer you anything but the original deal as specified by headquarters in New York?''

Kate nodded. Under those conditions she had no choice but to refuse. And it was clear without the editor in chief's express cooperation, the deal was off, since Alex would be returning shortly to the Middle East.

Nick stood, offering a hand wearily. "Ms. Ryker, it's been an experience. If you're ever in need of a job in marketing, let me know."

"I hope you're satisfied because by God I'd like to wring your neck!" Alex murmured tightly as they walked towards the coat check. Kate stood quietly as he paid the tip and retrieved their wraps.

"*Missouri Woman* is a regional magazine, Alex, known for its steadfast refusal to further sexist discrimination of any sort. We don't further the image of the woman who lives only for her man and the end of the day when he comes home and she gets to spray on her perfume!" Kate sighed, exasperated. "They did that in the fifties. There's a whole generation of displaced homemakers out there, Alex—a generation that once included my mother! I won't be part of creating another, not even for a half a million dollar account!"

Alex caught up with her at the elevators. Before she could stop him, he was in the paneled cage with her, slamming the ground floor button down before anyone could join them.

"Okay, Kate you've had your say and now I'm going to have mine." The dangerous set of his mouth prevented interruption. "That account in there would have made *Missouri Woman* solvent for a minimum of the next three years. Your staff could have had raises. You could have accompanied me back to Riyadh, or at least been able to afford periodic jaunts over if it was what you wished. I understand your reasoning. I let you blow it despite what it cost me professionally and personally."

As he spoke, Kate's amber eyes ran over the length of him. Alex had dressed all in black, the European cut of his suit enhancing the animal vitality of his lean form, the slender musculature of his waist and hips, the width and breadth of his shoulders. The white silk of his shirt gleamed against the darker tan of his skin, the jet black hue of his precision cut hair. Only the electric blue of his eyes, the confident nature of his faint smile, alerted her to something else, some extra card he had up his sleeve.

"Why did you do that?" Kate cut in impetuously. Why had he let her blow the account when he could have overruled her as publisher at any point? He could have even fired her on the spot.

Alex straightened as the elevator approached ground level. "Because there's something I want more than any revenue or advertising coup, and that's the pleasure of your company for the next two weeks."

"Now I know you're crazy!" Kate exclaimed. The elevator doors opened. People stared with unmitigated interest as Alex smiled, took Kate's elbow, and led her through the lobby and revolving doors to the street.

"Determined," he corrected, "and, yes, I am. So don't argue with me, Kate. You're going with me to Corpus Christi for a much needed vacation and that's that."

Kate dug in her heels, icy air assaulting her face as Alex hailed a cab. "What happens if I refuse to go?" She knew that self-satisfied look on his face. He had yet to even play his trump.

All affability vanished. Alex turned to face her with

all the heart of the steel skyscraper from which they'd just stepped. "Then I sue you for mismanagement of *Missouri Woman*, replace you with an editor who will do what I say, and run the Firebrand ads, all three years of them, exactly as Nick Santini suggested."

Chapter Ten

It came as little surprise to find that Alex had already
secured the necessary airline tickets and packed appropriate warm weather clothing for Kate.

"I should have known you'd find a way to get me to
go away with you," Kate muttered ferociously as they
boarded the 727 for Corpus Christi, Texas. She recalled the first night Alex had been back, his suggestion they go away together, his surprising nonreaction
when she had refused. For a man who'd flown thousands of miles for the express purpose of seeing her,
he had taken it very well, she realized belatedly. Too
well.

"You're right." Alex folded his long legs into the
cramped space in front of them. Dark blue eyes held
hers. "When it comes to something I want, I leave
very little to chance."

Kate spent the rest of the three hour flight drowning her sorrows in a liberal dosing of Fresca. Her
stomach rumbled relentlessly and the lunch she had
scorned in favor of arguing with the Firebrand account executive became the object of her fantasies.
Oh, to have just one more bite of that jasmine and

orange spiced rice or tender chicken. Instead, she got tiny bags of peanuts and pretzels from inhospitable flight attendants. Later, a mild case of pending airsickness.

"Should have eaten while you had a chance," Alex observed over the edge of his *Wall Street Journal.*

Kate kept one eye on the location of the airsick bags, closed the other, and prayed for a sudden air mass to send them back to Springfield. No such luck. They landed at the Corpus Christi International Airport shortly after four. A rental car was already waiting, their luggage dispatched immediately to the midnight blue Mercedes.

"Well, I guess this is it," Kate stared glumly at the clear blue sky and relaxed into the eighty-five degree temperature outside the crowded airline terminal. Why couldn't Alex accept the fact she didn't want to be alone with him, and certainly not in any place as close to paradise as Padre Island and the Texas Gulf Coast? Why couldn't they make a clean break, end the turbulent swirl of emotions between them once and for all?

They drove north of the city, towards Aransas Pass, and onto a concrete causeway connecting them to Mustang Island. Kate rolled down her window, let the warm subtropical breeze stir her hair and her senses as she took in the profusion of plush resorts. "I can see you're adapting already," Alex grinned.

The two-story condominium was located directly on the beach. After stopping in briefly at the hotel office, Alex parked the Mercedes at the rear of the complex, then carried their suitcases around to the beachside entrance. While he unlocked the sliding glass doors off the deck, Kate admired the warmth of the gentle breeze, the beckoning stir of the ocean against the expanse of deserted white sand. Off-season, it was wonderfully deserted. Kate's mind went back to the days of their honeymoon, the two wonderful weeks they had spent sunning and loving on the beach. Was Alex trying to recapture that? she wondered.

"Don't you want to see the inside?" Alex lounged against the door. Composing herself swiftly, Kate strolled past his beckoning arm. The interior was just as luxurious as she would have imagined. The spacious living room spanned out in a cool collection of off-white and beige. The dining room beyond was a soothing pale green and white, the kitchen completely concealed by swinging wooden doors. A carpeted staircase led to the two well-appointed bedrooms and baths.

"I'm a firm believer in freedom of choice, Kate," Alex assured. "You can have one bedroom. I'll take the other." He grinned. "Unless of course you change your mind."

Kate couldn't forget how he'd twisted her arm to get her down there. "Fine." She strolled back towards the wood deck jutting out over the sand. "You go your way and I'll go mine."

Alex studied her contemplatively. "I admit I'm no saint. My methods were less than gallant. However, now that we're both here and the vacation has begun, can't we call a truce? Have dinner out together?"

It had to be emotionally safer than staying there alone. Kate nodded reluctantly. "I suppose you packed something suitable from my closet?"

Alex affirmed he had. "I'll go shower and change."

As soon as he disappeared up the stairs, Kate tossed off her wool suit jacket, stockings, and shoes, and went down to the beach. Wiggling her toes in the warm wet sand she began however recalcitrantly to enjoy the enforced change of pace. *Leave it to Alex,* she sighed, *to first analyze and then decide what would be best. For Southwestern Oil's Riyadh office, the magazine, even her...*

"Smile, Kate, this is a much deserved vacation, not a wake," the low voice purred softly next to her ear. Alex had changed into pleated white linen trousers, silky blue shirt, and tie. The matching white jacket was draped over a chair on the deck. Kate noticed a carafe of white wine, glasses and a bucket of ice on the patio table. Alex was really making every effort, she mused. And the tantalizing way he was looking at her was going to make him that much harder to resist. His mischievous glance traveled down to her wiggling toes. "I wouldn't mind having dinner here if you're too tired to change or go out."

Kate read the speculative direction of his thoughts. She wasn't going to make it that easy for him. "And after you've gone to so much trouble to dress up? Don't be silly, Alex. I'll just be an hour... or two."

Clearly, Alex occupied the master bedroom. His clothes—mostly sportswear and casual evening attire— hung neatly in the closet. The adjoining bath was littered with shaving utensils, toothpaste, mouthwash, cologne, and other masculine personal items. Her suitcase had been left unopened in the carpeted hall, directly between the two luxuriously appointed bedrooms. The spectator pumps she'd discarded downstairs had been pointed, one in either direction, toward the doorways of the two bedrooms. Her panty-hose were left in between, arranged carefully in what Kate could only assume was supposed to resemble a rather filmy question mark of indecision.

Grinning at the symbolically eloquent display, Kate tossed all her belongings into the smaller bedroom. From somewhere behind her a masculine voice sighed, "I had a feeling after all that's gone on today you'd choose the prim route." Mumbling something Kate couldn't quite make out about firebrands and lost accounts, Alex tripped on back down the stairs. But it was clear his high hopes hadn't been entirely crushed. Filtering after him was a pointedly screeched rendition of "Some Enchanted Evening."

Kate was in the shower by the time he hit the high notes. Standing under the warm, stinging spray, she wondered how much longer she was going to resist Alex, even on principle or pride. True, he had black-mailed her into going away with him, but before that he'd asked her nicely innumerable times. And time was running out.

When Kate emerged from the steamy bath, all was quiet. Rapidly, she dressed in an off the shoulder powder blue dress and spiky silver sandals. Her hair was left loose and free, gently brushing her soft shoulders.

"You're just in time for the sunset," Alex murmured as she joined him on the deck. The ocean was bathed in a dusky glow from the poinsettia-red sky. The vibrant sun sank slowly into the horizon, dragging with it the light and tensions of the day. In silence Kate and Alex sipped at the wine. Never had it been more clear they both still felt very married, if estranged. Both were the victims of circumstances, career demands.

They drove to a popular oceanside restaurant. Built entirely on a barge and docked at the Corpus Christi marina, the floating restaurant was one of the main tourist attractions in the area and had built its reputation on the tempting array of fresh seafood it offered.

"Remember the first time we were here?" Alex whispered as they were seated in the dark candlelit restaurant.

"How could I forget?" Kate tried not to feel the coaxing warmth in the fingertips pressed possessively over her arm. "It was during our honeymoon. You promised me a fish, caught nothing on the boat, and took me here instead."

Alex grinned. "Remember the consolation prize?" That memory would have been even harder to block out. They'd still been up to see the dawn. "This could be our second honeymoon, Kate." Electric blue eyes caught hers. The tip of his index finger traced the trembling outline of her mouth. The sparkling lights of the city reflected beautifully off the water. In the distance, the occasional motion of ships could be seen, the blinkng of warning, shifting lights. The bay was so peaceful, different from anything they knew in Springfield.

"I thought you'd still be angry with me for botching up the Firebrand account," Kate remarked, slightly puzzled.

Alex shrugged. "We've put enough of ourselves into *Missouri Woman* the past few weeks, Kate. Let it go." He shifted closer, brushing his thigh against hers, drew a wandering fingertip from the curve of her bare shoulder to her wrist.

"I wish I could," Kate said softly. But her work there was too valuable, both in terms of the magazine and for women as a whole.

Alex moved even closer. Positioning his muscular thigh against hers, he draped a long suit-covered arm across her shoulders, let it slip down over her back possessively to cradle her in his cologne scented warmth. He ordered her favorite wine, requested the orchestra play her favorite love songs as well as selected numbers from his favorite, *South Pacific*.

"Alex—" Kate felt herself begin to blush as he pressed a feather light kiss into the nape of her neck. This was the kind of all out advance she had expected from him the first day back in Springfield. This was precisely why she had run. Realistically, she should have known better. Leave it to Alex to take care of business first, then assault her at nuke level in a place too romantic to resist, in a place that had all too many fond memories for them both.

"I missed you, Kate." Alex murmured, leading her onto the dance floor in the adjacent lounge. "And being with you and yet not is even worse. If you're honest you'll agree the feeling is mutual. You'll tell me you want to be with me every bit as much as I want to be with you."

There seemed no point in denying the rapid beat of her heart. Kate relaxed further into his arms, enjoying the dance to the end. Alex escorted her back to the table, ordered another celebratory bottle of wine.

"Come back to the Middle East with me, Kate," he murmured persuasively, abruptly breaking the spell.

"*Missouri Woman* will hold its own for a few months."

Kate froze, reality crashing in around her. "That's why you took over as publisher, isn't it, Alex? Worked so hard the past weeks to make sure *M.W.* is truly financially secure. You never did care about the magazine or the money you invested. You just wanted to make it possible for me to go back."

Alex shrugged. "I made it clear from the start, Kate, that I did not want a divorce. So yes, to be perfectly honest about it, everything I have done for you and *Missouri Woman* the past month was only to that end. I want you back with me in Riyadh, full-time if possible, until my assignment ends. It's just that simple."

Dinner passed in a maze of inane conversation, suitable for strangers. Kate barely tasted the fresh tender flounder, dripping in lemon and butter, the crisp green salad, or hot homemade rolls. Alex made no comment about the amount of white wine she imbibed with her meal, but the concerned slant of his dark brows mirrored her own recriminations. Yet, by the same token Kate seemed powerless to help it. Just when everything had been going so well, it was all falling apart, more rapidly than she had ever dreamed. They parted at the door of the condo without even a kiss. Alex walked off to explore the moonlit beach alone.

Kate spent a restless night in the smaller upstairs bedroom; she finally heard Alex come in a little after three. Pounding the pillow, she berated herself for caring, then forced herself to count sheep until she fell back asleep, and did not wake again until noon the next day. A letter left on the polished pine of the dining room table indicated simply that Alex had gone deep-sea fishing and would return later that day.

"Great," Kate muttered, padding out to the kitchen for a look into the refrigerator. Finding a carton of juice, she sloshed four ounces into a tumbler and placed a long-distance call to the magazine. "Liz! How are things going?"

"Kate Ryker, you're supposed to be on vacation!" the managing editor chided.

"So Alex told you," Kate ascertained, realizing he had made his plans long before she ever knew about them.

"Yes, several days ago. Now don't worry about a thing. I've got everything under control. Though now I've got you on the line there are a few messages." Kate could hear Liz rustling through papers. "Darrel Hendrix phoned, left a message about that *Missouri Woman* stock that was being so mysteriously bought up. He said Alex now has title to it all. Isn't that a surprise! And you were so worried that someone else might be trying to elbow in for partial control now that our fiscal picture is looking up."

"When did Alex acquire the stock?" Kate asked. "Did Darrel say?" And why hadn't he mentioned purchasing it to her? Unless of course he planned to use it to her distinct disadvantage.

"Yesterday morning." Liz paused. "There's more here." Liz made clucking noises about Marge's indecipherable scrawl. "Something about a legal tangle. Alex holds another twenty percent which would make your joint shares over eighty, though these new ones are in his name alone. His fifty to your thirty. Am I making sense?''

"More than you know," Kate reflected somberly. No wonder Alex had been unconcerned over the botched Firebrand account. If Liz were right and he did now hold a cool fifty percent as opposed to her thirty, he could veto her right down the line.

"When am I going to see you?" Liz chirped. "And how's that second honeymoon of yours going? You didn't say!"

So Alex had told them that too, Kate thought sourly. What else had he counted on? "Everything's fine here," Kate replied. "And I promise, you'll see me sooner than you thought."

Kate hung up the phone and turned to see Alex standing there, the morning paper folded under his arm. He was wearing tailored white tennis shorts and Adidas. His chest was already sporting the renewed darkness of his Riyadh tan. A matching short-sleeved white polo shirt was flung casually over his bare back. "Back to business already, Kate?" Alex asked smoothly, sauntering into the small galley kitchen. "And you accuse me of being the only one tied to a job."

Kate turned on him. "Why didn't you tell me you were buying up additional shares of *Missouri Woman* stock?"

Alex started slightly. "Who told you about that?"

"Darrel Hendrix."

Alex studied her thoughtfully, grimaced as if there were so much more he wanted to say. "How long have you known?"

"Just this morning. And you didn't answer my

question, Alex. Why didn't you tell me you had purchased an additional twenty percent of the magazine
stock?''

Alex frowned. ''Because I didn't want to argue
about it, or generate any more of a power struggle at
Missouri Woman than we were already embroiled in.''

''Then the stocks are in your name exclusively?''

After hesitating a brief second, Alex nodded affir-
matively. They were no longer equal partners, publisher to editor in chief. Alex could sell *Missouri
Woman* out from under her if he chose, a move that
vindictively done could completely change the scope
of *M.W.* if not destroy it.

''Planning to blackmail me into returning with you
to the Middle East?'' The icy accusation was out before Kate could stop it.

Alex paused, sent her a smouldering look that
covered her from head to toe. Upon rising, Kate
hadn't bothered to change or cover her white chiffon
nightgown. Now realizing how much the bare fabric,
skimpy spaghetti straps and low cut bodice revealed to
his penetrating stare, she wished she had.

''I could have done *that* weeks ago.'' Anger increasing, Alex put down his paper and removed a flask of
grapefruit juice from the refrigerator. Uncapping the
bottle, he drank straight from the container. When
the last of the juice had disappeared, he wiped the
grim lines of his mouth with the back of his hand. ''I
also could have sued you for mismanagement, had
you entirely out of a job, probably even the house if
I'd decided to go ahead with the divorce and ask the
joint property be put up for sale.''

''Why didn't you?'' Kate seethed.

"Marriage is a lifetime commitment, Kate. Frankly, you haven't begun to honor your half." His gaze slid back down over the length of her, softening desirously in the process. "Truthfully, I guess I was hoping you'd come around on your own. See how the magazine should be run, at least from a financial and organizational standpoint. Come back to me, be a real wife to me again instead of just a part-time drop-in whenever circumstances and *Missouri Woman* allowed."

"Supposing the time came to return to Riyadh and I hadn't come around. Then what?" Kate asked.

"I want you by my side, Kate," Alex admitted. His mouth twisted wryly as he forced himself to confront the ethics of the situation, the fact that he'd already blackmailed her into vacationing with him. "That's the one thing about our relationship that's always remained constant. If I thought for a moment those extra shares would—"

"I don't want to hear any more." Trembling, Kate turned away, desperately trying to hide the tears blurring her eyes. "How could you even consider doing such a thing to me?" And yet, knowing how important it was that she remain his wife, honor the commitment they had made to have and to hold, how could Kate have anticipated anything less? Particularly when all other means of persuasion had failed?

"We really don't know each other at all, do we, Kate?" Alex said succinctly at last. And on that note, he turned and walked out of the kitchen, out of the condo, taking both the keys and the rental car with him.

The rest of the day stretched out ahead of Kate like an abyss. Not having any idea when Alex would be back, she walked to a neighboring restaurant for lunch. Strolling back, the sun looked too tempting to resist. Kate changed into the white bikini Alex had packed, also another reminder of their honeymoon, and strolled barefoot back down to the padded chaise on the deck. For nearly an hour afterward, Kate read the latest bestseller by her favorite author, but soon even that bored her, and rolling over onto her stomach, she fell asleep on the chaise. Minutes passed. Kate awakened herself drowsily and shifted positions, promising in a few minutes she would get up and go inside. The next thing she knew it was nearly five o'clock and she had a peculiar burning feeling across the back of her neck. Getting slowly to her feet, Kate discovered the searing sensation encompassed nearly all of her, even the unexposed parts of skin beneath the suit.

Dizzily, Kate made her way upstairs. She was just struggling clumsily with the tie on her bikini top when she heard the door slam downstairs. Footsteps sounded in the hall and seconds later Alex's tall frame appeared in the open door to her room.

"Kate?" The questioning tone ended on a worried note when he took in the reddish flush to her skin. "My God, you don't fool around, do you?"

Dropping the collection of newspapers and magazines in his fiand, Alex strode quickly to her side. Kate's knees gave out and she swayed weakly against him, the pounding in her head growing more intense with every passing second. "Can't seem to get the stubborn suit untied," Kate whispered.

"How long were you out in the sun?" Alex helped her gently to the bed.

"I don't know." Kate pressed a trembling hand to her forehead, trying to think. "Four or five hours. Since noon." She winced as he fidgeted with the hopelessly tangled knot at her back, the tenderness of her skin stinging unbearably against the hair roughened surface of the back of his hand. Alex finally managed the knot against her spine, then the one at her neck. "Do we have any aspirin?" Kate asked. "I have a bass drum pounding inside my head. Either that or the whole Houston Philharmonic Orchestra."

"Stay there." Alex disappeared into the bath beyond. Typically, Kate was on her feet almost instantly, heading for the robe across the chair. Halfway there, dizziness engulfed her. She stumbled into strong hands. Sunburned skin was drawn roughly up against the cotton knit of his tennis shorts and shirt. "You stubborn little fool," Alex murmured exasperatedly against her temple. "Can't you rely on me this once to take care of you? Would it be so terrible, Kate?"

Kate was horrified to find tears pressing from beneath her tightly shut lashes. "I don't know. It's just that I feel so awful."

"You're probably suffering from a mild case of heat exhaustion." Alex swung her gently up into his arms and carried her to the bed. Kate landed against the cool comfort of rumpled percale. Obediently, she relaxed against the sheets. The next thing Kate knew Alex was beside her again, helping remove the rest of the swimsuit, handing her the requested aspirin and a cold drink.

"Thanks." Eyes shut, Kate lay back, gasped as an icy cloth slid across her face, forehead, neck.

"What were you doing out so long?" Alex asked

conversationally. Terribly fair skinned, Kate always burned at more than an hour or so of sun.

"Sleeping mostly." Kate winced and hissed with each new inch of skin he traversed. But eventually the cooling process began to work. Walking over to Kate's suitcase, Alex rummaged through the contents and returned with a jar of Noxema. "Guess I forgot the Solarcaine," Kate murmured, though even if she'd wanted to administer the soothing salve, the aching rawness of her skin and pounding head would have prevented it.

"Any type of lotion or moisturizer will do," Alex informed quietly, completing the routine first aid with tender, gentle strokes of his hand. Sometime later, Alex returned with another glass of icy soda. Kate sipped at the chilled Dr Pepper, was barely able to get her second dose of aspirin down before her stomach threatened to revolt. "Nauseated?" Alex was still hovering above her.

Kate nodded slightly, too sick to speak.

"Close your eyes. Take a few deep beaths." Alex took a seat next to the bed. "I'll be here." Alex pressed her palm tightly in the cradle of his hands. "Right here with you always. Now sleep."

Kate woke to utter silence. Alex was in the chair next to her, studying what looked to be Southwestern Oil business. When he saw she was awake, he smiled and stretched lazily.

"What time is it?" Kate's mouth felt as if it were stuffed with cotton but the nausea was gone.

"Nine o'clock. Feel like eating something?"

Kate tested the validity of her recovery by rising

slightly. Her stomach was okay but her skin tingled and burned with even the slightest motion. "Maybe a soda," Kate decided finally. "Some more aspirin." Groaning, Kate vowed never to fall asleep in the sun again no matter how much effort it took to get up and walk into the house.

A tray full of Dr Pepper on ice, beef broth and saltine crackers, pretzels and potato chips heralded Alex's return. "I called the first-aid station while you were asleep. The physician on duty said as long as there was no fever, and the burns were only first degree—no blisters—not to worry. Just to keep you quiet, cool, out of the sun, and feed you plenty of liquids and salty things."

"Sounds simple enough, thanks." Kate concentrated again on the soup. Alex went routinely back to his Southwestern Oil reports. Kate fell asleep again shortly afterwards.

The next thing she knew it was morning, and the sounds of ice cubes clinking sounded next to her ear. Kate looked up to see Alex standing next to the bed. Dressed only in a towel, he apparently had just finished his shower.

"Morning, sweetheart. How do you feel?"

Kate propped herself up on her elbows testingly. The headache seemed to have disappeared completely. Her slightly fiery skin felt as if it had been stretched tight across her bones, but was not nearly as uncomfortable as it had been the night before.

"I think I'm cured," she murmured, deciding she needed some clothes.

"This first. Then you'll be cured." Sprawling halfway across the bed, Alex lowered Kate back down onto the pillows. Kate was used to the ice water and lotion routine. A glance at the discarded Southwestern Oil portfolio of reports kept her resolve intact. But when Alex worked his way sensually down her thighs, lingered tantalizingly despite her efforts to free herself from his playful advance, she thought she would melt with desire.

"Alex—" The plea for mercy was muffled by his mouth. Alex kissed her more gently and lingeringly than he ever had before, drinking the love and passion from her even as he gave, drawing her near, tempting her with the promise, the completeness of body and soul only he could provide.

The pressure of his lips and hands moving over and against her were equally devastating, making her forget the tenderness of sunburned skin, the circumstances of their estrangement, the lack of an immediate future to share. Kate clung to him, wanting the moment to go on forever. Alex tenderly brushed tawny gold hair from her face. "You're not the only one who wishes my job wasn't in the Mid-East," he murmured.

Alex traced lazy erotic circles with his tongue, concentrating on first one taut rosy nipple, and then the other. Kate shifted desirously, wishing for more intimate contact.

"I thought you had decided you didn't want this." Alex laughed, his pleasure rumbling deep in his throat. Whispering the depth of his passion, he folded her tightly into his arms.

"I want you," Kate whispered, trembling as she felt the shuddering depth of his need. "I've always wanted you. There were nights—"

"Tell me," Alex urged, pressing the warmth of his mouth to the pulse throbbing wildly at the base of her neck. "Tell me what you're feeling, Kate. Make me understand. God knows I want to."

"I love you," Kate said softly, looking deep into his eyes. "At the moment nothing else seems to matter."

"The months I've longed to hear you say that," Alex murmured, gentle hands framing her face. His lips fit over hers once more, and this time there was no denying the passion, no stopping the ardor driving them both. Demandingly, he ravaged her mouth, then gentled his kiss, then tormented her again, forcing her to cling, to give to him sexually in a way she would never surrender her soul.

Kate moved against her husband wantonly, running her fingers through the crisp mat of hair feathering his chest, sinking her palms into the muscular surface of his thighs, caressing and exploring the lean width of his lower spine. Suddenly the tables were turned and it was Alex who was out of control, Alex who was making the muffled sounds of frustration and urgency deep in his throat. She could feel the evidence of his desire against her. Kate welcomed the plundering heat, the passion so out of control. She cried out with the depth and the ardor, then gave herself up to the building crescendo, the entwining of souls, the shattering climax.

Alex held her tightly to him on the long shuddering descent back to normalcy. Kate cuddled closer as he stroked her silky hair, whispered her name, and kissed the slowly ebbing pulse in her throat. Tears pricking her eyes, Kate wondered how she was ever going to live without him again.

They were still in bed when the phone rang half an hour later. "I'll get it." Alex reached for the receiver reluctantly, Kate still cradled languidly in his arms. Unfortunately, it didn't take long to discern it was his employer on the other end of the line. Kate rose silently from the bed, ignoring the wordless plea to remain with him, and walked into the other room to shower and dress.

By the time she had donned her robe and run a brush through her hair, he was off the phone, facing her unhappily. "There's trouble in the Riyadh office, Kate. Some sort of dispute about the new policies Southwestern is trying to implement in all their overseas offices."

Kate knew his job had been to see the new rules were implemented, and that the transition went smoothly. "When are you leaving?" As indispensible as Alex was, she had known it would not be long before Southwestern was banging on their door, leave of absence or no.

"I promised them I'd be on a plane to New York no later than the end of the week," he said quietly. From there he'd make connections to the company's Persian Gulf office.

"Why wait?" Kate asked, her icy indifference meant to cover her hurt. She walked into the master bedroom and reached for the phone. "I'm sure you can get a flight out tonight if you try."

The hand that closed over hers was rough with frustration. "Damn it, Kate," he gritted in her ear. "How can you be so cool about this after everything that's just happened? The start towards repairing our relationship finally made?"

"Because this has been inevitable from the start."

Kate blinked back tears. "We knew it would end. You would go back to your job. I to mine. The lovemaking was an added bonus. Something that shouldn't have happened," she added cryptically. The intimacy, as she had feared, was only making the inevitable break between them that much more difficult.

"I want you to come with me." His jaw had hardened implacably as he shrugged into a pair of low slung briefs and discarded white tennis shorts.

"I can't do that, Alex." Kate turned towards the door.

Alex caught her inflexibly, whirled her around to face him. Kate wasn't the only one being torn about by the news. "Kate I've sacrificed a lot to be here with you the past weeks. I've been as patient and giving as I know how to be. Now it's your turn to sacrifice something. Come with me."

"The magazine—" Kate began, thinking of the changes Alex had prompted, the overload of work still waiting.

"To hell with the magazine," Alex gritted. "What about us?"

Kate was silent. What about them? Had they ever had a future, one not underwritten by the emotional insecurity a troubleshooting job like his required? In his position as managerial consultant and corporate fire fighter Alex would always have to go where the company sent him. Kate's work would always be in Springfield, with her magazine.

"It's unfair of you to ask me to give up *Missouri Woman*, Alex," Kate whispered finally. "Even for a short time. With the changes you've helped implement—"

"Spare me the details." Alex's voice cut roughly across hers. The glacial indifference in his eyes chilled Kate to the bone. "I guess I've always known what was important to you, Kate. It just took today to hammer it through."

Kate drove Alex to the airport despite his casual insistence that it would be just as easy to take a cab. Graciously, he'd left her the rental car since she had no plans to return to Springfield until the next day. Alex thought it was to give her a chance to further enjoy the sunny break from wintry Springfield. Kate knew she would need the time to pull herself together. Once he left for Riyadh there would be a storm of tears. It was better no one else witness the devastation.

"What about the magazine?" Kate asked as they checked his bags through the appropriate airline counter. "Darrel's insisted we have a full-time business manager." And since Alex was no longer going to be there...

He pivoted to study her appraisingly. Her tawny hair fell in wild disarray around her shoulders, gleaming even lighter than usual against the sun-flushed hue of her fair skin. "Divorce or no, Kate," Alex said quietly, intimating that for the very first time he might angrily be considering one, "I'm not giving up my hold on *Missouri Woman*. It was an investment, one I've paid dearly for. I intend to see it milked to the end."

"Which brings us back to your purchase of the extra stocks." Kate's amber eyes flashed with unspent fury. How like Alex to arrogantly insist they continue on as unequal partners despite the demise of their marriage. He was probably just doing it to spite her. Either that, or to prove true his claim that it would never really be over between them, that it would always continue on one level or another.

White teeth slashed smilingly across the tan of his handsome face. "I was wondering when you'd bring that up."

He apparently wanted her to. "You knew Darrel was going to tell me you owned an additional twenty percent of the stock?" Kate guessed, realizing she'd been duped into thinking his motives were simpler than they were.

"I instructed Darrel to tell you," he replied lazily, taking his ticket and boarding pass from the uniformed airline clerk. "I just didn't expect you to call Liz for messages so soon."

"Why?" Kate allowed Alex to take her elbow as he ushered them through the crowds towards the metal detector.

"Several reasons," Alex admitted with an infuriating calm. "First, I felt you should know someone was trying to buy up the stock and that I had done something about it."

Kate recalled her initial meeting with Darrel over cocktails. "... I knew if I told you about it, along with my plans, we'd have a fight. Second, after the Firebrand fiasco, I didn't think it would hurt to let you know I meant what I said about turning *Missouri Woman* around fiscally. If you'd have continued on uncooperatively, Kate, I would have used that stock against you."

"And now?"

Alex glanced at her, for the first time looking as if
he were truly going to miss her as his blue eyes raked
over the slashing front placket of her midnight-blue
gauze shirt. "I intend to sign with Nick Santini anyway." Ignoring Kate's hiss of anger, he added blithely, "Naturally, it was my hope to be able to convince
you to come around while we were down here vacationing. I figured when you had time to think about it
you would realize the Beautiful You Cosmetics account was vital for the good of the magazine and your
employees."

Kate grinned superciliously. "You may be right,
Alex. But given the argument Nick Santini and I
had—"

"I've already smoothed things over with him,"
Alex answered dryly, his hand against her back as he
ushered her past security and towards the gate. "First
thing yesterday morning I promised him he wouldn't
have to deal with you personally anymore. I would
handle the account exclusively."

"But you'll be in Riyadh!" Kate sputtered.

"There is such a thing as long-distance, Kate. And
Darrel's been given written power of attorney for all
contracts, provided of course he checks with me via
phone first. I'll absorb the cost of long-distance. So
you see, sweetheart, we'll still be partners, just as tied
together as always. Unless of course you decide to sell
out..." The slant of his brows said he would be only
too willing to arrange the transaction.

"You're despicable!" Kate swore with a stomp of
her foot, ignoring the gazes of others around them.

"Determined to have you, Kate, one way or another, and yes, I am." Clasping her arm firmly, Alex

drew her over to a secluded spot next to the wall. "That's why I bought and am keeping the extra stock."

"I don't know how I ever could have trusted you!"

"This was more than just a power play on my part," Alex interrupted her tirade calmly. "Before, had there been a divorce, there would have been another forty percent of *M.W.* stock floating around free on the market. Someone like Gavin Hayes could have quietly bought in, vied for control—"

"What does Hayes have to do with anything?" Kate cut in bewilderedly.

Alex sighed. "You made an enemy, Kate. Though why Hayes was so determined to advertise in *Missouri Woman,* I still don't know. Just that he was, and decided to manage it one way or another even if it meant buying up your stock through out-of-town brokers. Hell, maybe you wounded the man's pride!"

"Then he was behind the sharp rise in prices?"

"More or less," Alex conceded. "I found out about it through Darrel, despite your initial decision not to inform me of the conversation the two of you had regarding the matter."

Kate blushed.

"And set Hayes straight. I told him if I found him or any of his surfer-boy lackeys in *Missouri Woman* offices I would personally have his head. Hayes believed me." Alex grinned, apparently relishing the memory. "Hasn't been around since, as you may have noticed. I don't imagine he will be. I trust you'll notify either Darrel or myself if he does."

The call for passengers on Flight 601 to New York sounded, circumventing their conversation. "It's still not too late to come with me," Alex urged, very low. "Even if you just stay a few weeks, Kate...?"

And make it harder to leave than ever before? "I don't want a long-distance marriage subject to the whims of Southwestern Oil," Kate said abruptly, her rudeness masking the emotion quivering just below the surface.

"But you're not willing to sacrifice anything for our marriage, either, are you?" Alex said roughly. One arm sliding about her waist, he drew her implacably near. Kate saw his passionate intentions and jerked her head to the side. They were enough of a display already. Not to be outdone, Alex dropped his briefcase to the carpeted floor beside him, used his other hand to cup her chin, draw her gold-flecked amber eyes up to meet his gaze. "I want you, Kate," he said softly, ignoring the tears shimmering just below the surface of her cool composure. "But if you won't put your stubbornness aside and come with me, then I'll just have to make due."

Alex's mouth lowered to hers, taking her slightly parted lips in less than a beat of a heart. Tasting the sweetness of his mouth, the distinct flavor and texture of his tongue and lips, Kate eventually yielded despite herself. Alex crushed his fingers through the thick layers of her hair as he felt her spiralling response, let his other hand stray to the succumbing pliancy of her spine, linger at her waist, and then come back up to cup her shoulders, draw her even closer. Without wanting to, Kate began to respond even more wildly. The firm insistence of his mouth sent shivers of desire sinking all the way down to the tips of her toes. Her hands went up to curl about his neck, entangle themselves in the soft fullness of ebony hair brushing the collar of his shirt. If only they'd had more time, Kate thought. Just one more day, one more hour...

"Sir?" The polite tapping on Alex's broad shoulder jerked them from their reverie. "The last call for your flight was just announced," the embarrassed ticket agent reminded. "If you still plan to board...?"

He did. Turning back to Kate, Alex pleaded impatiently. "It's still not too late to come with me, Kate. Please."

Numbly, she shook her head. Alex's eyes darkened and his mouth slatted out in exasperated displeasure. The ticket agent hovered nearby. Holding up a hand to circumvent another intrusion from the airline personnel, Alex stooped to pick up his briefcase, then leaned forward and gave Kate a perfunctory peck on the very top of her head. "You know where to find me, Kate. Needless to say, you're always welcome." And on that note, he pivoted and walked away.

Kate left the airport after the jet took off, then spent the next few days in a veritable river of self-pitying tears. But contrary to her secret hopes, Alex did not call or return. She was where she had started out, in a legal and moral limbo, loving a man she would never really have. Kate returned to Springfield and *Missouri Woman,* more desolate than ever before.

Chapter Eleven

Kate, I've been trying to get hold of you for days," Max Collins boomed over the phone lines. "Good heavens, woman, where have you been?"

"Inundated in last minute preparations for the March issue of *Missouri Woman*," Kate said dryly. "Before that, Corpus Christi." According to her calendar, Alex had been gone three weeks. It seemed like three years. During that time she hadn't been able to eat, sleep, or even think clearly, much less juggle the tons of messages pouring in with congratulations on their new format.

"Listen, about that article I promised I'd do for the magazine," Max began earnestly.

"I remember," Kate said wryly. "And since I've already lived up to my half of the bargain by printing something about your efforts to increase aid to dependent children—"

"Right." Max cut the recriminations short. "And I would have already completed something and sent it over had we not been so busy with this fraud investigation—"

"I read something about that the other day." Kate

had been too heartsick over Alex's departure to keep up with much of the statewide news, other than that which directly affected the magazine. "Have you really got something on Hayes Heaven Used Cars lots?"

"You bet your copy we do," Max said. "It's a good thing you didn't advertise for the shyster, Kate. But I'll tell you all about his scheme to use our friendship to halt the investigation into his car lot scams when I see you."

"Wait a minute." Kate backed up the conversation peremptorily. "You mean Hayes thought advertising in *M.W.* would stop your investigation of his fraudulent dealings?"

"He knew about our friendship," Max explained, "growing up together and figured correctly I would never want to do anything to hurt you. Naturally, if *Missouri Woman* was full of Hayes Heaven Used Cars ads just about the time the Senate investigation of his lots was about to begin..."

"I see his train of thought," Kate mused.

"When you continued to refuse him, and Alex more or less threatened him about harassing you again, Hayes decided to lay it all out on the table and come to see me anyway. Of course, he intimated there was an agreement between you to run the ads. I told him no deal regardless. He finally agreed to cooperate with the district attorney in exchange for lessening the charges."

"You have been busy!" Kate sighed.

"But not too busy to fulfill my end of the agreement," Max corrected. "The article's already roughed in and researched, Kate. All I need is your final approval and editing wizardry. I've got a clear slot tomorrow after five. How does that sound?"

"Okay, but we're going to have to meet at my house instead of the office. They're still installing a new test kitchen at the end of the hall. The noise and confusion here that time of day are incredible."

"Your place it is, then," Max agreed. There was another slight pause, this one more probing. "How are you doing otherwise, with Alex out of the country again?"

Truthfully, emotionally, Kate was falling apart. The second separation was ten times more painful than the first. "I'm managing just fine," she lied briskly. "And thanks for calling, Max. I'll see you tomorrow night."

Kate spent a restless night rethinking every moment of Alex's stay there, the changes he had made at *Missouri Woman,* then flew to St. Louis early the next day. It took a lot of persuading and the embellishment of a fictional high-priority transatlantic phone conversation with Alex granting her ad account authority to get the Beautiful You Cosmetics company account executive to meet with her. But once that gargantuan chore was accomplished, Kate didn't waste any time in apologizing for her less than tactful commentary on Firebrand's advertising the last time Kate and Nick had met.

"Look, Mr. Santini, I admit I was out of line." Kate swallowed, remembering Alex's intention to go with the contract regardless and the raises her employees desperately needed. "I promise to limit my observations from this point forward to *Missouri Woman* business only. We still have a lot of work to do, however, if we're going to get you top return for every dollar spent." Nick seemed to be listening, so Kate continued amenably, "As I mentioned before, the *Missouri Woman* readership is very discriminating. It would be advantageous to play up to that, rather than ignore it."

They were seated in the same St. Louis restaurant they had met in weeks before. Only the view outside had changed. A string of evergreen and festive holly, blinking colored lights, heralded the approach of the yuletide. *Christmas,* Kate thought. *Without Alex.*

There was a significant pause as Nick Santini mulled over Kate's last statement. "You're aware, of course, Ms. Ryker, that the copy cannot be changed. The ten-page layout is designed for national use."

Tactfully, Kate refrained from commenting on the sexist approach they used for their perfume. "It's the Firebrand ad I'm concerned about, the use of four photos instead of one on a single page. Couldn't we just go with a blow-up of the woman spraying on perfume?" Waiting for hubby or not, the woman was sexy and together. At least that would not offend or alienate her readers. "It just seems to me that a focus on the woman and the bottle of perfume would have greater impact, particularly after nine pages of Beautiful You Cosmetics."

"Well—" Nick paused thoughtfully.

"Of course, if you really wanted to hype Firebrand's image," Kate continued casually over coffee, "have it on the mind of every woman in this state, we could run some sort of contest. At *Missouri Woman*'s expense, of course. Ask the readers what sells a fragrance to them. We could select the ten best ideas, publish them in the magazine, again at our expense. Maybe run a concurrent article or two about fragrances and the added boost they can give a woman's morale. Give the winner a free trip to the advertising studio to see how the layouts are actually conceived and put together. Give the runners up free samples of Firebrand and Beautiful You Cosmetics, perhaps a consultation at a local department store."

"I'd have to check this out with marketing," Nick mused. "But perhaps if it were considered in the research budget . . ."

"Sounds good to me." Kate signaled the waiter for a check. "And, Nick, thanks for working with me on this."

Liz Shaw swept into the office as soon as Kate returned from St. Louis, oblivious of the triumphant look on her boss's face as Kate thought about what she had accomplished with Santini. "Have you looked at these detailed critiques Sally Hendrix has been writing up for the recipes you hired her daughter to test?"

Kate shook her head negatively. "No, I saw the note you left on my desk, though. Are they any good?"

"Good? They're terrific!" Liz tossed her a couple. Kate read down the list, grinning at the neat precision in the copy, the touch of humor underlying every detailed report, the indexed grocery lists of items needed for the recipe preparations. "We ought to run these adjacent to the recipe section."

"My thoughts exactly," Liz concurred. "For the record, she's already given her permission, though I told her salary and so forth would be up to Alex to work out."

Kate nodded her agreement. "Good."

"Has it occurred to you we could use someone like Sally Hendrix on our staff full-time?" Liz tapped a pencil restlessly on the edge of Kate's chrome and glass desk.

"I don't think she'd want to leave her toddler," Kate mused, thinking of Kristin's curly blond hair and wide blue eyes, the each-day-brings-something-new wonder Sally had once described. Yet Liz was right. Sally would be a great addition to their staff. They needed a woman who had been primarily a full-time homemaker most of her adult life, someone in touch with the demands of teenagers and toddlers alike. It would give a new dimension to their staff, and hopefully, to *M.W.*'s copy.

"She wouldn't have to leave Kristin. She could do almost everything at home," Liz said emphatically. "My God, Kate, the woman can really write. I've spoken to her several times when she comes in to drop off something particularly wonderful Angie has whipped up. Sally's bright, she's articulate, she's organized. And the swift professional way she and Angie are working, we're going to run out of recipes for them to test and write up, at least to the point where Sally's challenged. More specifically, we need someone here to help us wade through the fiction that's now pouring in."

Kate nodded agreeably. "You're right on every count, Liz. And I should have thought of that."

"You've been so busy worrying about *M.W.* finances and missing Alex, you haven't had a chance to," Liz said softly. "Isn't there any hope the two of you will work things out?" The staff had been equally dismayed to learn Alex had gone back to Southwestern. Though Alex's name had remained on the masthead, his office and power would again be as silently in the background as before.

"No. I knew when he left that he would be in Riyadh for at least another year or two," Kate said. And in the three weeks that had passed he hadn't attempted to get in touch with her once.

"Well, what do you say?" Liz got back to business promptly. "Do I have your permission to extend an offer to Sally Hendrix for a full-time editorial position here? We really need help with this March issue if it's going to go to press next week."

Kate nodded. "Have Darrel work out the details: salary, contracts, and so forth if Sal is willing."

Kate spent the rest of the day elbow deep in paperwork and problems and it wasn't until nearly five she remembered her appointment with long time friend and state Senator Max Collins. He was waiting for her in the drive when she got there.

"Still cutting it close, I see?" he quipped when she emerged from the car to unlock the front door and let him into the wintry chill of a deserted house.

"Sorry. I got hung up at the office again, this time refereeing a dispute between our food and decorating editors over the color of the new test kitchen. I left them still hassling it out, though with the arrival of the subcontractors and the drills, I doubt they can keep up the shouting match for very long."

Still catching up on one another's news, they

walked into the kitchen. Max lit his pipe while Kate put on a pot of coffee and removed a walnut and raisin cake from the freezer, and put it briefly into the microwave. Dinner, as usual, would have to wait. Probably, Kate thought, that would be her dinner, even after Max had left. With Alex gone, it was once again hard to get psyched-up to cook.

They spread the papers out over the coffee table in the living room and between nibbles of the rich frosted cake went over the basic structure Max had set up for the article. Kate reviewed the typewritten pages in their entirety, scribbled a few notes in the margin, did some restructuring and simplifying of the opening paragraph.

Max concurred with all the minor editing changes. Leaning forward to make a point, and at the same time put down his pipe, he accidentally hit Kate's arm. The cup of lukewarm coffee in her lap overturned. Coffee spread darkly across the white wool of her tailored skirt.

"Oh, Kate, I'm sorry!" Max dabbed helplessly at the stain on both her blouse and skirt.

"It's all right." Kate righted the cup and dabbed at the murky brown mess. What was one more small disaster in the mangled frame of her life? she thought wryly.

"Look, Kate, just take the skirt off, wrap it up for me. I'll drop it by the cleaner's on the way home."

"Don't be silly, Max! It was my fault as much as yours. I'll just go change."

Back in the bedroom, Kate could hear her friend fiddling with the stereo system in the living room. Static, soft music, country and western, more static.

"How do you get the news?" Max shouted eventually.

"Just keep punching the buttons!" Kate stuck her head around the master bedroom door. "One of them is bound to be the right— Alex? Alex!" Kate froze, ruined skirt and blouse still in hand. She blinked, figuring she had to be hallucinating the tall, ruggedly virile male, then she stepped cautiously around the door. Putting out a hand, she touched the fabric of his dark business suit. The wool was real all right. So was the heartbeat beneath her hand.

"Walks, talks, and kisses pretty good, too," the figment of her imagination replied.

"You are here," Kate breathed, leaning weakly against the door.

His eyes raked familiarly down the length of her slip-clad frame. "Expecting someone else? You know, Kate, that coffee on the lap routine went out with sis-boom-bah."

"You were spying on me?"

Alex shook his head negatively. "Sleeping off jet lag, in the guest room. Though it would have been pretty hard to snore through all this subterfuge."

"Kate! Kate, did you get that skirt off yet!" Max Collins could be heard to yell impatiently from the living room. "I've been trying but I can't seem to—" The senator's steps halted just short of the other end of the hall. Max turned almost as white as the wool on Kate's skirt. "Ryker—"

"That makes it unanimous," Alex purred with a warning smile that would have slain a shark. "Everyone here remembers my name."

Max recovered slightly, removed the stub of his

pipe between his teeth. "I thought you were in Riyadh."

"Apparently so did Kate." Alex turned back to Kate. Suddenly aware of her dishabille, she shut the bedroom door with a thump and began to pull on a shirt and pants. Why had he come home so unexpectedly? It couldn't be he'd changed his mind about working overseas, could it? But there was no stopping the wild rush of joy flooding her heart.

Moments later, after a steady drifting of low, surprisingly amiable masculine voices, the front door shut. Alex walked back into the bedroom, confronted Kate as she leaned weakly against the bureau, running a brush haltingly through her gleaming hair.

"I got as far as New York when I realized no job was worth the second demise of our marriage," Alex began, strolling over to join her. Arm around her waist, he walked her into the living room. The music Max had accidentally turned on made a nice relaxing backdrop. "But I had a commitment to fulfill just the same. I went back, worked night and day for three weeks getting things straightened out again, then told personnel they still owed me two more weeks leave of absence. They didn't like it, but eventually relented. I still have to go back, Kate, but this time only for five months."

"And then what?" She was almost afraid to discover.

"That depends on you. Do you still want to make another go of our marriage, full-time? Are you willing to wait the additional five months I have to go back to Saudi Arabia?"

"You're not demanding I go with you?" Before he

had stated the only way they could be together was if
she gave up her position at *M.W.* at least temporarily.

"I want you with me. But I realized the moment I
left it was unfair to expect you to give up your work at
Missouri Woman, even for a short while, particularly
when you'd be so out of touch. The only solution is
for you to wait for me here. I'm bound by contract,
Kate, by obligation, and by honor. I can't walk out on
the middle of a very crucial hierarchical change
there."

"I understand." Kate knew how important his
work was. "But what happens after that? Southwestern doesn't have any offices in Missouri."

"I'd have to quit the company," Alex said bluntly.

"I never meant for that to happen!" Kate exclaimed, face ashen. Alex laughed and drew her
nearer.

"I know, sweetheart. But it's inevitable. My assignments with Southwestern would be overseas continuously because that seems to be where most of their
fire fighting problems crop up. Granted, it's challenging to be able to walk in and make sense of their organizational messes, but so was the revitalization and
restructuring of *Missouri Woman*."

Kate frowned warily. "You're not coming back as
publisher full-time, are you?"

Alex grinned. "No, Kate, not full-time. But I also
have no intention of letting you run it single-handedly
again, either. You're a bit too laid-back when it comes
to policy and organization. You need a full-time business manager to keep things in line fiscally. I'll continue to play the heavy as needed."

"And the rest of the time?" Kate asked. "What will you do?"

"Open my own consulting firm," Alex said quietly. "I'll still have to travel wherever I'm needed, but only as far as Houston, Dallas, St. Louis, Kansas City."

"Actually," Kate qualified, "I think I could live with any assignment within the continental United States."

"As long as we're together two or three days a week," Alex said.

"Absolute minimum," Kate agreed.

"Then it's settled?" Alex asked. "You still love me and want to work things out? Heaven knows I love you more than words could ever relay."

"Then why didn't you tell me?" Kate asked after a very lengthy kiss.

Alex shrugged. "I didn't think you'd believe me, after the months of separation, anger, and silence. And then, too, there was always the creative challenge of conveying the message in other ways."

Kate grinned, thinking of his more interesting moves. "Yes, Alex, I love you. I always have." She was silent, remembering much of the past months. "And as for Max Collins—"

Alex laughed. "I'm aware the two of you were just friends. I couldn't resist, though."

Which reminded Kate. "He does seem to have a way of cropping up at the worst times. Including your first day back in the city, the time I was painting the house and nearly killed myself falling off the ladder. When *are* we going to paint the trim?"

"Considering our respective schedules, probably

never. I guess we'll have to hire someone to do it, because I certainly don't intend to waste one moment of the time we have together." Slowly, he lowered her back onto the sofa, sheltered her slender form with the desirous warmth of his own. "The rearranging you prompt me to do . . ."

Kate paused, trying hard to ignore the hands gliding from shoulder to thigh. "Are you sure you're not going to regret your decision to resign from Southwestern?" She knew Alex wanted to be with her now, but in six months or a year, would he still feel the same?

"Kate, I love you." Alex directed her amber gaze to his. "I realized the first months overseas that our marriage was really the only important thing, that I'd chuck everything if I had to."

"Why didn't you tell me the moment you got back?"

"I meant to," Alex said dryly. "But somehow in that downtown Springfield car chase, I got side-tracked. Later, realizing just how deeply I had hurt you when I walked out, I knew I'd have to win you back again, start from scratch. And, as they say, actions speak louder than words."

Kate caught the impish grin spreading over ruggedly masculine features. "And your takeover at *Missouri Woman*?"

"Part of my desire to protect my investment," Alex admitted. "Mostly a way to get close to you."

"And you did," Kate added thoughtfully, recalling tripping over him at every turn. "Why did you stay away so much, though? Always running around out of town?"

"Because living with you and not sleeping with you

was sheer torture. Yet at the same time, I couldn't bear the questions, doubt, and hurt in your eyes later. I knew I was just going to to have to hold the passion at bay until we worked through our problems and came up with some sort of solution. Naturally, I hoped you would be the one to chuck everything first. When that didn't happen, I realized it was my turn to give. After all, I can get a job anywhere, doing work I enjoy. You can't simply begin another *Missouri Woman*, or offhandedly desert something that has been your life's work."

"You're right, though," Kate added reflectively. "I have been a little too stubborn and idealistic at times." Briefly, she filled him in on the Firebrand renegotiations, her hopes to eventually de-discriminate their copy.

"It's hard to believe, but we finally seem to have worked everything out." Kate snuggled closer, nuzzling her face along the crisply scented underside of his jaw, feeling the warmth of his chest, the steady beating of his heart. How she had missed him.

"Right, with only a couple of cut fingers, a tumble in the creek, and a bad sunburn to show for it," Alex laughed, reaching for the zipper to her slacks. "Remind me to put Solarcaine in the first-aid kit in the suitcase. I've got until after the Christmas holidays before I have to go back to Riyadh so we might as well go somewhere exotic."

"And after that?" Kate speculated, thoughtfully undoing his tie and the buttons to his shirt, helping him struggle out of the rest of his well-tailored clothing. "Maybe a midpoint rendezvous in Paris after another two or three months? Something to keep us going until after you're permanently back in the States. After all, if we can take a second honeymoon, we can certainly take a third or even a fourth."

"Speaking of which," Alex cradled her snugly in his arms, touched his lips lightly, persuasively to hers, "let's continue the second one right now..."

These books are
already available
from

HARLEQUIN
Love Affair

HARLEQUIN *Love Affair*

Now on sale

FLIGHT OF FANCY   *Dorothea Hale*

Frank Andrews thought it was a whim. He loved his wife, Carol, he insisted, and wouldn't let her go. But Carol had never had any opportunity to be anything but Mrs. Frank Andrews—and she sought freedom. Now, despite the tiny flat and the routine job in the dress shop, Carol was uncovering hidden abilities, long buried talents, and something unexpected—a love for Frank that could not be denied!

TREASURES OF THE HEART   *Andrea Davidson*

Pine Lake Lodge, Colorado, was no ordinary resort. Luxurious and secluded, it was where the rich came to play, to think, to forget the world. Senator John Ryan had come for all three reasons. And Lana Munsinger was determined to discover why. Lana needed this story; her reputation and her job as a journalist were at stake. Yet from the first, Lana sensed a vulnerability, a weariness, in John Ryan that melted her determination and her heart. Lana's choice was impossible—between her love and her life . . .

TOUCH OF FIRE   *Cathy Gillen Thacker*

Kate Ryker considered her two-year-old marriage over. Her husband Alex had taken a job in Saudi Arabia and Kate refused to move with him. She had her own life to live—as editor of *Missouri Woman* magazine. Kate took control of her situation and filed for divorce, and when seven months passed without any word from Alex, she thought her actions were final. But obviously Alex did not . . .

Next month's titles

MIRRORS AND MISTAKES *Kathleen Gilles Seidel*
They were very proper Bostonians who worked hard, dressed conservatively, and ate and drank in moderation. Suzanne Lawrence, secretary to the vice-president of Southard-Colt, and Patrick Britten, the firm's most brilliant consultant, hid behind polite, cool facades—and led lives of exquisite loneliness. Identical in taste, temperament and habit, they drew together in the belief that they would always remain friends. Neither anticipated the powerful instinct that would overwhelm Patrick . . .

LOVE IS A FAIRY TALE *Zelma Orr*
Ami Whitelake had surrendered her dreams long ago and took satisfaction in hard work, pleasure in the wonder of nature and love where she found it—rescuing an injured mongrel dog, taking in a homeless boy. For Ami, Wagner's Ranch became her sole source of joy. It was a chance to practise her veterinary skills in a land of spectacular beauty. She never expected to find love there, until she met Jeff Wagner. But Jeff barely noticed her. Surely he would never return her love . . .

MUSEUM PIECE *Anne Stuart*
James Elliott thwarted her at every turn, scooping up art treasures before she could acquire them for San Francisco's Museum of American Art. It was unethical and Mary Lindsay McDonough decided she'd better do something about it. She would send him a cool letter of protest. But not before she had written an extremely nasty poison pen letter—the letter she would have sent if she didn't have her reputation to consider. Unfortunately, she slipped the wrong letter into the envelope . . .

These two absorbing titles
will be published in January
by

HARLEQUIN
SuperRomance

THE RIGHT WOMAN Jenny Loring
Lia Andrews was a blackjack dealer. Flint Tancer
was a gambler. At least that's what it looked like to
the patrons of Lake Tahoe's Goldorado casino.

In fact Lia was a psychologist working on her
master's thesis. And Flint—all Lia knew for sure
was that the word *love* had had no meaning until
she met the charming high roller from San Francisco.

Lia had once been engaged to a gambler and vowed
never again. But how could she keep her resolve
when a moment shared with Flint Tancer sparked a
promise of paradise?

NOW, IN SEPTEMBER Meg Hudson
Dirk Van Der Maas had the power and style of a
Madison Avenue executive yet an artist's soul—a
combination Andrea Campbell found alluring.

But Andrea couldn't let personal feelings affect her
work—not when she had to design a critical ad
campaign for Dirk's company in Holland, Michi-
gan.

She wanted to do the account justice, but as soon as
it was over she would return to Boston—and say
goodbye to Dirk. It was going to be a challenge
putting her heart into a project that would separate
her forever from the one man she could love.